DEAR AMERICAN BROTHER

Joe J. Elder

BASED ON A TRUE STORY

DEAR AMERICAN BROTHER is a work of fiction. Except where actual historic events and characters are blended into the story, any resemblance to places or persons, living or dead, are purely coincidental.

ISBN 978-0-9939936-1-9 (Paperback book)

ISBN 978-0-9939936-2-6 (Electronic book)

ISBN 978-0-9939936-3-3 (Audio book)

This captivating novel of endurance and love intertwines Soviet and Nazi era history with Hans Gerein's struggle to immigrate to America.

Forced starvation, internment in a gulag camp, and a series of difficult choices strengthen his resolve to do whatever is necessary for survival under the oppressive regimes, no matter the cost to his heart or his humanity.

Reviews

A riveting blend of historical detail and fictional drama.

— *Kirkus Reviews*

A chillingly vivid tale of communism, country, and salvation that deftly captures a bygone world and a protagonist changed by the difficult choices it presents.

— D. Donovan, Senior Reviewer, Midwest Book Review

For Mike:

Great to share the ball field with you.

Joe

PROLOGUE

Berlin - July, 1945

"Come out!" barked a gruff voice from behind the powerful beam of light. "Give yourself up."

Sonovabitch. I had let my guard down. Darkness surprised me with its swiftness, and the Allied curfew patrol closed in. Pinned in the shadow of a rubble pile in war-ravaged Berlin, I calculated the distance to the alley, my only chance of escape; I could make a run for it and hope to avoid a bullet if caught in the beam of the spotlight. Decision made, I sprang to my feet and ran, a determined soldier hot on my heels. Damn! I stumbled, clambered, clawed over mounds of broken bricks and mangled beams. My lungs threatened to explode when, without warning, bright headlights shone from the far end of the alley, ending my sprint and, perhaps my freedom.

Two American soldiers leapt from the jeep to block my escape. The one chasing me wrenched my arm behind my back. *"Achtung*! You're coming with us," he hissed.

My mind raced. 'You bastard,' I thought. 'You're in for a hell of a fight!' I twisted my upper body to upset the soldier's balance and slammed him into a bullet-scarred brick wall. Spittle on the rush of his expended breath spattered my face, then his knees buckled and he flowed to the ground like warm honey. As I grabbed the next soldier, his partner bashed my head with a nightstick; an explosion of stars clouded my vision.

I regained consciousness sprawled on a dirt floor, a ring of inquisitive faces staring down over the edges of multi-tiered bunks. A scrawny man stretched out an arm and pointed to a lower bunk. In the flicker of light cast by a kerosene lantern, I crawled across the floor, my brain throbbing in time with the beat of my heart, pulled myself upright against the rough timber frame and flopped onto the thin mattress.

Although my eyelids drooped, my predicament kept sleep at bay. How could I search for my precious seventeen-year-old daughter, Ami, from the confines of this refugee camp? Near the end of World War II, the Soviet Army had swiftly pushed Hitler's demoralized ranks back from Poland to Germany and I lost contact with Ami during our flight from the communist onslaught. For sixty-two wretched days, I scoured the countryside and the German towns bordered by Poland, then combed the destroyed streets of Dresden and Cottbus before moving on to Berlin. My thoughts, my energy, *my everything*, had gone into searching for her—she was all I had left to live for.

While tallying the suffering that had shaped my life, it seemed as if I were cursed. What did the future hold for me—more hardship, more pain? Triggered by self-pity, my life escaped the confines of my soul and played out in my mind as a vivid dream, a dream beginning in the bliss of my youth.

1

SAY YOU'RE SORRY

South Russia - April, 1914

Good fortune shone upon me on July 10, 1903, the day I came into this world. My family loved me, although I questioned the affection of my father when he would correct my behavior. I had a cozy home in South Russia, where, strictly speaking, the majority of people in the village of Chornov and the neighboring communities were German immigrants, 'foreigners.' Our ambitious, hardworking ancestors had lived in relative peace and harmony on the vast steppe north of the Black Sea after settling there more than a century ago.

None of it mattered to me at the moment. The idea to search a linden tree for crows' eggs had seemed exciting while I stood on the ground, but high in the tree, and eager to prove myself to my older friends watching from below, I mumbled, "I can do it … just a little higher." I wrapped my left hand around a thin overhead branch swaying in the breeze and leaned closer to the nest than the laws of equilibrium would allow. My leather-soled boots loosened a patch of dead bark, slippery as goose grease, tumbling me from my precarious perch. I landed with a 'thud' on the bed of dried leaves and twigs, stunned, unable to catch my breath.

My older brother's voice rang in my ears. "Hans! Open your eyes, you idiot. Mama will kill us if you're dead." He held out a mud-streaked hand. "Here. Get up."

"Twelve years old and still a *Dummkopf*," Lothar blustered. "See if he's breathing."

Kurt brushed away a sharp twig, then knelt and placed his ear to my lips. "I can hear his guts working." Of their own volition, my arms shot skyward and locked around my brother's slender neck. We writhed on the damp soil until he wriggled free.

Fritz Ripplinger, our timid friend, bent over me. "Hans, are you hurt? Maybe we should carry you—"

"That sissy's alright," said the bully Lothar, watching me struggle to my feet. "Come on, guys. Let's go home."

We paraded down the gentle bank and my companions crossed Chornov Creek by leap-frogging on moss-covered rocks. Still dizzy from the fall, I teetered precariously on the first rock, then slipped into the shallow water, tiny geysers erupting from the lacing eyelets on my ankle-high boots.

As we crested a low hill, Saint Gustav's Church steeple came into view before the entire village spread out in the shallow green valley. The bright sun reflected off the horse-drawn carriages in front of the shops on Church Street, the main boulevard. Squat thatched-roof houses on long narrow lots lined two secondary lanes, while the homes on River Street, including ours at the far end, had somewhat larger yards and faced the creek meandering along the opposite side of the road.

The church bell pealed six notes as we, four disheveled boys, scattered toward our homes. My brother's pace matched that of his friends; being the youngest, I brought up the rear—*slosh ... slosh.*

The rusty hinges of the wrought iron gate creaked, but held firm in the stone fence when Fritz entered his yard. Lothar left us at the next intersection, while Kurt and I continued to our yard. 'My home is the nicest place in the village,' I thought, as I followed the irregular-shaped flagstones past a row of blooming plum trees. A sturdy barn formed the rear of a dated single-story house of limestone blocks, the thatched roof draped over the eaves obscuring the tops of multi-paned windows in the kitchen and the living room; a single-seat wooden outhouse, often considered our most important building, stood near the porch. A short distance beyond, crushed oats and barley filled a small granary, while between the old threshing floor and three mounds of dusty hay, a weathered chicken coop leaned precariously to the east. Mama's vegetable garden, partially hidden by the summer kitchen, fronted onto the orchard, really only six rows of cherry and apricot trees stretching across the rear of the yard. A high stone fence encircled the one home I had ever known.

Our older sister Loni's auburn hair bounced as she skipped rope to meet us. "You boys didn't do your chores after school. Papa's gonna box your ears 'til the dust flies." She turned up her nose in disgust. "And Hans, you're filthy. Boy, I pity you."

My stomach knotted. I knew from experience Papa's reaction to dirtied school clothes.

We hung our jackets and caps on a hook in the enclosed porch before Kurt pushed me ahead of him toward our modest kitchen. Although not a large man, Papa dominated the room. His full dark hair, showing a tinge of grey, covered one side of his furrowed forehead, and a prominent nose projected above thin, colorless lips that seldom parted in a smile. "*Warte mal*," he bellowed from his chair at the head of a wooden table pockmarked from years of use. "Why isn't the henhouse cleaned out? He slammed his fist on the table with such force the silverware rattled. "Johannes! Where did you get so dirty? And look at me when I talk to you."

Kurt bolted out the door. My knees quivered as I raised only my eyes and answered in a small voice, "I-in the creek."

His face clouded over as he sprang from his chair, took two long strides, grasped me by the collar and dragged me to the porch. I stifled a groan when his huge calloused hand reached for the strap, a torn length of horse harness hanging on a metal hook high in a corner. The initial surge of pain forced a moan from my lips; the second blow landed with a loud smack where the legs of my short pants still seeped creek water.

"Karl!" Mama called in a sharp voice from the kitchen.

Papa took hold of my suspenders, unceremoniously dumped me into the yard and swung shut the door.

I brushed a snotty drip from my nose and rubbed the sticky hand across my throbbing bum. Why was it always *me* in trouble? I limped to the henhouse to help Kurt shovel chicken manure into a wheelbarrow.

"How many did Papa give you?" he asked.

"T-t-two."

I picked up the short-handled pitchfork and squirmed under the wooden roost. Suddenly, Kurt grabbed my arm and whispered in my ear, "We've still got our school clothes on and we'll really get a licking if there's chicken crap all over them."

"Then you go in the house to get our work clothes. Y-you haven't been licked yet."

"He wouldn't belt you twice, would he?"

"Sure, he would."

Darkness had settled like a winter fog when my brother and I finally sat down at the kitchen table to eat a cold supper. Papa frowned, tapped out his pipe in the ashtray and, without a word, went to the barn to repair a harness.

A look of pity for her sons filled Mama's bright brown eyes. At thirty-four years of age, and the mother of five children, she was a short, plump woman with hair drawn flat into a tight bun. A blue-checkered apron that drooped over her ample abdomen and hung straight to her ankles partially hid her full-length black dress. A small golden cross, a wedding gift from her parents, dangled from a delicate chain around her neck. Her life had not been easy; a few years ago, she had buried Daniel, a six-year old son, and Lilli, a two-year old daughter, typhoid fever the culprit. "Now, off to bed with both of you," she ordered after applying goose grease salve to the welts across my buttocks.

A privacy curtain separated our simple wood-framed bed at the far end of the chilly room from Loni's smaller version in the corner nearest the kitchen. My brother and I curled up on the corn-straw mattress and pulled the goose tick comforter to our chins. Papa's hammer echoed from the barn. *Tap, tap, tap.* "I h-hate him," I whispered through chattering teeth. "Wasn't my fault I slipped in the creek. Besides, we could buy eggs from Hoffer's Store instead of looking after those shittin' squawkers."

When heavy footsteps sounded in the hallway connecting the house to the attached barn, we cowered like cornered mice. "Shh, pretend you're asleep," my brother whispered.

The door creaked open. Papa paused at the foot of our bed and cleared his throat as if to speak.

'Say you're sorry,' I thought. 'Say you didn't mean to strap me so hard.' Instead, he continued on to the kitchen, closing the door behind him.

Our rooster, for no particular reason named 'Sammy,' crowed moments before Mama drew back the heavy drapes from the bedroom window. Loni, always enthusiastic about school, was already in the kitchen. Afraid of our father's wrath if we were late, Kurt and I hastily pulled on our red plaid cotton shirts, brown short pants gathered below the knees, and long wool socks. Had Kurt been slightly heavier, we could have passed for twins, although his hair was fairer than mine, and his eyes were a deeper shade of blue.

When the church bell rang eight times, we gulped our porridge, grabbed our brown narrow-brimmed caps and headed out the door. My buttocks, sore from yesterday's strapping, throbbed as we dashed down River Street. Our neighbor, Herr Gus Vetter, a slight man, only his temper outmatching his quick movements akin to those of a weasel, flicked a hand in greeting from behind his gate.

The strong odor of tobacco drifting from our grandparents' yard at the end of the block indicated that Grandfather Wilhelm Gerein, or perhaps Uncle Heinz, unmarried and living with his parents, was enjoying a morning smoke. Heinz was my grandparents' youngest child, with Papa in the middle; the eldest, Pius, along with his wife, Francisca and their sons Barnie and Erwin, lived in Mannheim, a large town thirteen miles south of Chornov. On the other hand, my mother, an only child, suffered the loss of her parents due to influenza several years after she married Papa.

Grandpa, leaning against the stone fence, tipped his black

military-style cap in our direction. Sleek white hair accented his weathered features. "*Guten Morgen*," he said in a groggy voice. Deep wrinkles spiderwebbed from the corners of his eyes and mouth.

I forced myself to sound cheerful. "Good morning, Grampa."

His pipe waggled between sparse yellowed teeth. "Well, off to school. And listen to the teacher so you'll be smart when you grow up"

That was our grandfather—always giving a lesson. Although I loved my parents, he was my favorite person in the world, next to Kurt. But that was different—Kurt was my brother.

At age ten, I was in Form Five. Kurt and his classmates, one year ahead of me, shared our spartan room. When we aligned ourselves according to age in the schoolyard, Kurt immediately whispered in Lothar's ear, and I knew he was relaying my misfortune of the previous evening. "He can't be that sore," Lothar mocked, kicking my left buttock.

A sharp cry escaped my lips. That bully! I tolerated Lothar's arrogance only to be part of the group. Last summer, the government paid a small bounty for crows' feet, apparently to rid the area of the pests. When my friends and I explored the grove of linden trees near the creek, I climbed to the highest branch, the one supporting a crudely constructed nest. Two immature crows turned their beady eyes to me, hopped off the edge and fluttered to the ground. Without hesitation, Lothar grabbed their tails and clubbed the helpless creatures with a rock. I felt queasy when he ripped off their legs and waved them above his head like trophies. At that moment, it became clear why he and I were not close friends.

Headmaster Slava Blokin peered over his glasses. "There is to be absolute quiet and order during assembly. Johannes Gerein, why did you shout out?"

I fought to stem my tears. "I-I don't know, sir."

Katie Frey, a shy freckle-faced girl in my grade, raised her hand. "Please, sir, I know. Lothar kicked him."

The stern man waved his gnarled walking stick. "All students into class! You, too, Johannes. As for Mister Troublemaker, you come with me."

One of the older students held open the outside door of the schoolhouse, and Lothar, grim-faced and trembling, followed the headmaster into his cluttered office, while the rest of us filed down the hallway to our respective classrooms. I heard, "Hold out your right hand," before three distinct smacks and three escalating wails echoed into our classroom. I cringed, afraid the headmaster would call me next. Katie sat poker straight in the front row. Why had she been so foolish? Tattling on a classmate was frowned upon—tattling on Lothar Degenstein was a grave error in judgment. Certainly, he would seek revenge on Katie … and me, more for his humiliation in front of his classmates than for the pain of the lashes.

The day dragged on, and I closed my ragged-edged notebook the minute the dismissal bell rang. Fritz begged Kurt and me to come see his newborn puppies, adding that afterwards we could look at motorcars in a magazine his father received from America. I didn't care much about the puppies, but anything to do with motorcars and America interested me.

At the first corner of the street just past the church, we saw Katie struggle with Lothar, who had a firm grip on one of her braids. "Stop it! Let 'er go," I yelled, feeling my face flush with anger. I clenched my fists and squared off in front of him, putting all my energy into one blow. Lothar, a year older and a head taller than me, did not expect my swift attack. Stunned, he released Katie's hair and fell to the ground, blood gushing from his nose.

After he rose to his feet and staggered down Middle Avenue, he turned and with a nasal drawl threatened, "I'm gonna ged you, Hans Gerein, and damn good!"

"He really *is* gonna kill you now. You know that, don't you?" Kurt said.

Katie stepped forward, a smile exposing the gap between her front teeth. "*Danke Schön*, Hans," she said, then kissed my cheek. She blushed and ran toward home.

Fritz slapped me on the back. “Kisser, that’s what we’ll call you from now on. Hans Kisser!”

I scrubbed my assaulted face with the back of my hand and muttered, “Stoopid girls.” However, in that moment, a strange revelation arose within me: girls were different from boys, and they possessed an indescribable power over us—and I liked it! I liked Katie.

2
DON'T TALK TO ME ABOUT REASON

May, 1914

Grandma and Uncle Heinz followed Grandpa inside as he opened our porch door one warm, windy Saturday. When the men paused beside my father, I noticed that Grandpa and Papa matched in height and breadth, their posture stooped. Uncle Heinz, taller and thinner with a skinny caterpillar mustache, stood more erect. To me, he was the most handsome man in Chornov.

"I heard talk today at Squeaky Hoffer's store," my grandfather said. The shrill voice of Herr Hoffer, a man of short stature, indeed nearly as wide as he was tall, had gained him the nickname 'Squeaky.' Grandpa continued, "Something about the trouble between Austria and Bosnia starting a war in Western Europe. What do you think, Karl?"

"If it does, you can bet your boots Germany will side with Austria. And if France gets involved, Russia will take their side. With so many of our boys in the Russian Army, Germans would be fighting Germans."

Grandma's face turned white. "If Russia goes to war, Heinz might be conscripted and he wants to get married …"

Uncle Heinz had announced last week that he intended to ask Monica Kraft from Mannheim for her hand in marriage, but her father didn't like him. "For one thing, compared to the Krafts, we're penniless," my uncle had said. "For another, he considers me a physical weakling, not strapping like his son." Kurt and I had laughed when our uncle flexed his muscles and puffed out his chest. "The only thing going for me is that I love Monica and she loves me." Grandpa had replied that if her father is rich, every eligible man in Mannheim must be eager to marry her, too. "The wheat of the poor and the daughters of the rich are soon ripe. If you're serious, you shouldn't wait to ask her," he had said. My uncle announced a few days later that he and Monica would be married on May 25 in Mannheim.

Grandpa reached over and patted his wife's arm. "*Ya-naih*, don't worry so much. There won't be any war."

Uncle Heinz deftly changed the subject. "Karl, I heard that old man Andrew Boser and his sons Young Andy and Rochus are selling their land so they can move to America in October. I'm sure Benedict Bauman's going to buy the thirty acres along Pototski Road, but if we buy the twenty south of—"

"Talk about business at a better time, not when we want to visit," Grandma grumbled. "In fact, why don't we have dinner at our house after church tomorrow? Hans, come over later and help me catch some chickens. Kurt, bring the small axe … and the chopping block."

After our relatives returned home, my family relaxed on a bench in the shade of an apricot tree. Papa stretched out his legs and leaned back. "Rosina," he said, "I think it would be good for us to own more land. I can't believe Kurt is twelve and Hans is almost eleven, but they are, and someday we'll want to give them a start in farming, too."

'Leave me out of it,' I thought, 'because *America* will one day be my home.'

"There's both Heinz and me to make the payments. We each have a hundred roubles for the down payment, and only need to borrow fourteen hundred from the bank. Herr Boser wants to sell now, and if we don't hurry, somebody else will take it."

"We have enough to eat and everybody's clothed," Mama said, sounding skeptical. "What if we don't get a crop and still have to make the payment? But Karl, if you think you can manage it, I won't interfere."

"Then Heinz and I will meet with Old Andy this afternoon." He rose from the bench and hooked his thumbs under his suspenders. "Let's hope we can agree on the terms."

When Uncle Heinz and Papa came through our gate later that day, I prayed Herr Boser had sold the land to someone else, however, my uncle playfully caught me under the arms and swung me in a circle. No doubt, he was a happy landowner.

Papa beamed as he told Mama that the deal, although

unconventional, was sealed. "The Bosers need the money within ten days to pay for their passage to America," he said, "but we'll only take title to the land when they leave in October."

Mama's frown confirmed she did not share Papa's enthusiasm.

That Friday, Papa and Kurt combed the horses' manes and tails, and polished their hooves with a dab of axle grease. Loni, Mama, and I entered the summer kitchen as Grandma rolled out a lump of dough. "What's a wedding without *Kuchen*?" she said. "And when my mother baked cakes for special occasions, she added a little brandy to the cream filling. Hans, go and bring up the bottle of apricot brandy. You can read which one is apricot, can't you?"

I hurried across the yard and dragged open the heavy plank door of the limestone block passageway, then eased my way down the creaky stairs into the root cellar, where shadows cast long gnarled fingers across the rough timbers. Next to the potato bin stood a large earthenware sauerkraut crock and a wine barrel on the packed-earth floor, perhaps with monsters hiding behind them. On the opposite side, Grandma had aligned various flasks on a low shelf, her writing on each barely legible. "Plum," I read aloud and pushed the bottle aside. "Gooseberry." An acrid taste arose in my mouth. "A-p-r-i-" I pried the cork from the amber bottle with my thumb and index finger and held it to my nose. "It smells like apricots … better try a sip." I downed a large swallow, burped loudly, then scampered up the stairs without checking the sauerkraut crock's shadow.

"Sorry I took so long, Grandma," I said as she snatched the bottle from me. "The words, they're kinda rubbed off."

"Did you take a drink?"

"*Naaiiih.*"

She slapped me. "Don't lie, Johannes. That's a big sin."

I nodded, but dared not rub my burning cheek.

She caught me by the ear and led me to the corner behind the stove. "Kneel here for an hour, you rascal."

"Please, can I move to a different spot?" I asked. "It's too hot here."

"Not nearly as hot as you'll be in hell if you keep telling lies."

After Kurt and I crawled into bed that evening, I began to recite my prayer for a second time. "What are you doing, Kisser?" Kurt asked. "We already prayed."

'Mind your own business,' I thought, before continuing, "When I lay down to sleep on the Good Mother's lap, I ask her to tuck me in and make the sign of the cross over me." I fluffed my feather pillow. "Kurt, how hot do you think it'd be in hell?"

"Hot as being in the sun all day, I bet. *Naih*, it'd prob'ly be hot as a *Backofen*. Or maybe hotter than a blacksmith's fire. Or even …"

I poked him in the ribs with my elbow. "Shut up already."

"Well, you asked." He turned and faced the wall. Soon his breathing settled into a deep steady rhythm, however, I lay awake trying to rid my mind of horned devils and red-hot pitchforks.

Early the next morning, Grandpa, who appeared tired and sweaty, carried wooden crates of food to his wagon. "Genoveva, if you add one more item to the list, we'll need *two* wagons," he said.

Grandma sniffled into a white linen handkerchief. "We don't want to seem stingy to the new in-laws. They already look down their noses at us," she said, while Uncle Heinz and I spread an old bed sheet on top of the bulging wagon to protect the precious cargo from road dust.

We set out for Mannheim, a family sharing the excitement of the day. Papa laughed heartily and ruffled my hair when I declared that this was going to be the best day ever. Why couldn't he always be in such a good mood?

After the lengthy wedding service in the Catholic Church of Mary, the well-wishers formed a procession to the Kraft yard. An impressive house sprawled behind the manicured lilac hedge, a monstrous threshing machine stood next to three towering granaries, and five wagons occupied the space beyond the water trough.

Overwhelmed, I wondered how people got the money to buy all that stuff. I wandered around the back yard admiring the opulence of the property when the sound of voices from the rear of the house attracted me to an open window. I peeked in and saw Grandpa and Grandma seated on matching wingback chairs in a spacious room. They faced Monica's parents, who were relaxing on an elegant royal blue sofa. Uncle Pius and Aunt Francisca stood to one side near a teakwood cabinet with lion heads carved into the legs.

"Did you hear that the Archduke of Austria was murdered in Bosnia not long ago?" said Herr Paul Kraft, taking a sip of wine from his glass. "I'm afraid that might mean trouble for us. Russia has problems too, and the politicians have been saying for years that the Germans are to blame. And they mean *us*, not the ones in Germany."

Grandpa shrugged his shoulders. "But what can we do—"

Uncle Pius stepped in front of him. "We wouldn't have to worry about that if you hadn't been so damn stubborn ten years ago when so many families moved to America. I thought we should go with them, but you refused." He slammed his clenched fist into his hand.

"You want to go to America," Grandma said, raising her voice. "And if Heinz is taken into the army, I can't see what reason they—"

"*Ya-naih*, Heinz and Monica are young and in love," Grandpa said, reaching for his wife's hand. "Genoveva, remember when we were that age? Good reasoning was the last thing we used. So just let them have—"

Frau Kraft jumped to her feet. "Don't talk to me about reason! If you had used some reasoning with your son, he'd have seen the craziness of getting married now. What if Monica gets pregnant, then he's taken away and never comes back? You should have just told Heinz he can't get married, and that would be …" Frau Kraft trailed off, then pressed her apron to her mouth and fled the room.

Grandma's blazing eyes followed her. "Wait a minute! Did that kind of thinking work with *your daughter*?"

I rested my back against the cool wall of the house. The argument was alarming, but the talk of America excited me. I returned to the wedding celebration, and decided that when the time was right, I would swear Kurt to secrecy before telling him about Uncle Pius and America. If Papa learned of my eavesdropping, he would certainly punish me.

3

NO LOVING GOD WOULD BE SO CRUEL

July, 1914

I lay in bed, every muscle relaxed, my hands folded behind my head. Summer vacation had begun and my friends and I could play stickball all day at Pototski Field, a playground at the edge of Chornov. And it was only a week until my eleventh birthday. The one small cloud over my life was that Kurt merely shrugged his shoulders when I repeated the conversation about America.

My fantasy of a leisurely summer ended when Papa announced that our family's assignment was to cut the hay on the communal property a mile beyond Chornov. All German villagers shared the proceeds from the crops on communal land granted to the village by the Czar a century ago, but throughout the years, the more progressive farmers purchased their own property from Russian Counts.

Several times over the course of the hot day, Papa guided the horses pulling the mushroomed wagon to our yard. Eventually, we formed a round stack of hay next to the old threshing floor. The dust created from stomping down the hay made me cough, but I wasn't excused from the job. Though I supposed Papa was proud of his boys, of how hard we worked, we knew better than to expect any favors or words of praise.

Shortly before sunset, we took the last load of hay to the local inn as payment for Loni's friend, Alma Goldstein, helping her with chores on the days we were busy in the field. On the way, Papa explained to us that Herr Ira Goldstein's grandfather initially shared a land grant in Neufeld, a distant town, but Ira didn't like farming, so he forfeited his share in any communal crop and built the Goldstein Inn in Chornov. When I asked if they didn't come to church because they weren't from Chornov, he replied they were Jewish, not Catholic.

"Jewish? What's that?" I said. "They look the same as us. And

I thought everybody in the world was Catholic."

I failed to see the humor, but Papa threw back his head and laughed.

One Sunday morning in September, Father Heisser climbed the creaking stairs and laid his horn-rimmed glasses on the ledge of the pulpit. Twice he began to speak, and twice he hesitated. Finally, drawing a deep breath, the good priest said, "Brethren, I do not know a gentle way to tell you this, so I will be blunt. Germany and Austria have declared war on Russia!"

In the ensuing bedlam, men shouted at the priest, at each other, at the Lord Himself; the women cried that we were doomed, that we would all die. Frau Vetter rushed forward and dragged her sons, Albert and Josef, from their seats next to Kurt. She flew down the aisle, chanting a litany of regrets: "Why didn't we go to America with my brother? Why didn't we *all* go? Now it's too late to get visas."

Father Heisser shouted above the din. "Quiet! Everyone!" A hush settled over the congregation. "This is terrible news, but we must remain calm. Germany and Austria are far away. We will be safe here. The Lord will not forget us if we are fervent in our prayer and truly believe." He bowed his head. "Our Father, who art in Heaven …"

I moved my lips in prayer, but worried the army would come for Uncle Heinz, just as my grandmother had suspected.

On the following Saturday, the bright sunshine seemed to bless the German villagers as they set aside their concerns and carried on with the yearly tradition of husking corn for pig feed. In an adjoining field, Oleg Golubov, a Russian laborer, waved to us from an iron-wheeled tractor towing a plough across land privately owned by Benedict Bauman of Pototski Estate. Due to his large landholdings—and pompous sense of superiority—Herr Bauman did not participate in the communal harvest.

"Damn noisy contraption," Papa muttered. "Just like that motorcar of his."

Papa was referring to the day last week when he and I stepped out of Hoffer's Store and heard a soft *putt, putt, putt* interrupted by an occasional muffled boom. Black metal reflected the bright sunshine at the intersection of Church Street and Middle Avenue. A motorcar! Most of the villagers had never seen a motorcar and the commotion drew a large crowd. Herr Bauman sat tall behind the steering wheel, while his son Hubert, one of my classmates, smiled at me from the back seat. The arrogant man slid from the seat and strutted into the store. Upon returning, he spun a shiny crank mounted low on the front of the motorcar until the engine chugged to life, then jumped into the vehicle and flapped his hat. "Get out of the way, you gawkers," he said to the curious onlookers, his eyes gleaming with contempt before speeding down Pototski Road toward his estate.

"Karl, just forget about Showman Bauman. He'll never change," Mama said as she selected corncobs from a huge pile beside the communal granary.

A male's voice sounded from across the yard. "Mathias found a red ear of corn! Now show us your sweetheart!"

Mathias Klatt's shoulders twitched as he searched for Margot Hoffer. When he found her sitting on the ground next to Loni and bent to kiss her burning cheeks, she pushed him away and covered her face with her hands. The tradition complete, the huskers cheered loudly.

"I hope you find one of those cobs," Kurt said. "Can't you see it now, Hans Kisser? Katie would be so happy."

I wrestled him to the ground, but, in truth, I had hoped to see her today.

My brother broke loose, and his mouth dropped open as he pointed over my shoulder. "H-Hans …"

I jumped to my feet and watched five uniformed men, their horses cantering alongside the stone fence. My heart fluttered and I swallowed hard when the expressionless soldiers brought their mounts to a halt near the gate. They dismounted and snapped to attention, polished rifles high on their squared shoulders. The captain, a row of medals adorning his tunic, remained straight-backed on a glistening black horse and silenced everyone with the intensity of his gaze. "I am Captain Stransky of the Czar's Imperial Army. I have draft orders for several young men from this village."

A murmur like buzzing bees rippled through the yard.

"When I call your name, step forward." He withdrew a paper from his saddlebag. "Alois, Jacob."

The crowd fell silent. A heavy-set young man shuffled nervously beside his weeping mother.

The officer rose in his stirrups. "Step lively!"

Jacob sprang forward.

The captain surveyed the paper. "Blatz, Johannes. Faust, Georg. Gerein, Heinz."

Aunt Monica gasped and clung to Uncle Heinz, who had to pry her fingers from his arm before stepping into line.

My eyes filled with tears. At my uncle and aunt's wedding, Frau Meier had said he might not come back from the war.

"Vetter, Jacob."

Gus stomped toward the captain. "My son's only turning twenty-one next week. He's not old enough to recruit."

The captain's face turned dark. "One lousy week? You dare sham the regulations on a technicality? Private, shut that man up!"

A burly soldier lifted his rifle butt and struck Gus on the head, knocking him to the ground. When he kicked Gus in the face, a knot of angry village men immediately pushed forward, but the captain drew his pistol and shot once into the air. The shoving stopped. Bile rose in my throat as Gus dragged himself back to the crowd, spitting broken teeth and gobs of blood.

Jacob glanced first to his father, then to the impatient captain, and hurried over to the other reluctant recruits.

"All of you report at the train station in Karpowa at seven o'clock tonight, or face a court-martial," bellowed the captain so loudly that his horse flared his nostrils and pranced in a circle. He jerked on the reins and ordered the soldiers to their horses. Within seconds, they had trotted out of our sight.

Despondent beyond words, Grandpa and Uncle Heinz packed a duffle bag, while Aunt Monica and Grandma prepared lunch to take along on the journey. Uncle Heinz kissed each member of my family before he climbed alongside his mother and his wife on the rear seat of the carriage. With a wave of his hand, he was gone. I would miss him, his jokes and his antics, but I looked forward to hearing the exciting war stories he would tell when he returned home.

Kurt cocked his hand like a pistol. "I wish I was old enough to go. It would be fun."

Papa twisted Kurt's ear until he moaned. "Don't ever talk of war as a game. It is deadly serious."

When he walked away, my brother rubbed his sore ear and whispered, "Hans, I'd still like to go to war. I wanna shoot a big rifle like those soldiers had."

After evening chores, Papa, Kurt, and I first stopped at the Vetter yard, and then went to Grandpa's house. "Come in," he said without his usual cheerfulness. "Grandma and Monica are lying down. Heinz's conscription really took a toll on them."

Papa slowly nodded his head. "It was a rough day all the way around. We just helped the Vetter boys with chores. That soldier kicked Gus in the face pretty hard and there's permanent damage."

"What's the world coming to when innocent people are just taken away, or kicked around like stray dogs?"

"Did you talk to our Russian friend Viktor Lebedin when you were in Karpowa? Can he come to help with harvest?" Papa asked.

"He's too busy with his own land. And the other Russians are working for Benedict Bauman or in the ammunition factories." Grandpa bowed his head and studied his work-worn hands. "I don't know what we can do. Heinz is gone …"

Aunt Monica emerged from her bedroom, drawn and red-eyed. She assured Grandpa that she would fill in for Heinz. "I didn't have to do outside work at home, but I'll give it a try."

"Monica, that would be appreciated very much," said Grandpa. He turned to Kurt. "Do you know the philosophy of life that every good German should practice as if it were Gospel? 'Work hard, take care of your own, have pride in your family, never bring shame to your name, and do all for the glory of God.' My father always—"

Suddenly, Grandma flung open the bedroom door. The evening sun through the bedroom window cast her short, plump figure into silhouette. Her rumpled white hair shone like a halo. "That's bullshit, you old goat! How in hell can you sit there and tell the boys things like that?"

My jaw dropped. I had never seen her like this.

Grandpa began to rise from his chair. "Come, you're upset. It's been a—"

"Sit down and listen for a change. And quit being such a damn holy holy!" She tromped across the kitchen floor, her hands planted on her hips, and stopped directly in front of Grandpa. "What good did all our hard work do? We should have had more fun with our *Kinder* when they were growing up instead of working all the time. Now here we are, crying about a son we'll never see again. And Pius wants to leave us, too." She leaned forward and waggled a finger in Grandpa's face. "No loving God would be so cruel, so heartless, so …" She whirled around, crossed the room, and slammed the door behind her. I heard the bedsprings creak, and her muffled sobbing saddened me, but I didn't know how to ease her pain.

Erasmus Goldstein parked his threshing machine in a wheat field south of the village and over the next few weeks, my family settled into a work pattern: Kurt, Loni, and Papa joined other teams in gathering sheaves for the thresher, while Grandpa, Aunt Monica, and I helped cart away the grain. We returned to our yard one particularly hot morning, the wagon bulging with bags of wheat. Aunt Monica used the spokes of a front wheel as a ladder and climbed to the ground. "Now that the blisters and aches have improved, I rather enjoy field work.

And it gets me away from Mother's depressing attitude," she said.

Grandpa stood to stretch his back. "I know what you mean. Maybe she's in a better mood today. Hans, go with Monica to get lunch. Grandma might have some cookies for you."

Aunt Monica led the way to the house. "Mother?" she called into the kitchen. When Grandma didn't reply, my aunt sent me to see if she was picking vegetables for supper.

In the garden, my grandmother lay on her side, one hand reaching for a melon. I had seen her stooped over several times that summer to pull weeds from around the tomato plants, but now, she stared with glassy eyes, her jaw slack. The initial terror deep in my gut loosened its grip. Grandpa heard my sharp scream and came running, Aunt Monica close behind. "What's wrong, Johannes? Did you hurt yourself?" he asked anxiously.

I pointed toward the melon patch. Grandpa fell to his knees and placed an ear on his wife's mouth, then on her chest. "Genoveva! Not like this, not yet!" he pleaded, desperate for a pulse, for any sign of life. He brushed closed her eyelids and wiped the soil from her nose before spreading her apron over her face. "Please, Monica, can you tell Karl? And Hans, run get the priest to give her the Last Sacraments." His voice broke into a sob.

I leaned against the fence to clear my mind and my eyes before dashing to the rectory. Father Heisser gathered his stole, two small bottles of Holy Water, anointing oil, and an incense burner suspended on three brass chains. As we hurried along the street, I wondered if he wore anything under the ankle-length black cassock that billowed around his legs. Thoughts like that at such a time worried me, but at least they diverted my attention away from the crisis at hand.

That evening, the air in the house dripped with grief. We hugged Grandpa and quietly went into the living room, where the single candle on a small table flickered shadows across the ceiling. A white lace tablecloth lay draped over the open edge of the simple box resting on two low stools. I stood on tiptoes and leaned forward, careful not to touch the casket. Grandma, her face peaceful, was dressed in her best taffeta dress. A black rosary entwined her fingers and a small bible lay open next to her folded hands.

"Does somebody have to stay with Gramma all the time, even at n-night?" Kurt asked, suppressing a sob.

"When a person dies, a prayer vigil always has to be kept, so the devil doesn't steal the soul," Papa said in a hoarse whisper.

On the way home, the inky darkness frightened me—a demon might jump out at any moment.

Our somber family crowded into Grandpa's house on the day of the funeral. Uncle Pius led us in prayer before the six pallbearers arrived. *Bang. Bang.* The casket lid was nailed shut. I crept away, feeling as if that sound would ring in my ears forever.

The three Russian families stood in silence when the procession to the church passed their homes, the men holding their caps to their chests in respect; they had often enjoyed Grandma's meals at harvest time. After the service, we trailed the casket to the cemetery, Grandpa's head sagging between his shoulders as he gripped the funeral wagon. I recalled my grandparents dancing at their son's wedding a short time ago. Now …

Against the wishes of her parents, Aunt Monica remained in Chornov. I expect she wanted to be there when, or rather, *if* Uncle Heinz returned from the army. "Monica's a great help to me," Grandpa said the next Friday when Kurt and I helped him cement one of Libby Epp's wrought iron crosses into a square hole at the head end of Grandma's grave.

"Can she bake cookies as good as Gramma did?" Kurt asked.

"*Naih*," he replied with a twinkle in his eye. "But don't tell your aunt. I don't want to be my own cook."

4

I JUST WISH BOTH OF US COULD GO

October, 1914

One crisp morning in early October, three rugged wagons, arched wooden frames covered with torn canvas, clattered down our street. A noisy horde of children sat at the rear of each wagon, dangling their legs. The riotous colors of the men's shirts contrasted with the bright sashes around their heads, and beaded belts gathered the women's full skirts at the waist. Papa jammed his pitchfork into the manure pile near the barn and nervously shuffled from one foot to the other. "Hans, those goddamn *Zigeuner* wander around the countryside to peddle stuff and steal whatever they can get their hands on. They're sure not welcome here."

Still, the gypsies intrigued me. Minutes after one of the wagons stopped in front of the yard, two women with dark complexions and flowing coal-black hair opened our front gate and followed the flagstone path along the row of trees. I started toward them, but Papa grabbed my suspenders and muttered, "Stay behind me, Hans. I'll ask what the hell they want."

Kurt, Loni, and Mama edged out from the house in time to see the women lower colorful cloth bundles from their backs onto the ground. A variety of wares—cooking utensils, scrub brushes, bangles and beads—enthralled my family. The younger woman spread her arms wide. "Don't you agree that we have something for everyone?"

When Papa informed her that he had no money, they struck a deal to trade a variety of goods for one of the fat young pigs squealing in our barnyard. Mama fancied a shiny copper pot, Loni a silver crucifix on a beaded chain. Papa picked a currycomb for the horses, and then approved Kurt claiming a little red pocketknife. My breathing turned shallow. Papa had allowed everyone else in my family to select an item. Was he purposely keeping me in suspense? Perhaps he thought

I didn't give an honest effort in the field, or Mama had told him about the brandy incident at Grandma's house. Or maybe … maybe. To my disbelief, he tossed me a slingshot fashioned from a lilac branch. Through teary eyes, I thanked him for the gift.

After the gypsy women folded their wares into the bundles, the *babushka* summoned her husband, who was waiting in the street. He drove their wagon to the barnyard and loaded the pig into a crate at the same time as our flock of white geese waddled from the village pond and into our chicken coop. "Nice birds," he commented.

Papa's disdainful glance assured him they were not for sale.

Once the gypsies had departed, my brother fondled the little red pocketknife. "I'm keeping this forever."

"And this slingshot will be with *me* forever." I ran my finger over the intricate pattern carved into the wooden handle. I searched for suitable pebbles to use in the slingshot. Kurt, his tongue wedged out of a corner of his mouth, tested the pocketknife's sharpness by carving his initials in the trunk of a cherry tree. In no time, at all, we were arguing over who had received the better reward that day.

The next morning, we observed the chickens and geese flutter from the coop. "Dammit!" my father yelled. "Those *Zigeuner* sneaked back here after dark and stole two geese! They're probably camped at Pototski Field."

I had seldom seen him run, and never so fast. I struggled to keep pace and nearly tripped over my own feet. When we arrived at the deserted encampment, Papa angrily kicked the cold campfire ashes. "At least they didn't take a pig," he said, trying to console himself.

The day was not yet finished with us. The *clop*, *clop* of horse hooves awakened Kurt and me late that night. We crawled from bed, careful not to wake our sister, and tiptoed to the bedroom window. I pulled back a corner of the curtain and squinted into the moonlit yard. "Looks like Grampa and Uncle Pius," I whispered.

Papa answered the knock on the porch door and we heard

kitchen chairs scraping across the floor. My brother and I edged from the window and crouched beside Loni's dresser near the partially open bedroom door. "If we get caught eavesdropping, we're dead," Kurt murmured.

"Go back to bed, you chicken, but I'm not." I sidled closer to the door.

Uncle Pius spoke first. "I'm sorry it's so late, but we've just come from the Bosers."

"Couldn't this wait 'til morning?" said Papa as he lit the kitchen lantern.

"There's not much time, so hear us out. I talked to Old Andy Boser today. You remember that he and his two sons Rochus and Young Andy and their families are leaving for America next week?"

"*Ya*, and sorry to say, I wish we were going, too." Papa exhaled deeply. "I'm afraid there could be trouble here."

Maybe my dream of going to America would come true! I poked Kurt, but he only rolled his eyes.

"And there might soon be a ban on us Germans buying more land. Guess the government figures we're getting too powerful," my uncle added.

Grandpa spoke again. "It's good your mother can't hear us talk about America, Karl. I don't know why it took me so long to realize it's the smart thing to do. Anyways, now one of Young Andy's boys has trachoma and can't get into America with that eye disease, so his family won't go at this time. Now listen closely, Karl. Since there are no pictures on the passports, do you think it would be a good idea if Pius and Francisca pretend to be Young Andy's family and go to America with Old Andy and Rochus?"

"Certainly not!" Papa said, without hesitation. "Imagine what will happen to them if they get caught."

"Maybe no worse than what might happen if they stay here and this political stupidity carries on. I think they should try to get to America." I heard Grandpa's sigh. "Karl, I'd give you the chance if your family matched the Boser's."

Papa delayed his response, then finally said, "Of course. I'll help anyway I can."

'Ask Grandpa how we can get to America, too,' I thought. 'You'll help your brother, but not your own family.'

I heard the shuffle of feet before Grandpa said, "Here's the situation. Young Andy will trade his family's emigration papers for the land you and Heinz bought from him and—"

"That devil Boser!" Papa's voice shook with anger. "That's not a fair exchange. Those papers couldn't cost nearly as much as we paid for his land."

"I know it's not really even, but Monica is certain Heinz would give up the land, and Pius will give you back right now the hundred rouble down payment you put on the land."

"Even if Heinz and I give the land back to Young Andy, we're still responsible to re-pay the bank loan," Papa said. "And Pius, if you don't get past our customs agents, or the Americans won't let you in, you'll be back here, or in jail, with worthless papers."

"That is true, Karl. And I won't be offended if you don't agree with the plan," said Uncle Pius. "But Young Andy told me they waited over two years for those papers. With the war and all, I don't have that much time." Excitement built in his voice. "You should apply right away for passports, too. Include Father, Heinz, and Monica. I'll write a sponsorship letter for you as soon as we're settled there."

Mama came out of her bedroom rubbing sleep from her eyes. "I overheard what was said and admit that I wasn't keen on buying the land anyway." She placed a hand on her husband's shoulder. "So Karl, you make the decision."

"*Ya-naih*, I've had second thoughts, too." Papa sighed deeply. "Pius, if it's the only way, take the land."

"I am very thankful to both of you," our uncle said, and then cleared his throat before continuing. "Karl, maybe we can do each other a favor here, since you also want to leave Russia soon."

My heart leapt. I dared not look at Kurt for fear of shouting with joy.

Uncle Pius elaborated. "My family matches Young Andy's, except for his twin boys. I need a boy that could pass as a twin to my Barnie. Would you let me take one of *your* sons?"

"What? You're not serious!" Mama exclaimed.

My throat constricted and a small cough escaped my lips. Papa crossed the room and drew our bedroom door shut.

"You idiot, Kisser. Why'd you cough?" Kurt whined under his breath.

"It just came out. I'm sneaking up closer to hear them again."

Kurt grabbed my arm. I jerked free from his grip and crept forward, my brother following so close behind me that I felt his warm breath on my neck. We quietly went down on our hands and knees and then stretched out flat on our bellies with our ears to the gap under the door. The voices seeped through and we plainly heard Uncle Pius say, "If you agree to send him along, I'll let Old Andy and Rochus know first thing in the morning before going back home to Mannheim. They're already leaving for America next Wednesday."

I could imagine the strained look on Mama's face when she asked, "But what if he doesn't want to go?"

Papa's voice softened. "He's too young to decide for himself, Rosina. We'll have to make the decision for him, and God help us if we are wrong. I guess we could always bring him back if things become normal here again."

"I don't know what normal is anymore," Mama sobbed.

"Rosina," our uncle said before he and Grandpa went out into the night, "I swear we'll treat your son like he's one of our own."

The house settled back into silence. My brother and I crept into bed. "Who's it gonna be? You or me?" I asked.

Kurt didn't answer. Instead, he wriggled close and wrapped his arms around me.

In the days that followed, my brother and I spent as much time together as possible. We played stickball with our friends, searched for pebbles to use in my slingshot, and whittled tree branches into crude animal figures with Kurt's pocketknife, all the while keeping the deception secret. Why didn't our parents say which one of us was going with Uncle Pius? Which one might never see his friends again? We studied our features in the mirror to determine who most resembled our cousin Barnie. "My nose is short like his, but you and him both have Gramma's funny squinty eyes," said Kurt.

"What d'you mean? I'd rather have funny eyes than big ears like you."

Kurt plunked himself on the bed. "Mama and Papa are being so nice to me. I bet they'll send me. But I really don't want to go."

"They're nice to me, too." I sat beside him, our shoulders touching. "I just wish both of us could go."

Monday after school, Mama called Kurt aside. "Come, we'll go over to Great-uncle Schwengler's," she said. "Hans, you stay here, please." Herr Schwengler was the village shoemaker.

That evening at the pond, Kurt and I decided that since Mama had ordered new shoes for him, he was the one who would emigrate with Uncle Pius. "But it's *you* who thinks America is heaven," he lamented, skipping a pebble across the water. "I'd rather not go. It'll be a lot of trouble to get there and I might not like it anyway. And what if none of you come over? Then what?"

I couldn't help thinking it should have been me who was chosen, but I understood my brother's feelings. I looked him in the eye and said, "Kurt, for sure, some day I will join you in America." To seal the vow, I spat on a large rock at my feet.

All too soon, it was the morning of the dreaded departure. A somber Kurt and I already knew why the family had gathered in the kitchen earlier than usual, our parents' puffy eyes brimming with tears. My brother, seated on the bench between them, appeared small and fragile when they broke the news as gently as possible. “Promise all of you will come to America,” Kurt said, his bottom lip quivering. “I won’t go unless you *promise*.”

Mama dabbed her tears with the edge of her apron. “We’ll be there before you know it,” she said softly.

Loni clasped her hands over her mouth and stared at Kurt; his place at the table would be vacant tomorrow. I felt dizzy and leaned against a wall; it all seemed like a bad dream. My pulse quickened as Kurt, stoop-shouldered, walked one final time through his home. He trailed his fingers across the furniture in the living room. He paused at the open bedroom door, as if to memorize the details of where he and I slept since we were toddlers, where we had snuggled together on cold nights, scaring each other with horror stories, where we often peeked from the window late at night to investigate mysterious sounds.

On the way to Grandpa’s house, our sister stayed tight beside Kurt, her uncustomary silence relaying how she felt. In an unusual display of affection, Mama and Papa held hands and walked behind them. Despondent, I ignored everyone and kicked a pebble down the street.

Uncle Pius was already piling three bulging burlap sacks in his carriage. Next, he tied two large wooden boxes onto the luggage rack of Grandpa’s carriage while Papa slipped Kurt’s luggage—Mama’s pair of prized leather bags—under the rear seat.

I wasn’t ready to give up Kurt and begged Papa to take me along to meet the train in Karpowa, a predominately Russian town in the opposite direction from Mannheim. When my head drooped, he relented and said, “*Ya-naih*, Hans. Come along then. You can practice driving Cookie and Ghost on the way home. I traded Uncle Pius his outfit for the down payment I put on the Boser land.”

I joined my distressed mother and Kurt on the back seat of Grandpa’s carriage before he could change his mind. Papa and my grandfather sat on the front seat as we rode to the Boser’s yard, where anxious horses harnessed to three overloaded carriages stomped their iron-shod hooves. Fritz and Lothar watched the confusion from atop the stone fence.

"Kurt! Hans! Get over here. You're not going to America," Lothar yelled.

Kurt slowly got out of the carriage and braced himself against a wheel. "I am going, but I don't want—"

Fritz hopped off the fence and grabbed Kurt's shirtsleeve. "What'd you mean you're going? *Ya*, to the train station?"

"I mean to America."

"When are you coming back? Without you, there aren't enough guys to play our games."

"Ach, Fritz. He's only teasing us," Lothar jeered from his perch. "He'll ride to the train station, then come back with his Papa and laugh at us for believing him."

Kurt started blubbering. "I'm really going to m–miss you guys."

Before his friends could reply, Grandpa announced from the driver's seat that it was time to leave for Karpowa. A tearful Loni helped her brother into the open carriage, where he flopped in a miserable heap between Mama and me. I wanted to scream, "Kurt, don't go to America! Let's get off the carriage and go play stickball." Instead, I laid my head against my brother's back and tried not to let my emotions run wild.

It seemed the entire village gathered to say goodbye. Young Andy clarified why Uncle Pius would emigrate now, and his own family would go to America later. The onlookers trudged behind the carriages to the edge of Chornov, all the while chanting the same sorrowful dirge I had heard at Grandma's funeral:

> "No one is exempt from their fate
> Death rules over scepter and crown
> It is vain to think otherwise
> Everything, everything goes back to earth."

As was the custom, Father Heisser sprinkled Holy Water over

the travelers and offered his blessing for a safe crossing of the salt water. The poignant moment matched the agony in my heart. I wondered if I would have the courage to do what Kurt must.

Aunt Monica and my sister jumped, waved, and yelled as we receded into the distance. Kurt stood on the carriage seat and waved, then buried his face in Mama's breast. I curbed my melancholy by counting the *click*, *click*, *click* of the carriage wheels as the seams of the iron tires met the road.

The locomotive at the rail station, much bigger than anything I had ever imagined, smelled of oil and hissed a cloud of steam. Under different circumstances, Kurt would have made a silly comment to get me to laugh. Grandpa and Papa piled the luggage on the platform, while Uncle Pius and the Bosers arranged their tickets with the conductor. Mama drew Aunt Francisca aside and gave her a tablecloth with fine embroidery at the edges. "R-remember us when you use this," Mama said, tears choking her words as they embraced tightly. "And now you'll be Kurt's American mother. Please take care of my boy. I'm so afraid this'll turn out bad and—"

Uncle Pius, wary of drawing suspicion, apologized to Mama for cutting the conversation short and hustled his family aboard the waiting train. I stood tight beside my brother, clinging to the faint hope that he would not leave. Our distraught parents both spoke at the same time to dispense last-minute advice and instructions, but mostly, they smothered their son with hugs and kisses.

The conductor called, 'All aboard.' Kurt threw his arms around my neck, our tears mixing on our cheeks. "I'll be waiting for you in America," he whispered before Uncle Pius grabbed his arm and whisked him away. "Mama! Don't make me go!" Kurt pleaded as the rail car door slammed shut. Papa waved with both hands. Mama sank to her knees.

The train began to move and I raced along the platform when Kurt leaned out an open window. I pulled my slingshot from my back pocket and thrust it into his outstretched hand. A moment later, a red and silver object flashed through the air. I caught it as easily as if playing stickball, then frantically waved Kurt's little red pocketknife above my head. Through my sobs I yelled, "I will, Kurt! Cross my heart! I *will* come to America!" I wasn't sure if he heard me, but at the end of the platform, I stopped running.

5
THERE WOULDN'T BE ANY TEARS FROM ME

November, 1914

Though I swore it could never happen, life did go on, but nothing was the same. I wanted Kurt at home terribly. When my melancholy reached its peak, I knelt at the base of the cherry tree where he had carved his initials and added my own with his pocketknife. Mama plodded through her daily chores, cooking meals and laundering clothes. Her mind, however, I'm sure was with Kurt.

One thing that didn't change was my seemingly innate ability to attract trouble. One pleasant Sunday, my family clambered aboard Uncle Pius' carriage to visit my parents' friends, Lizbet and Dieter Guttenburg, the overseer at Pototski Estate. The estate horseman's son, Ivan Kurganov, and I roamed the huge yard until Hubert Bauman joined us and promptly sent Ivan away. "Ach, he's just a Russian. We don't need him hanging around," Hubert scoffed. "And he doesn't even go to school." Though Russian children could attend school, most of their families were impoverished or didn't value an education. I had not met Ivan previously, but he seemed quite likable and I felt a sense of shame that Hubert shunned him.

We soon wandered to the storage area and Hubert balked when I asked to see his father's motorcar. "We're not s'posed to play in it, but I guess we can *look*," he said, glancing around the yard before we entered the carriage house.

I ran my fingers along the curve of the vehicle's fender and envisioned myself a driver of a fancy car in Fritz's American magazines. Before long, several spare tires and inner tubes hanging on wall pegs caught my attention. "We could make us each a slingshot," I said excitedly.

I tore my short pants on a thorn while unsuccessfully sawing at a branch of an acacia tree then decided, instead, to hack two perfect

Y's from Frau Bauman's groomed lilac hedge.

Back at the carriage house, we cut rubber bands from an inner tube with the little red pocketknife. "Kurt should be here with us," Hubert said.

Somehow, it was comforting to know his friends also missed him.

We heard Dieter's voice as we tied the rubber bands onto the second lilac branch. "What are you doing in here, boys?"

My friend beamed. "We're making slingshots. Hans knows how."

Dieter's face lost all color as he grabbed the slingshot from my hand and peered at the items on the wall. "Hubert, thank God you've only cut one tube. Your father would kill somebody if both of them were ruined. And he still might!"

Upon hearing what we had done, Showman Bauman condemned the 'miscreant' who led his boy astray. While unsure of the meaning of the word, I was sure he meant me, and that I was a troublemaker. Papa reluctantly paid Herr Bauman one rouble—half the cost of the inner tube.

The trip home seemed endless. It would take the money from fifty pairs of crows' feet to repay my debt. I only got four pairs all last summer, and since then Papa had forbidden me to climb trees. However, the loss of Kurt's little red pocketknife bothered me most. I studied the bulge in my father's pocket; the confiscated item was out of my reach for the first time since my separation from Kurt. I envisioned the day I could escape Papa's strict shackles and join Kurt in America. There wouldn't be any tears from me, that's for sure.

One week before Christmas, the first winter storm blew in from the north, but that evening the porch door swung open accompanied by a rush of cold as Grandpa and Aunt Monica hurried inside. We laughed at our aunt's hair sprinkled white with snow. Grandpa waved a long brown envelope above his head. "It's from Pius. They made it!"

Kurt was safe! I danced on the spot. Mama rushed over to Grandpa, her hands trembling as she opened the envelope. She reluctantly passed me a small, carefully folded note with my name printed in bold letters across the back. I shuffled to the kitchen for privacy and propped my elbows on the cupboard. This little note had found its way from America to Chornov. I held it to my chest and imagined Kurt awkwardly forming the words, his tongue wedged in a corner of his mouth; he had always loathed writing assignments. My eyes blurred as I unfolded the single sheet of unlined paper and slowly read:

Hallo Hans,

I sure wish you were here. It's fun most of the time. In Russia, I got tired of riding the train after five days, and I got tired of the ship, too. But then we took another train across a country called Angland. They don't eat the same food as us and I was hungry for Mama's noodles. Back on a ship again, we were all down low in one big room, no beds or nothing. We slept on the floor in our clothes. I got sick from the rocking boat for two days and then was better. In America they eat ice cream. It's so good and kinda tastes like the stuff on cream Kuchen but it's frozen. And the Statue of Licorice is a big woman holding a burning stick, and it's even taller than St Gustav's Church. They have little stones on the railroads too. I shot some with your slingshot once when the train stopped.

Tell Fritz and Lothar and the other guys hallo.

Your American brother, Kurt

Mixed emotions clouded my mind. I had selfishly hoped the officials would turn him back, but now found myself wishing him happiness in America. I wiped my eyes and slumped toward Mama as she finished reading Uncle Pius' letter:

All along the journey, we were pushed through line-ups and had few problems. We were possibly the last passengers to cross the Atlantic for some time, as the war effort is claiming all available ships. I'll never forget your sacrifices for us and will send you money when I'm able. I pray for Heinz's safe return every day.

After an awkward pause, my family heaved a collective sigh of relief. Mama dabbed her eyes on her sleeve. "Hans, can you read Kurt's letter for us, or is it only for you?" she said.

I stood on the worn hemp rug in front of the sofa, and read aloud, my voice shaking. Loni decided something frozen couldn't be delicious and Kurt must still be seasick. The adults laughed at Kurt's reference to the 'Statue of Licorice.' When I read, 'Your American brother,' Papa silently walked to the porch.

We celebrated a subdued Christmas without Kurt, Uncle Heinz, and Grandma; no colorful paper streamers, no fruit tree twigs blooming in water-filled jars. That evening, the *Kriskringel* presented us with paper baskets constructed by Loni earlier in the week. The enclosed treats—two cookies and a thick slice of halvah—had seemed tastier when I had shared them with Kurt. And he had always joked that the cookies were fresh because the generous visitor carried a *Backofen* under her long flowing skirt. We would throw ourselves on the floor, rolling and laughing until our sister complained that we would embarrass her forever.

After Loni and I recited a popular verse to Grandpa and Aunt Monica on New Year's Day, our grandfather gave each of us a rouble. With a long face, I placed mine in Papa's outstretched hand as repayment for destroying Herr Bauman's inner tube. It didn't seem fair; Herr Bauman had claimed both the slingshots and the payment, even though the damaged tube couldn't be replaced because of the war.

"*Ya*, and I know an old New Year's verse, too," Grandpa said cheerfully, perhaps sensing the heavy mood:

> "We wish you a Happy New Year
> A pretzel and a beer
> And a candy as big as a platter.
> Give us a shot of whiskey
> And we'll scatter."

I glanced around the room filled with laughter, and realized that despite feeling sad, one could act happy.

6

DON'T EVER THINK LIKE THAT

March, 1915

One evening during mealtime, Grandpa stomped into our kitchen, immediately lit his pipe, and pointed the stem at no one in particular. "When my usual *Eureka Rundschau* wasn't in the mail today, Herr Ostertag told me our government won't allow American newspapers into Russia anymore, not in English or German," he said. "And the Russian one from Odessa isn't allowed to report on the war or politics. Worst of all, a unit of the Czar's army wants to billet here in Chornov. Apparently, they're going to conscript every healthy male over eighteen. Cannon fodder for the collapsing Western Front, I'd say." He shook his head in disgust and flopped into a chair.

"Surely they wouldn't take a man who has children at home," Papa reasoned.

Indeed, the conscription soldiers *did* take Papa away. For days, Mama confined herself to her bedroom with the door closed, the loss of Kurt and now her husband unbearable. Her sobs nearly broke my heart, and the tray of food I set beside her bed every evening often went untouched. Loni, though also saddened, performed the household duties. For my part, I missed Papa terribly. I missed him sitting at the kitchen table. I missed his habit of brushing the hair back from his forehead. I even missed him correcting my behavior. Moreover, his importance with the outdoor chores soon became apparent. Though I had helped care for the animals, he had performed the most strenuous tasks. Now I struggled to keep the trough filled with water and carried mounds of hay with my small pitchfork. Before long, I realized how tedious adult responsibilities really were.

As time allowed, once their own chores were finished,

Grandpa and Aunt Monica came to my rescue. One evening, over the sound of milk spurting into the metal milk pail, Grandpa railed against the Czar's wartime policies, the most recent a ban on speaking German in public. "*Ya*, I can talk Russian, but who will report me for talking our own language? *Bürgermeister* Redekop? He's our town mayor and German to boot."

"But not everybody living here is German," Aunt Monica retorted. "What about the Yablonskis, Headmaster Blokin, and the two teachers who came after our German ones were fired? They're all Russian, and might like a chance to get one over on a German. And the Jewish Goldsteins speak German, but aren't really part of our *Volksdeutsche* community."

While listening to the conversation, the reality of the situation sunk in: each member of my family played a different role. Grandpa stewed over the war, my aunt worried about her husband and acted as Grandpa's sounding board, my sister helped Mama, who tried her best to be cheerful, and I did the chores and asked God's forgiveness for all the bad thoughts I had harbored toward Papa.

Later in the summer, our family received what we considered a gift from God—Uncle Heinz returned from the army, albeit his left arm missing below the elbow, the circumstances of which he didn't relate to us. We were overjoyed to see him, but disappointed that he had not seen or heard about Papa.

Though Uncle Heinz's injury hindered his farming abilities, his return gave Grandpa free time to join an informal deciphering pool. He and his friends collected personal letters the villagers had received from foreign countries, and then pieced together political information from sections overlooked by the censors. They soon learned Czar Nicholas II had recently signed a truce with Germany and Austria. My uncle feared some of the newly discharged soldiers might be far from home and would scavenge in our area, so he insisted my family move in with Grandpa, while he and Aunt Monica would move into our smaller house. That way there would be a man in each household. Mama felt sure Papa would soon return from the army, but she agreed to the move to please her brother-in-law.

Loni occupied the smallest bedroom and Mama slept in the second room. My grandfather and I shared the master bedroom and often had enjoyable conversations while snuggled in our beds separated by Grandma's large dresser. One morning we discussed the land loan. "The bank gave us money to buy the land from Young Andy Boser," he responded to my question. "But since we gave the land back to him in exchange for the emigration papers, if I don't make the payments, the bank will claim it from him."

"Sooo, not paying the loan wouldn't hurt you none. Uncle Pius is in America and no—"

Grandpa bolted upright in his bed. "Johannes! Don't ever think like that. I promised Herr Boser that either Uncle Pius or I would make the loan payments, and by God, it will be paid, even if it takes everything I've got. I gave him my *word*."

The passion in my grandfather's voice reminded me of the last time I saw my father. He stumbled through the kitchen early one morning before he opened the porch door to confront two noisy soldiers in the yard. I remember peeking out my bedroom window and hearing their heated argument. "Damn it, I've got two children to feed! For the love of God, listen to me," hissed Papa, still dressed in his nightshirt.

The captain's gruff voice sounded forbidding. "Every able-bodied man has to go fight the damn Germans."

Papa waved a fist in the officer's face. "If the Germans win, maybe we'll be—"

I shuddered as a private lunged forward and smashed the butt of his rifle into Papa's lower back. He slowly pulled himself to his feet and, prodded by his escorts, staggered through the porch and to his bedroom. Mama stifled her cries while Papa dressed, then stuffed clothes and provisions into a duffle bag. I jumped back into bed and cowered beneath the covers, my heart racing wildly.

When he came into our bedroom, a soldier followed, blocking the hallway door. Papa hugged and kissed Loni, who clung to him until he promised to come home soon. When he spoke in German, the soldier ordered, 'Russian!' but Papa ignored him.

Next, my father knelt at the edge of my bed, large tears rolling down his cheeks. "*Ya-naih*, Johannes. I have to say goodbye, but it won't be for long. *You* are the man of the house now. Mind your mother and keep up your chores." He reached into his pocket and then placed Kurt's little red pocketknife in my trembling hands. "I know you'll behave yourself while I'm away." For the first time in memory, my father pulled me close and kissed me on both cheeks. He rose to his feet and snarled at the guard, "Let's go, so you're out of my house."

I heard the porch door slam and rushed to the bedroom window, but he and the soldiers had already disappeared into the morning haze. Papa! Would I ever see him again?

7
WORK MAKES LIFE SWEET
July, 1916

Spring rains gave way to clear weather and the crops ripened, however, the army had confiscated all gasoline in the area the previous autumn and, consequently, Herr Bauman's tractors stood idle. Grandpa sold him the team of plow horses for a premium price, leaving the two carriage horses, Ghost and Cookie, to struggle with Papa's old mower; our draft horses, Henry and Herta, easily pulled Uncle Heinz's mower.

One afternoon as the teams plodded around the communal field, I fought boredom by considering the recent changes in my life. When Ivan Kurganov's father died in the war last winter, Herr Bauman insisted the family leave Pototski Estate, so Ivan and his mother moved into a barely inhabitable house next door to Yuri Yablonski. Fritz, Ivan and I spent leisure time with Georg Frey, often playing tag on the frozen pond. During very cold spells, we huddled inside the house, appreciative of the warmth cast by the compacted blocks of manure and straw smoldering in the stove. The bonus was that whenever we stopped at the Freys' house, Katie had a timid smile for me.

The noise from Erasmus Goldstein's threshing unit passing by on the road brought me back to the present. Grandpa jerked the horses to a halt. "I wonder where the hell he's going. He should be setting up here to start harvest for us in a few days."

We joined a group of village men already on the road, where Herr Klatt, the Communal Land Coordinator, waved for Goldstein to stop. Erasmus heaved his bulky frame from the steam tractor towing the threshing machine. His bushy mustache twitched like a squirrel's tail as he spoke. "Showman Bauman offered me double what you were giving me. I'm a businessman, not a charity, and I gotta go where I get the best deal. Now get out of my way."

The usually mild-mannered Herr Klatt accosted Goldstein.

"You bastard! We've hired you for years, and now you run off to a higher bidder. Where's your goddamn loyalty? Besides, when Bauman gets the parts to repair his own machine, he'll fire you and—"

"He won't get any parts," Erasmus shot back. "Every farm implement factory in this godforsaken country was re-tooled to make equipment for the army. If my machine breaks down, I'll never get to your crops, and nor will anybody else."

The Chornov farmers' had no choice but to use their outdated threshing floors. I led Herta as she dragged the threshing wheel—a heavy implement the shape of a fluted log—across the stalks spread out on the circular floor of packed earth. Next, I raked away the straw and gathered the shelled grain kernels into burlap sacks while Grandpa cut the binding twine and spread more sheaves on the floor. When he apologized, saying that the job would last all winter, I told him that thirteen-year-olds did not need more schooling. Although I put on a brave face so Grandpa wouldn't feel guilty, I secretly wished to be with my friends and would gladly have gone back to class.

Soon, Uncle Heinz, Aunt Monica, and Yuri Yablonski, our hired hand for the duration of harvest, halted beside the threshing floor with another bulging load of sheaves. My uncle appeared both smug and worried. "Now Erasmus Goldstein's outfit has broken down, too." He nudged Yuri on the shoulder. "And tell him your news. Go on."

Yuri, a raw-boned man with a weathered face and crusty elbows that poked through holes in his sleeves, nervously cast his eyes to the ground. "Mister Bauman will give me a lot more than you are. I don't wanna leave you, Wilhelm, but I've got six kids to feed."

"That crook Bauman! First, he steals our machine, then he tries to steal our worker." Grandpa broke off abruptly. "Sorry, Yuri. You're just back from the army and have no money. Do what's best for your family."

Yuri managed a nod before trudging toward our gate. He seemed to regret letting us down.

"*Ya-naih*, we'll have to finish the harvesting ourselves.

Besides, work makes life sweet and laziness rots your bones. You don't want to grow up with weak bones, do you, Hans?" Grandpa said.

"I want to be strong and go to America." I threw back my shoulders and stood so erect that my chest bulged.

That evening at supper, Loni, having completed Form Eight, the highest level attainable in Chornov, told Grandpa about a milkmaid job at Pototski Estate. His response was predictable. "No relative of mine is gonna work for that crook!" he yelled, pacing circles around the table.

Mama told him that my sister could work for Ira Goldstein as a chambermaid, but he was only paying half as much. "And you already said your family's never again going to help that Jew Erasmus or anybody remotely related to him," she added.

"And nobody's going to."

Mama relished her triumph. "Then that leaves Showman's offer, and he'll even supply her with work boots."

Grandpa flopped into his overstuffed chair. "*Ya-naih*, I'll agree to it, if she really wants to work there." He paused and rubbed his stubbly chin. "I wonder how he can get boots when nobody else can?"

One afternoon in early 1917, Grandpa returned home and proudly announced the letter-deciphering pool discovered why the Czar recently declared all assemblies illegal, including church services, corn-husking day, and village meetings at the town hall. "A quarter million people in St. Petersburg got together to protest poor wages, and he doesn't want any other big groups to form marches and cause him more trouble," he said, throwing a scribbled-in notebook on the table. "And his advisors, especially Alexander Kerensky, are encouraging them to unionize. There's bound to be some changes."

Sure enough, Saint Gustav's Church bell chimed loudly one mid-afternoon the following month. A sudden chill passed over me. Perhaps some of the recruited men, including Papa, had come home. Although he had been away two years, it seemed much longer. As Grandpa and I left our yard, we met Uncle Heinz and Gus Vetter, who carried an old shotgun under his arm. "No damn soldier's gonna surprise me again, Vilhelm," he said, responding to Grandpa's raised eyebrows. Ever since being kicked in the face by the recruiting soldier, Gus spoke with a slight impediment.

Herr Hoffer shrilled above the din in the churchyard. "Can you believe it? The Czar gave up and ran. He's gone!"

The ecstatic villagers slapped each other on the back and noisily followed our priest into church. When Ira Goldstein slipped into a rear pew, Whiskey Wolff, the local drunk, shouted that a Jew had no place in a Catholic church.

Father Heisser retaliated that Herr Goldstein had a right to stay to hear the news. He cleared his throat. "Our bishop in Odessa has informed me that on March eighth, the revolutionaries forced Czar Nicholas II to abdicate. Alexander Kerensky has assumed control of the provisional government and he has rescinded the Czar's restrictive wartime measures. We can once again hold regular Mass, speak our language in public, and our German teachers are allowed to resume their classes."

When Herr Goldstein slipped out from the pew and quietly closed the church door behind him, I wondered if Jews ever prayed.

After several months, Kerensky re-committed the Russian Army to fighting the Germans, but faltering discipline within his own troops forced him to negotiate a truce that allowed German soldiers to occupy our country. Only a few of the men conscripted from Chornov struggled home from the front lines. I was hopeful somebody had seen my father in the army, but all they related were harrowing stories of the scarcity of food, inadequate clothing, and filth and rodents in the trenches. Nightmares of a rat chewing on Papa's feet disturbed my sleep for weeks.

A much-anticipated letter from Uncle Pius arrived shortly before harvest. “This letter doesn’t have sections censored out,” Mama said with delight, but when she read further, she frowned. “Now America is in the godforsaken war, too. It’s a blessing that Pius’ boys and Kurt aren’t old enough to be recruited.”

She handed Grandpa the letter. He read, “*Father, my crops are poor and I can’t send the loan payment for the land,*” then shook his head and slowly folded the paper.

If our uncle had no money, did Kurt have boots to wear? Maybe America wasn’t heaven after all.

“I guess if we sold Ghost and Cookie to raise money for the payment, we’d still have Herta and Henry. And the money would pay more than half the loan. Imagine, Hans. I’ll get at least a thousand roubles for the team, the same as what the Boser land is actually worth now. But two years ago, horses sold for only two hundred roubles and the land was sixteen hundred. Maybe this upside-down pricing will straighten out soon.”

His melancholy was akin to my own; I had learned the loss of someone or something one loves can be painful. Despite the time that had passed, thoughts of Papa and Kurt still popped into my mind when least expected.

8

MIGHT NOT BE YOURS FOR LONG

November, 1917

My grandfather said he could feel it in his aching bones that something was about to happen, and not for the good. Less than a week later, a mounted contingent stormed into Chornov. I stood near the back of the crowd on Church Street and admired the studded saddles on the groomed horses. A tall imposing man with slick black hair and piercing eyes swung off his steed and marched up the church steps. "We Bolsheviks have ousted Kerensky and his provisional government. The Revolution of 1917 will be pivotal in the history of our country!" he shouted in Russian, while pumping his fist in the air. He identified himself as Igor Kronchin, a college student from Odessa, and then introduced his well-armed party of young communists. "We are the new political force. There will be a special announcement in your town hall at two o'clock this afternoon. Everyone over the age of twenty—male or female, Russian or German—must attend. And don't be late!"

Herr Redekop plodded up the steps and confronted Kronchin. "I'm the *Bürgermeister* of this village, and will not allow—"

Kronchin looked down his nose at the plump man. "And now *I'm* the administrator here. And don't you ever again wag your fat finger in my face. Understand?"

"B-but I was elected—"

"Where is Pototski Estate?" the Bolshevik shouted louder than necessary. When no one answered, an assistant tapped Redekop's chest with a bayonet and ordered, "You! Make sure the owner is at that meeting!"

At the designated hour, I settled myself into a large tree beside the hall, now nearly filled to capacity. Fifteen minutes later, Lothar's older brother, Martin Degenstein, the Bauman's current horseman, halted a team of matched blacks nearby. The door of the enclosed carriage with tassels dangling from a padded leather roof swung open. The Showman stepped out, threw his hat on the seat, and adjusted the lapels of his jacket. Frau Bauman, wearing a bright purple hat with a large bow and a white feather angled to one side, accepted Martin's hand as she descended the metal steps. The Baumans entered the hall arm-in-arm as if they were royalty.

I edged along a branch to peer into the hall through an open window. Frau Bauman took a seat in the last row beside Frau Klatt, while her husband marched forward to address the administrator. Igor Kronchin, flanked by two armed men, drummed his fingers on an old desk at the front of the room. "The meeting started at two o'clock!"

"I'll get here when I damn well please," Bauman said as he motioned to the assembled villagers. "You can play Lord of Chornov if these people won't stand up for themselves, but you will not rule Pototski Estate." He smirked and sauntered to the back of the hall.

Kronchin pursed his lips and raked the crowd over with his eyes as he opened a small leather-bound notebook. "The new policy of the Communist Party will affect all of you. According to our dogma, from this day forward, all farmland in Russia, whether communal or privately owned, belongs to the State. No landowner shall be exempt. The government of 'The People' will take control."

A sound like a huge deflating lung filled the room, the occupants staring at one another in disbelief. Benedict Bauman's voice rang out in indignation. "Who the hell do you think you are to say we have to donate our property? My grandfather was a colonist from Germany, and shared in the original communal land grant from the Czar. My father bought hundreds of additional acres to produce grain for Russia's exports, as I am doing. We paid for that land with sweat, hard work, and good money, and now you communists want it for *nothing*?"

Igor Kronchin jumped up from behind the desk. "You're right. You and your despicable ancestors acquired that land with sweat—the sweat of your laborers, your house servants, and your milkmaids. You barely gave them enough to eat while you grew fat," he thundered.

"I'm gonna like your communism," Herr Bauman's senior driver Oleg drawled, rubbing the scars on his cheek. After a tedious day of plowing last spring, he had fallen asleep at the wheel and had driven the tractor into a tree. His boss, incensed, had rained cutting blows on the hired man's head and shoulders with a riding quirt.

Showman glared at him. "You're fired! *All* you lazy Russians are fired! Don't any of you ever again set foot on Pototski Estate."

"Might not be yours for long. Maybe I'll get more use out of it than you will." A grin flooded Oleg's face.

I heard Gus' voice. "I'm not givin' any government bastards my land!"

Grandpa bellowed above the crowd. "What the goddamn hell are you talking about, Kronchin?"

Kronchin waited a considerable time for the dissent to cool before speaking. "Furthermore, to aid in the modernization of our new communist state, every landowner will pay a tax of six roubles an acre on his former holdings. And to provide the funds, we will allow you to continue with this year's harvest." Two guards drew their pistols and glared at the protesting villagers when the leader's voice turned bitter and cold. "Now listen, and listen closely! One month from today, I will return to collect the tax. Failure to pay will result in incarceration until the debt is settled."

Herr Ripplinger surged forward. "This is preposterous! You *steal* our land, then expect us to *pay* you for the privilege?"

The frustrated administrator straightened in his chair and said, "I don't make the rules, I am only here to enforce them."

Showman Bauman spun around on his heel. "Let's get out of here, Irma. These jokers have no jurisdiction over me. Martin. Untie the horses!"

Kronchin began to raise a hand, then seemed to change his mind and declared the meeting over. His troops hustled behind him from the hall, leaving us to digest our new prospects.

I scrambled down the tree and ran to the front step. Ivan's mother, Katya, a lithe woman I thought would be quite pretty if she combed her hair more often, invited Oleg to stay with them. He accepted her generosity before they joined the landless Germans crowding around the vocal Whiskey Wolff. Meanwhile, the landowners whispering in small groups were well aware of their impending losses; even I understood the severity of the decree.

Desperate to finish his harvest without the Russian workers, Showman Bauman rode his horse into the village early the next morning and hired able-bodied Germans, offering twice the wage if they owned a gun. By late afternoon, he had posted armed men along the perimeter of Pototski Estate on twenty-four hour watch.

Mama and Loni had already gone to bed when Uncle Heinz arrived home after checking on Aunt Monica's family in Mannheim. "They're not happy about the communists' ruling, either, but everybody's all right," he reported.

Grandpa anxiously related to him the solution proposed by the Chornov Civic Council. "Those Bolsheviks don't know the strength of our Kutschurgan colony," he said, puffing furiously on his pipe. "We Germans in this area always stick together to the end. Four of us landowners and Philip Klatt are going to Odessa on Monday along with representatives from the other six villages to protest this new land policy. What do you—"

Suddenly, the door porch rattled and Gus Vetter poked his head inside. "Quick, guys. Come see this."

We dashed down our flagstone path to the gate. A long line of men, rifle barrels glinting in the moonlight, reined their steeds onto Middle Avenue and cantered into the night along Pototski Road. "I bet that arrogant *Arshloch* Kronchin is going out to knock Bauman down a peg," Gus stated.

Grandpa shook his head. "Benedict's already got most of Chornov's men as guards, and a lot of our guns, too, so there's no way we'd be much help to him."

Nevertheless, Uncle Heinz and Gus rode to Pototski Estate while Grandpa stayed behind, pacing the floor. He neglected to send me to bed and I certainly wasn't going to leave the room voluntarily. Peering out the window reminded me of the time Uncle Pius asked our parents if Kurt could go with them to America. I realized that my thoughts over the last few days hadn't included my brother. Did Kurt still think about us—about me—every day?

Uncle Heinz finally stumbled into the kitchen in the middle of the night. He dragged himself to a chair, his forehead beaded with perspiration. "We didn't go too close because of the shooting. Then we saw the workers' quarters go up in flames and …" He put his hands over his face and fell silent.

I hoped that my friend Hubert Bauman was safe.

Grandpa patted my uncle's shoulder. "Thank goodness Lizbet went back to Elsass when Dieter was called to the army. God help me, who would have thought it'd get this violent? And Heinz, were any of the village men that Bauman hired hurt?"

"Apparently they grabbed their guns and abandoned their posts when Kronchin's men rode up and started shooting."

"*Ya*, the problem is there's no other road out of Pototski, except through Chornov. I think we should warn everybody, just in case Kronchin and his bunch want to push their weight around here." Grandpa turned to me. "Hans, run to as many houses as you can. Start with the Freys and go all the way up our street, then back down Church Street. Heinz, you go the other way. I'll take the east end."

Uncle Heinz pulled me to his side. In his eyes, I saw panic barely restrained. "And tell them to hide the women and girls."

Were the women and girls, but not the boys, in danger?

Mist from the pond drifted across the street in eerie black shapes as dawn crept over the horizon. Near the far end of my assigned route Herr Bauman's carriage, trailed by a dozen armed men, appeared on Pototski

Road. Something inside me screamed, "Run for home!" but there wasn't time. I quickly climbed a linden tree and disappeared among the autumn foliage.

The closed carriage made a wide turn in front of the church and came to a halt below me. I slowly, quietly, climbed higher, my fingers fumbling for grip. The door burst open and two burly men wrestled Herr Bauman from the carriage. His hands were bound behind his back, a torn sleeve of his stained rumpled shirt flapped at his side, his left ear hung loose. Dark red seeped from an open wound on the top of his bald head. He blinked coagulated blood and morning sunshine from his swollen eyes as one of the men forced him up the steps to the elevated luggage platform at the rear of the carriage. Igor Kronchin climbed onto the platform and stood beside the captive. "Kuzma, go ring the church bell," he ordered one of his men. "And Attila, do you still have that rope in your saddlebag?"

My heart pounded as the one called Attila climbed onto the carriage roof. He knotted the thick rope to a sturdy branch above Herr Bauman's head and dropped the other end to the platform. When the administrator slipped a crude noose around his prisoner's neck, my right hand involuntarily clutched my throat.

The ringing church bell attracted the bleary-eyed village men. They jostled with the guards and shouted for the release of Bauman, who appeared confused and steadfastly gazed at the white cross on Saint Gustav's steeple. Yuri, Oleg, and the other Russian harvest workers banished by Bauman gathered near the carriage, but Ivan stood leaning against a tree at the fringe of the crowd. I saw Grandpa and Uncle Heinz, their heads turning in every direction, but dared not call out to them.

Father Heisser hurried from the rectory as quickly as his arthritic hips would allow, shouting as he approached the carriage. "Keep your men out of my church! And release this man! He is a child of God."

Kronchin glared down from his position beside Herr Bauman. "There's no place for your God in the Soviet state, just as there is no longer any place for this ruthless capitalist."

The mounted men formed a circle around the carriage, forcing back both the villagers and the agitated priest. Herr Bauman teetered on his feet as the nervous team caused the carriage to sway. He tried to grasp the edge of the roof behind him, barely able to stay upright. I prayed someone would undo the noose.

The administrator seized the opportunity to condemn Herr Bauman and all estate owners. "These rich men, these *kulaks*, are nothing but parasites and must be removed from Soviet society," he said. He spat on Showman's dusty boots. "This … this despicable person's land and all his possessions are now the property of The People. And his family has been disinherited by the government. Anyone who aids them will be judged guilty of this man's crimes and sentenced to a similar fate—banishment to hard labor in the Arctic." After a pause, Kronchin's face opened in a grin. "To save me the bother of taking him to Odessa, who wants to lay the whip to this fine pair of horses? Come on, surely this man has enemies."

"*I* have reason to do it," Katya Kurganov screamed. "My Boris was so proud to be your horseman and you wouldn't pay a measly bribe to keep him out of the army. He died there and you *owe* him … and you owe his boy Ivan!"

Herr Bauman worked his lips as if to answer her. At the same moment, I heard a distinctive whir and saw a small stone ricochet off the rump of one of the horses in the team. As the frightened animal plunged forward, Kronchin and Herr Bauman lost their balance and tumbled from the platform. The rope around Herr Bauman's neck emitted an angry hum and snapped taut. The thick tree branch bent under his weight until his feet almost touched the ground, and then it re-bounded, flipping Herr Bauman into the air. A shower of yellow leaves fluttered around his twitching body as he bounced at the end of the rope like a rag doll.

A collective "*Naaaih*!" hissed from the lungs of the stunned villagers; they had witnessed the unimaginable. After a staunch-faced guard calmed the rearing horses, Kronchin slapped the dust from his trousers, jumped into the carriage, and led his men away from Chornov at a gallop.

From my vantage point, I saw Ivan stuff a slingshot into his back pocket and run to his mother's side. My mind reeled. Where did he get a slingshot?

Two men clutched Herr Bauman's waist and lifted his body to relieve the strain on his neck. "Somebody get a knife! Hurry up and cut that rope off," one of them yelled.

I shook the fright from my legs and shimmied halfway down the tree to the branch securing the noose. Praying for strength, I hacked with Kurt's pocketknife until the rope fell free. The men below me gently placed Herr Bauman's body on the ground, his neck kinked at a sharp angle.

As Father Heisser administered the last sacraments, a wailing Irma Bauman staggered into the village on the arm of Hubert; her youngest son and two older daughters limped behind them. Frau Bauman dropped to the ground beside her husband and gently wiped blood from his bloated face with her mud-spattered skirt. She was barely recognizable as the woman who only two days earlier had swaggered into the town hall. Hubert knelt beside his mother and placed a hand on his father's chest.

In spite of Kronchin's threat, the old priest guided the family to the rectory, while four village men trailed them carrying the body. If the priest had not sheltered the Baumans, perhaps someone else would have offered their home. Although concerned for Hubert, I was relieved Grandpa had not taken the risk.

When my grandfather ran to the bottom of the tree, I slid from my perch and collapsed into his arms. "Too bad you had to see what happened," he said, brushing leaves from my clothes and hair. He pressed my face against his chest and offered me his handkerchief. "There was nothing you could have done to help Herr Bauman."

The Russians shouted ugly threats and curses, angry that we Germans accused one of them of throwing the stone that startled the horse. Afraid the tempers might create a riot, I tugged at Grandpa's arm and, reluctant to tattle on my friend, said, "Maybe Ivan didn't have anything to do with it, but after the stone hit the horse, I saw him put a slingshot in his back pocket."

"Hans, are you sure about what you're saying?"

"Th-that's what I saw from up in the tree, but maybe—"

"We should tell Herr Redekop. He might not be *Bürgermeister* anymore, but he'll know what to do."

Herr Redekop listened to my observation. "Come on," he said to us. "We'll find out if there's anything to it."

We walked to the Russian group. Ivan, hiding behind his mother, immediately broke into tears. "I-I hit Mister Bauman's horse, but it was an accident. I wanted to hit *him* for what he did to my family. He should've paid the bribe—"

"Give me the weapon. It will be destroyed," the former *Bürgermeister* said. Ivan's mother handed over the charred slingshot. "Now, the way I see it," he continued, "since you did not intend to fatally injure Herr Bauman, you are not guilty of a crime. But if you were an adult, the situation could be quite different." He glanced around. "Does everyone agree?"

A murmur of approval spread through the crowd. As I turned to leave, Ivan tapped my shoulder. "My mama said that you told what you saw. I'm not mad at you, just so you know."

"I'm not mad at you either, Ivan, but where did you get the slingshot? Hubert's father took them away from us."

"I grabbed one from the fire when the workers were burning the garbage. The other one was already in flames." Ivan dropped his gaze to the ground. "I'm sorry I didn't tell you. Are we still friends?"

"We are, Ivan. I know how hard it is when something happens that you didn't intend in the first place." I truly regretted constructing the object that caused Herr Bauman's death.

The priest arranged the burial service held the following day for Herr Bauman. I stood beside Mama, recalling the pain of Grandma's death as the pallbearers lowered the casket into the ground. Before we left the cemetery, Hubert told me the priest had given his family a few roubles to start a new life in Odessa, where no one would recognize them as *kulaks*. The Landowners Commission, going to the city to clarify the land policy and have Igor Kronchin charged with murder, offered them a ride. I realized my fondness for Hubert when he bade me goodbye as the carriages rolled away. I selfishly did not allow myself to dwell on how Hubert must feel—he had lost everything.

The Landowners Commission returned home three days later. Grandpa was beside himself with fury. "Even after we petitioned along with Mannheim and Selz and the other Kutschurgan villages, the Minister of Agriculture still insisted the State has a right to take our farm land, and that's the final word."

Uncle Heinz's features darkened. "And I have news for you, too." He related the events of the previous day. Word had spread around Chornov that Oleg Golubov rode to Karpowa and announced the news about Showman Bauman's possessions. A parade of wagons headed toward Pototski Estate, and returned a few hours later. I had watched from atop the stone fence at the side of our yard as Oleg proudly waved from the driver's seat of Showman's large wagon. Four black draft horses pulled the load of beds, tables, and dining chairs; a delicate sofa upholstered in green brocade teetered on top. Six milk cows tethered to the rear of the wagon struggled to keep pace, their full udders bouncing off their back knees, while Yuri followed close behind with a buckboard piled high with booty.

"*Ya-naih*, that happened because Krochin said Bauman's property now belongs to The People. The next thing he'll say is that ours does, too, and there's not a goddamn thing we can do about it." Grandpa hardly took a breath before continuing to speak. "But the first thing is that tax they claim we owe on our former land holdings. If that makes any sense—"

"I thought about that while you were in Odessa. We should finish the harvest, pay their tax, and hide the rest of the grain. I don't trust those communist bastards for one minute."

"I agree about the tax, there's no way out of that, even if we won't have enough wheat to roast for *pripps*, as much as I hate that drink."

"*Ya*, it does taste like dishwater, not coffee," Uncle Heinz chuckled, then turned serious. "But what about the murder charge? Is Kronchin going to trial for Bauman's hanging?"

"That was the worst of it. The head of the state police cursed us for being insolent. He said our administrator is the absolute law in our village. It pisses me off. A good-for-nothing Russian instead of our German *Bürgermeister* is going to run Chornov?"

The former landowners spent two stressful days hauling grain to the brokers in Karpowa; they were unwilling to test Kronchin, with Benedict Bauman's demise fresh in their memory. On the day the land taxes were due Grandpa, my uncle, and I walked to the town hall a few minutes before noon. This time, ten men, each with a pistol strapped to his hip, accompanied Kronchin. The line extended out the door, and every landowner approached the table in turn to pay their tax. Franz Frey had chosen to be last for a reason. He wrung his cap in his hands and said, "Sir, I'm sorry, but I simply don't have the money."

Kronchin slammed shut his ledger and without looking up ordered, "There will be no favors or extensions. Get him out of here right now." Two of his men marched out the door, a distraught Herr Frey between them. The administrator rose to his feet, his voice filled with confidence. "As you know, all farmland now belongs to the State. To ensure it is put to good use, ten acres will be allotted to each family, and any surplus land can be leased from the State."

Families that previously farmed large tracts pounced on the opportunity to lease additional land and make use of their machinery; smaller farmers and the former landless—Whisky Wolff, several other families, and the Russians—settled for their allotted plots. Before the day was over, Grandpa managed to lease an additional ten acres of quality land, much smaller than his previous holdings, but the best that circumstances would allow.

Outside the hall, Gus kicked a hitching post with his worn boots, losing his balance and falling to one knee. I dared not laugh—the mood was dead serious. "I overheard that prick Kronchin tell his men to take Franz to the Mannheim jail, an' if the taxes aren't paid in a veek, they'll send him to a *konzlager*," he said, brushing manure from his pants. "You know, one of those damn vork camps in the far north."

"Maybe we should pay Franz's taxes from the Chornov Emergency Fund," Young Andy said.

Whiskey Wolff thrust forward his pitted red nose. "That money's for all us citizens. If we rescue every farmer who can't pay his debt, it'll be gone and the rest of us won't have got anything out of it. I say we take a vote."

It was determined that Whiskey had the right to demand a vote. The former landless group lost by a small margin and huffed away, hurling insults over their shoulders.

I dreaded the thought of Katie losing her father, and breathed a sigh of relief when Herr Frey's taxes were paid and he returned to his grateful family the next day.

The November Eleventh Armistice in 1918 ended the war in Europe, and the occupying German forces withdrew from Russia. The communists disbanded the Czar's Imperial Army and formed the Red Army, enforcing the slogan that the poor had the right to demand justice from the rich. Factory and industry employees—The Workers' Columns—were permitted to collect foodstuffs from farmers, even by raiding granaries. Grandpa's response was one of fury and concern. "That's the same as when the government stole our land! And the sham of the law we have now actually encourages it."

9

NOW YOU HAVE A SECRET

December, 1918

On Christmas Eve, every Catholic in Chornov attended the most celebrated Mass of the year. I polished the family's shabby footwear with a mixture of coal dust and goose grease. Loni primped her hair in front of the mirror in the hall and happily confided to me that yesterday Martin Degenstein had tried to kiss her. Our conversation ended when Grandpa yelled from the kitchen, "*Hahnah*, Apallonia, we'll be late for church. Besides, it's only the devil's arse you're seeing after looking in the mirror for that long. Let's go!"

Before Mass, Herr Reinbold removed a bundle from under his coat. The recent ruling that religious possessions belonged to the state had prompted Father Heisser to place a bag of cherished items—the chalice, incense burner, and a small golden crucifix—in the sacristy following each Mass. After Father left the church, an unidentified parishioner would take the bag home for safekeeping until the next service. As such, the priest, if interrogated, would not know the location of the bag.

In the midst of Father Heisser's encouraging sermon on the salvation of mankind made possible by Christ's birth, Ira Goldstein burst open the church doors. "Raiders! Raiders!" he yelled, his nightshirt flapping as he ran up the aisle. He panted and spun around to face the congregation. "Raiders are stealing horses and everything."

In the pandemonium that followed, I avoided Mama and lost myself among the men jostling out the door. Gus Vetter grabbed a long, narrow bag propped in a corner and pulled out his old shotgun. When an orange streak flashed from the north end of Church Street, the report echoing like thunder, Gus threw his weapon to his shoulder and emptied both barrels in response. Hoof beats on the frozen ground faded into the distance.

Kaspar Reinbold, Young Andy Boser and Franz Frey joined the knot of anxious men heading to check their properties; Squeaky Hoffer hurried to his store. "Come on, Hans," Grandpa said. "Rather than doing like them, we're better off in church praying the raiders don't come back."

Grandpa's presence gave me a feeling of security—even though his logic didn't always make sense.

The next morning, I ran my fingers across the sleek brown coat of Cookie's colt, Jake, while my grandfather and Uncle Heinz compared losses. Although the raiders had stolen Henry, our Herta and the two cows remained tied in the stalls, thanks to Ira's warning. "The bastards only got a few bags of grain from me, but this might just be the start," my uncle said.

"I hate to say it," Grandpa replied, "but I think so, too. Those raider bands will really get brazen if nobody stops them."

We left Uncle Heinz to finish his chores and walked along Church Street. Herr Goldstein swung a final blow with his hammer as he nailed a board across the side entrance to his inn. "It's enough trouble guarding one door, much less two," he said, then rubbed together his freezing hands. "Come into the dining room. I'll bring some wine to warm us." We sat at a small round table in the empty establishment exchanging holiday greetings and small talk until Grandpa shifted uneasily in his chair and said, "Ira, I was wrong to shun you because your brother Erasmus harvested Bauman's crop instead of ours, so thank you for the warning last night. But why were you outside after midnight, for God's sake?"

"It's the getting old that's the problem." He cast me a sheepish grin and turned back to Grandpa. "I went outside to pee and heard noises next door. I figured Louis would be in church, so something wasn't right. I looked over the fence and saw two guys leading a horse out of his barn. It was too dark to make them out, but they weren't talking German. I ran through those vacant lots toward the church and went over the back fence. Can you see me climbing out there in the dark? And in my nightshirt?" Herr Goldstein drew up his pant leg to reveal a large scrape. "My legs are too short and my ass too fat for that kinda stuff!"

The thought of the portly innkeeper scaling the fence brought a grin to my face.

"I wouldn't tell this to many people, but I trust you, Wilhelm. And the boy," he continued, glancing at me, "Can he keep things to himself?"

Grandpa gave Herr Goldstein an approving nod before we leaned closer across the small table.

"*Ya-naih*, when I came around the corner last night, there was somebody standing on the church steps by the door, but I couldn't see his face. Then, a guy on Middle Avenue waved and called 'Martin.' With the light shining through the church windows, I could see it was that Russian, Oleg. The one by the door ran down the steps and the two of them took off along Church Street. That's when I gave the warning." Ira wet his lips with wine and straightened in his chair.

Grandpa's eyes widened. "I bet the guy on the steps was Martin Degenstein! Oleg used him as the lookout so the raiders would know when Mass would be over. They've been friends ever since Martin worked as the carriage driver for Bauman at Pototski. Damn those traitors!"

"I'm not certain the one on the steps was Degenstein, but when you press charges, I'll swear it was Oleg on the road."

"We can't press charges! The Police Commander in Odessa clearly said the poor and landless have the right to take whatever they want from us."

Ira pushed back his chair. "Well, Oleg and Martin will eventually incriminate themselves and then we'll figure out how to deal with them."

Grandpa leaned across from his bed to mine and poked my shoulder.

He had something important on his mind and we were going to Uncle Heinz's house immediately.

He refused Aunt Monica's offer of a cup of *pripps* and raved to his yawning son, "I'm really upset about the political bullshit in this country. Those damn looters have permission to take whatever they want. I won't stand for it!"

"*Ya*, and apparently Kerensky isn't giving up easy, either. He got together the White Army, but if they don't beat the Bolshevik Reds, we'll have even more problems," said Uncle Heinz. "It's certain there'll be a civil war."

"It's all a downright danger for my family," Grandpa said. "If I ever get my hands—"

"Hold on, Father. There's a meeting tonight at the hall to see what can be done to protect ourselves."

Grandpa's voice lost its edge. "I have an idea of my own and Rosina already approved it." He outlined his plan to hide foodstuffs for emergency use and then added, "Heinz, you go to the meeting. Hans and I will start our project."

Several years earlier, Papa had quarried limestone for an addition to the small house now occupied by Uncle Heinz and Aunt Monica. Grandpa and I found the blocks hidden under a thin layer of snow behind the barn and estimated there were enough to build a false wall in our bedroom. Grandpa wiped sweat from his face as we loaded the wagon. "These are pretty heavy, Hans. It's good you're so big. You're a good helper," he said.

To be honest, I helped him not because I enjoyed working, but because I wanted to please him.

After dark, we slowly, quietly, led the team down River Street and turned into Grandpa's yard. We dusted off the snow and stacked the blocks in the master bedroom. "Hans, if we build our false wall three feet out from the old one, and the whole length of this room right up to the back of the *Backofen,* do you think anybody would realize it is not the original wall?" my grandfather said.

I trusted he knew what he was doing, and replied that it should be okay, if we can get the plaster color to match the old wall. We measured three feet from the existing wall and mortared blocks along the mark on the floor. When Uncle Heinz arrived near midnight, he marveled that the new wall already reached a third of the way to the ceiling. He immediately rolled up his sleeves and grabbed a trowel.

At three in the morning, we sat on the remaining blocks and passed around the water jug. Grandpa lit his pipe while my uncle recapped the meeting. "Everybody will pool their grain and sell it to the brokers in Karpowa, then deposit enough money in our local bank to buy seed next spring. We'll divide the leftover funds, and each man will be responsible for his own share. Hopefully ours'll be enough to pay off Pius' bank loan."

Grandpa drew heavily on his pipe. "It sure will be a relief to get that loan out of the way."

"*Ya*, I agree," my uncle said. "And there were more decisions at the meeting. The herders will bring the livestock in earlier than usual and once the milking is done, a different group will take them far into the pasture for the night. That way, the cattle and horses will be away from the village if raiders strike again. As for the Home Guard, starting next Tuesday, there'll be eight men patrolling the outskirts of Chornov in twelve-hour shifts to at least give us some warning that trouble's coming. Hans, you and me are on the day shift every Wednesday and Friday. We'll have to be at the town hall seven in the morning for the change of guard."

I wondered if Fritz, Georg, and Ivan were on the Home Guard list. I hoped we wouldn't be expected to shoot, maybe *kill* a raider.

Morning began to invade the room when, the wall completed, we tramped through the hallway and up the stairs leading to the attic. Uncle Heinz helped me pull the nails and lift the floorboards from a small area adjacent to the chimney. Next, we sawed a square opening through the dusty ceiling plaster below, creating the only access to the new room. He bent over, his voice echoing in the dark void. "This hole should be big enough for a man to fit through. Hans, get that short ladder from the barn so we can get down to the floor." He stood upright.

"When we're finished, we'll put back the floorboards and cover them with a few old tools for camouflage."

Grandpa grasped my shoulders in his sinewy hands and looked me in the eye. "Hans, now you have a secret. You must not tell anybody about this space, not even your friends. If our situation gets much worse, it could be the difference between life and death."

"I'll never tell." I crossed myself and spit on the floor before remembering the attic was part of the house.

The following day, Grandpa mixed yellow manure brine into a plaster solution until it matched the faded color of the other bedroom walls, then he and Uncle Heinz troweled a thick layer onto the new wall while I stirred the smelly mixture to keep it moist. My uncle dubbed the new space 'The Pantry.'

On The Pantry floor, we stacked three sacks of grain and a small crock of sauerkraut beside the jars of canned fruits and vegetables. "Don't forget some smoked sausages," Grandpa quipped. "Those are my favorite."

Uncle Heinz grinned. "Don't you get enough smoke from your pipe?"

In the end, it wasn't the raider gangs we should have feared the most. We thought it was only his strategy the day General Petliura led a White Army contingent into Chornov and held an enlistment rally in front of the town hall, cautioning our eligible men to enlist with him, and not with the Red Army. "You'll be damned sorry if you go with those buggers," he said. "They treat their recruits like shit, give them nothing but rags for clothes, and their attitude toward civilians is barbaric."

No one took Petliura's words seriously until a division of the Red Army rode into Chornov one chilly evening when the Home Guard was changing shifts. Other than the red insignias on their drooping shoulders, the soldiers were nothing more than a shabby array of hollow-cheeked men, their knees protruding through holes in pants caked with mud. "I can see trouble riding with that bunch," Fritz whispered, as we cowered behind the Ripplinger house.

My feet blurred as I crossed their orchard and cleared the back fence in a single bound. When I met Georg and Katie Frey on the road in front of their yard, my breath rattled in my throat. "Hide! The Red Army's here." Georg bolted toward their house, while Katie stood rooted to the spot. I grasped her arm, nearly yanking her off her feet, then ran to our house and flung open the porch door. "Where's Grampa?" I shouted to a surprised Mama and Loni sitting in the kitchen.

"He's visiting Herr Goldstein," Mama said. "What's the—"

"The Reds are coming! Should we hide in The Pantry?" I suddenly realized my error in revealing the existence of the secret space to someone other than family. Katie's sweaty fingers squeezed my hand tighter. "We can't just turn her away."

My mother grabbed the rifle from under a bench in the porch and motioned for us to follow her. "*Ya*, The Pantry's quite full, but there's still space for all of us. Come on, everybody. Hurry!"

A wave of heat escaped the *Backofen* as Loni opened the door and rolled a loaf of fresh bread into her apron. We frantically ran through the hallway and up the attic stairs. I dragged the old hand tools aside and removed the loosened floorboards from above the access hole. Loni and Katie nimbly descended the wooden ladder and crawled to the sacks of grain at the far end of the cramped, narrow room. I sat on a box of preserves, while Mama stood on the ladder to replace the floorboards above her head as best she could, and then settled down beside me, propping the rifle between us.

We waited in near darkness, with only a faint light seeping through the floorboards, apprehension our companion. Suddenly, *thump*, *thump*. Heavy boots clomped on the attic stairs. "I'm not lookin' through all this damn junk," a man said. "Let's go down and get that wine and fresh bread, just like Mama used to make."

"Where'd these *Nemetzis* go so fast?" said a second voice, his tongue already heavy with wine. "If we don't find 'em now, we'll come back later. There's girl clothes in a bedroom. Christ, I'm getting hot just thinking about it."

Loni and Katie huddled closer together.

"Forget about the girls," the first voice replied. "Jesus, there's gotta be money in this damn fine house and I'm gonna find it."

We sighed in relief as they started down the stairs, but cringed at the sound of furniture toppling and dishes breaking. Only the thickness of the new wall separated our tiny space from the assailants. Finally, an authoritative voice called from the porch, "Attention, you drunks! Captain wants everybody in the town hall in ten minutes. Bring any food and men's clothes you found."

Silence enveloped the house. My tense muscles relaxed and my breathing slowed. Deep down in my gut, I ached for Papa; though sometimes he judged and criticized me, I wanted him home now more than ever.

The fire in the *Backofen* burnt itself out and The Pantry cooled. I assumed that Mama and Loni, breathing deeply, were asleep. When Katie stirred, I wriggled close to keep her warm, and inhaled the sweet aroma of her hair as she whispered in my ear, "We don't have a secret room at our house. They'd have found me there, no matter where I hid. You saved me."

I had a sudden urge to kiss her. Not much more than a hen's peck, but in that one kiss, I showed Katie my feelings for her. If Kurt knew what I had done, would he have teased me, perhaps calling me Hans Kisser? Maybe not. I was fifteen, my brother would be almost seventeen and probably had a sweetheart of his own.

Shortly after a rooster's crow signaled daybreak, the hinges on the porch door squeaked. My pulse pounded as footsteps sounded on the floorboards above our heads. I gripped the cocked rifle in my sweaty hands until Grandpa called, "It's me. Come out. The army's gone."

No news had ever been more welcome. We scrambled up the ladder and nearly suffocated him with hugs. "I'm okay, I'm okay," he said, waving us off with his hand. "With all those drunk soldiers roaming the streets, I stayed the night with the Goldsteins. I figured you would be safe in The Pantry."

I returned from escorting Katie home and was relieved to hear Uncle Heinz had hidden Monica under a manger in the barn during the raid and she was fine. "But the Reds took almost everything, and your situation isn't any better," he said. "I checked your root cellar; there're only a few potatoes and the crock of sauerkraut."

"If things turn really desperate, we'll share what's in The Pantry," Mama said, while arranging the scattered silverware in the drawers that she had slid back into the cupboard.

Uncle Heinz sighed. "*Ya*, it was a rough day. All the bank accounts are empty, even the one set aside for buying seed in spring. And the bastards threatened to shoot whoever didn't voluntarily give them any money stashed at home. The leader said we can do it that way or have them come looking themselves. You know what *that* would mean."

I glanced around the room, still in an upheaval. We *did* know what that would mean; we had heard them through The Pantry walls.

Uncle Heinz continued, "He sarcastically thanked us for the donation, and his men packed the stolen food and clothes on their horses and rode off."

"There's going to be a lot of trouble," Grandpa said, his face haggard. "Somebody must've tipped off the Red Army about the communal account and that some of us hid money at home, too. And they rode in while our Home Guard was changing shifts. Now that's not just a coincidence."

Heinz's brow furrowed. "You're absolutely right, Father. For sure, somebody told them, and people are damned mad about it. In fact, the men are meeting shortly at the town hall to look into this mess."

Loni suddenly emerged from her bedroom and ran outside. There was someone at the gate—Martin Degenstein! Grandpa and I noticed him at the same time and followed Loni.

"Get off my property," Grandpa yelled, pointing the stem of

his pipe in Martin's face.

Martin glanced at Loni then retreated. Grandpa's narrowed eyes reminded me of Papa, of the times he spanked me as a child. "Apallonia, I forbid you to ever see that man again," he shouted. A puzzled expression flickered across my sister's face. "I mean it," he said and stormed back into the house.

Loni dared not ask for an explanation while our grandfather was in such a foul mood. I knew why he was upset, but couldn't tell her—I had given him my word.

Uncle Heinz and Grandpa didn't exactly invite me to accompany them to the meeting, but when Grandpa noticed me tag behind, he said I should hurry up, we were late. Before we joined the milling crowd, the blacksmith Herr Epp approached my uncle and Gus Vetter. After a hushed conversation, Gus said, "That's enough evidence for me. Come on, Heinz. Let's find them skunks."

The villagers busily compared losses until Herr Redekop pointed down Middle Avenue. "Hold on! Somebody's coming," he yelled.

A swaggering Gus prodded Oleg with his old shotgun, while Martin and Lothar slunk ahead of my uncle. "Ve got the stinkin' bastards. They couldn't hide from us," Gus said proudly.

"What's this about?" Oleg growled, his gaze fixed on his shoes.

Herr Goldstein stared at Oleg, his anger building. "You two helped the raiders on Christmas Eve. I heard you call to Martin on the church steps."

"And you were in a hurry yesterday for me to fix your horse's shoe. Was it so you could ride out and signal the Red Army?" Libby Epp shouted. "What did they pay you, Oleg? A few measly roubles?"

"Martin's the one you want! Him and his brother."

Lothar nervously rolled the hem of his jacket. "I-I don't know nothing about it. And when the two of them were gone for the night, I wasn't even with 'em."

"Did ya' hear that?" Whiskey Wolff pushed his way through the crowd and grabbed Lothar by the hair. "This little piss-ant pretty much admits Oleg and Martin were the ones who told the Red Army that we had money." He swayed on his feet, then steadied himself against Herr Redekop's shoulder. "If there's one thing I can't stand, it's a goddamn rat! Who wants to hang the bastards?"

Herr Redekop brushed Whiskey's hand from his shoulder. "Let's not be hasty. We'll take them to jail in Mannheim and let the court decide on a punishment."

Whiskey loosened the pistol tucked under his belt. "Ha! The same court that said anybody has the right to take our grain and *we're* the ones breaking the law if we stop 'em? I say get rid of 'em right now!"

Herr Goldstein confronted Whiskey. "I'm certain that Martin helped Oleg, but I can't say anything about the young fellow."

"He's only a boy. Let him go. We've got the other two, *gehl?*" Herr Epp conceded.

Lothar broke loose, dodged through the crowd, and disappeared behind the town hall. Before anyone could react, a hysterical female voice echoed above the clamor. "What are you doing to my boy?" Philomena Degenstein, her ankle-length skirt fluttering behind her, shouldered her way toward Martin. "Let him go. I beg you."

Whiskey waved his pistol in the air. He turned to the street, to the faces contorted in anger. "Hang 'em! Hang 'em!" he shouted. The angry mob surged forward and muscled Martin and Oleg against the stone fence, knocking Philomena off her feet.

Bam … Bam. Two shots rang out. An intense silence enveloped the crowd.

Philomena was the first to recover from the shock. She crawled between the forest of legs and fell in a dead faint beside her son. Martin lay on the ground, gripping his side; blood trickled between his fingers. Oleg had escaped injury, but his face was white as chalk. His eyes searched for a way out.

Gus, furious, ripped the smoking pistol from Whiskey's hand. "*Yop filla mut*! Vat the hell did you do?"

Whisky showed no remorse. "Get some rope. Hang 'em for what they done."

Uncle Heinz's facial muscles tightened with rage. "Whiskey, shut up! And Oleg, you goddamn traitor. You and Martin get on your horses and ride the hell out of here. And if you want to stay alive, don't ever come back to Chornov."

Oleg supported Martin on his shoulder and headed toward his yard, red splotches staining the ground behind them.

I dropped to my knees. How could decent, God-fearing people have become such a vengeful mob no different from the Red Army?

My uncle crouched beside me. "I don't like what happened either," he said. "But Whiskey was right. They'd be let off by the courts. And, no doubt, they should've been punished somehow."

The truth of his statement calmed me, but, nevertheless, I wondered whether the disdain we *Volksdeutsche* showed toward Oleg—toward most of the Russians—helped instigate this animosity.

As I rose to my feet, Loni rushed toward us and seized Uncle Heinz by his arm. "Tell me *you* weren't the one who accused Martin, that you're not the reason I'll never see him again!" She pounded her fists on his chest. "You don't know how much I loved him. We were going to be married."

Married? I had no idea their relationship was so serious. Poor Loni. What words could convince her that she was better off without Martin? Although Grandpa's proverb, 'Given time, a sorrow is often regarded as a gift in disguise,' seemed hollow, she brushed loose strands of hair from her eyes and allowed him to take her hand.

For months, all talk in the village centered on the ostracizing of Oleg and Martin. A few villagers wanted Whiskey Wolff charged for the shooting but, in the end, they agreed that justice had been served, and they simply went on with their lives—except for Philomena, who developed a deep hatred for Whiskey. Every Sunday after Mass, she reminded him that a man with attempted murder on his soul should not receive Communion. I couldn't fault her; he had grievously wounded her son.

10

NOTHING NEW TO THEM

February, 1919

Pius Gerein
Devils Flats N.D.
USA

February 8, 1919

My son and family,

I greet you from Russia with prayers that the Grace of Our Lord will be granted to you always.

We received your answer to our letter of last autumn. I applied for emigration papers. Heinz is eager to leave Russia, but Rosina is hesitant. She hopes Karl will return someday. I also have that hope, but realistically, it is only that—hope.

We're grateful that you've begun the formalities for us with regards to American immigration. Now I must impose upon you even more, as our financial situation is grave. I have paid cash for our passport applications and have no money left since the Red Army raid. We hope to sell our houses and farm machinery when we leave, but most people here cannot pay hard currency for these things. In any case, we need money to buy our exit papers and book our passage once our passports are granted. I ask that you please send what you are able. There is a Wells Fargo Office in Odessa that will accept a money gram. Or I can cash a bank draft in Mannheim, though these aren't always honored.

Your loving father, Wilhelm

I sat cross-legged on the bed with my back to the headboard and scribbled a note to Kurt to enclose with Grandpa's letter. As I wrote, 'Dear American Brother,' I reflected on how quickly time passed. It was more than four years since we lay whispering under these covers. Though their faces seemed hazy whenever I thought about them, the absence of my brother and my father still caused me pain.

In the coolness of an early March morning, Loni and I, a rifle at our feet, rode out to Pototski in our old wagon to check for manure to use as heating fuel. Cotton-ball clouds partially obscured the blue expanse of sky, and brown seedpods still fluttered on the acacia trees that encircled the abandoned estate. I reined Herta and a gelding borrowed from Gus toward the skeleton of the barn and was dismayed that the manure was already gone. We were about to leave the yard when a ragged figure climbed over chunks of brick and plaster torn from the ransacked house. I grabbed the rifle and raised it to my shoulder.

"Hans, don't shoot," he yelled. "It's me, Hubert Bauman."

I had never seen Hubert without fine clothes and a haircut; he looked every bit a stranger, but yes, it was he. I propped the rifle against the seat of the wagon and ran to him. "You old devil! You're nothing but a bag of bones," I said as we shared an embrace.

Loni crawled into the back of the wagon. "Come to Chornov, you vagabond. Sit in front with Hans. You two have lots to talk about."

"*Ya*, for sure. Come along. Lenin needs more workers, and he's letting *kulak* families apply for re-instatement into the community. And since Herr Ripplinger died last year, Fritz and his mother need extra help in the field."

Hubert retrieved from the house a small sack and a greatcoat. "This was buried under some junk in a corner of the upstairs bedroom." He patted the coarse leather of the garment his father had worn with pride while driving the motorcar.

On the journey to Chornov, I updated Hubert on our friends, and then he told us his two older sisters had disappeared while scavenging in Odessa, and his mother died of heartbreak after his younger brother starved to death. "I had nowhere else to go, so last month I came home and survived on raw corn and a few mushrooms growing where the manure pile used to be. You don't get fat on that," he laughed, then asked whether my father had come home.

"Not yet," I said with a sigh. "But I'd sure take a lot of the lickings he used to give me to find out what happened to him."

A steady rain began to fall as Grandpa and I worked the field one morning in early spring. Back in the comfort of the house, I complained that the weather had ruined our day. "Don't worry, Hans," Grandpa said with a chuckle. "Spring rains and old ladies dances don't last long."

Sure enough, the shower soon ended and I followed him down to Epp's Blacksmith Shop to assess Herr Bauman's motorcar abandoned alongside the building. The roof was in tatters, and someone had slashed the seats. I stomped down the high dead grass around the partially inflated front tires as my grandfather lifted the hood. Herr Epp stepped into the yard, wiping his greasy hands on a rag. "Somebody took a sledgehammer to the motor," he said, picking a twig off the car's rusty bumper. "You don't want me to fix this old wreck, do you, Wilhelm?"

"*Ya-naih*, Libby. Do you think you could build a cart using pieces from this car?"

"I never thought of that; it's really just scrap iron." I smelled forge smoke on his hair when he squatted on both heels to survey the undercarriage. "If I unbolt the front axle and add two shafts to hook into the harness, it would make a nice frame for a one-horse cart. And those rubber tires will give a smooth ride even without springs. But where will you get a box for it?"

"Maybe Andy Boser would give me his small open carriage. You know, the one with the broken frame. With a few changes, that box could be fitted onto this unit." Grandpa looked at me with a sparkle in his eyes. "What do you think, Hans? Should we go ahead with it?"

I smiled in approval.

On the walk home, Grandpa confided in me. “You know, Hans, that cart is more important than you realize. Ever since I sold Ghost and Cookie, I’ve been thinking it doesn’t make sense to own a nice carriage when it’s pulled by a mismatched pair.”

I craned my neck and observed him. Our financial situation must be dire if he was willing to sell such a fine carriage. He and Grandma, dressed in their finest attire, had ridden in it with pride on special occasions. “I’d hate to see you sell the carriage you like so much, Grampa.”

“Ach, it’s only a …” He closed his eyes and drew heavily on his pipe. “The new one will be just fine.”

Grandpa awoke in the morning in his usual good mood. We cleaned and polished the prized carriage, and by noon, we were on our way, Herta plodding along with Jake prancing at her side. Initially, Grandpa had considered going to the outdoor market in Strassburg, but he had opted instead for the smaller Karpowa market. “There’s more easy money there than in Strassburg. Easy money gets spent a lot quicker than earned money.”

“How can there be a difference in money? All roubles look the same to me.”

“With earned money each generation of a wealthy family works to make the pot bigger. Since they grow up rich, having money is nothing new to them and they don’t spend it on foolishness. Do you follow me so far, Hans?”

“I think so.”

“But people with easy money have a novelty. Like the Karpowa people who looted Pototski Estate, the money just fell in their lap. They didn’t have to sweat for it, so they get addicted to the good feeling of spending it.”

I recalled Grandpa’s quip from a few years ago. “Are those the kind of people who wanna piss with the big dogs but can’t get their leg that high?"

"You got it, my boy. You hit the nail on the head." He laughed so hard I worried he would choke.

By mid-afternoon, a pompous young man had made an acceptable offer, hitched his neatly groomed team to the carriage and proudly driven away. After Grandpa and I somberly mounted the bare backs of Jake and Herta, he stuffed the small wad of money into his pocket and I swung a canvas sack filled with fabric over my shoulder. Mama would be happily sewing clothing for some time.

The following Wednesday, spry Jake easily pulled our new cart along Church Street, curious shopkeepers eyeing the two-wheeled contraption. It could accommodate several people on a front bench, and a few more facing each other in the rear. If there were no passengers, the space between the back seats served as a cargo hold. We stopped at the post office, and then continued home to read the letter from America. Mama gasped when she opened the envelope and a bank draft from Uncle Pius, sufficient to pay half the family's ship passage to America, fell from a neatly folded letter. "Pius hopes we can be there before fall so he has help with the harvest," Mama said excitedly, after reading the letter. "Write him immediately to thank him for the money."

Grandpa inspected the bank draft. "I always knew Pius would do well in America," he said, pride reflecting in his voice. "He's got a good head on his shoulders."

Mama handed me the enclosed note from Kurt:

December 1, 1918

Hallo Hans,

I wish you the Grace of God. There has been a sickness here called the Spanish Flu and many people died. One family not far from our farm lost all five of their children. I was sick for two weeks, but then was okay.

I can't wait until all of you come here to live. The war is over now, so there should be room on the ships for you. I miss you and pray every night that Papa comes back before you leave.

There's so much to do. And the girls are pretty. They don't wear such long dresses or all put their hair up in buns.

Merry Christmas and Happy New Year to all of you.
Your American brother, Kurt

"Merry Christmas?" Mama questioned. "That envelope took a long time to get here. It's already April."

Grandpa tilted back in his chair, a halo of smoke around his head. "So, Kurt's noticing girls? I'd say he's almost grown up."

Loni, her arms akimbo, confronted Grandpa. "He's only just had his seventeenth birthday. I'll be nineteen at the end of May, and you still won't let me visit with boys. Kurt might have a girlfriend in America, but he sure wouldn't have one if he was living in this house!" She stomped to her bedroom.

Grandpa cocked an eyebrow and Mama's face darkened, but neither commented on Loni's rudeness. She still harbored bitterness toward Grandpa and Uncle Heinz for their role in Martin's exile from Chornov.

The next month, Katie's father Franz Frey and Lothar's mother Philomena Degenstein, both widowed, announced their intention to marry, but neither could afford a lavish reception. Following a simple dinner in the Frey's backyard, the men sat smoking their pipes in the shade of the fruit trees. Herr Frey noticed Georg, Hubert, Lothar, and me standing to one side and waved for us to join the circle. I started forward and tripped over Lothar's foot, his smirk suggesting it was intentional. With great effort, I squelched the urge to punch him. Anxious to be alone to collect my thoughts, I crossed the yard and ducked behind the summer kitchen. While standing in the high grass with my head against the stone wall and my eyes closed, a soft hand wriggled into mine.

"You look so handsome today, dressed in your Sunday best," said Katie, revealing the slight gap between her upper front teeth.

I squeezed her hand. "You l-look nice, too."

A gruff voice shattered the moment. "What're you two doing here, Hans Kisser?" Lothar, his hands jammed in his pockets and grinning like a horse chewing on thistle, stood at a corner of the summer kitchen.

The hair on my head prickled. "If you don't get out of here—"

"If *I* don't get out of here? I came to protect my new sister."

"Don't you dare call me your sister." A tear dropped on Katie's check.

I lunged forward and grabbed his collar. "If you bother her, I'll knock your head off. I won't let you get away with it."

He broke my grip and a button flew from his shirt. "You're going crazy, " he yelled and slipped around the corner.

Katie pressed slender fingers to her eyes. "I hate him so much. Why'd Papa have to marry his mother, of all people?"

At a loss for what to say or do, I edged past the summer kitchen and out the gate to the solitude of my own home. Upon hearing about the wedding, I had worried he would move into the Frey household across the street from us. Fortunately, Herr Frey ruled that his stepson would stay in Philomena's house at the other end of the village. Perhaps he also had no liking for Lothar.

11

DON'T STOP FOR NOTHING

August, 1919

A horrendous bang jolted me from my dream. Grandpa threw back the covers from his bed when the floor shook and the glass rattled in the windowpanes. "Rosina! Apallonia! Lightning hit the house. Get out!" he yelled in desperation. I grabbed the back of his nightshirt and we groped our way toward the porch. Through the haze of dust and smoke, I could barely distinguish Mama and Loni as they struggled to free the wooden bolt securing the door. "Damn state of affairs when we have to lock our doors," Grandpa muttered.

We huddled against the stone fence next to the lane, shadows dancing across our faces as flames licked at a corner of the bone-dry thatched roof. The static in the air from black thunderheads grinding out tongues of lightning caused our hair to rise. "Apallonia! Get pails from the barn!" Grandpa shouted, tension cracking his voice. "Hans, you draw the water. Rosina, call the neighbors and Heinz."

My uncle came running toward us with a ladder under his stump of an arm, his unbuttoned shirt flapping behind him. Herr Frey and Georg followed with a pail in each hand. I frantically dumped water from the well into the trough, while Mama and my sister filled pails for the men on the roof. Thoughts of our furniture, our clothes, our food, but especially Kurt's little red pocketknife in my trousers hanging beside the bed, crossed my mind. I pulled hard on the rough hemp rope, fighting the urge to rush into our burning home.

Grandpa and Herr Frey used twine to secure a section of canvas they had flung over the soot-scarred hole in the roof after extinguishing the last of the fire. The wheezing men climbed down the ladder, and Grandpa collapsed onto an upturned bucket. "How can I thank all of you? The house would be gone if you hadn't helped," he said, bracing himself against a sudden swirl of ash and dust. Raindrops mixed with hail pelted us. The Freys scurried home without retrieving their buckets, and we covered our heads with our hands and ran inside. Though the acrid smell of smoke permeated the house, Uncle Heinz lit the lantern and determined the only visible damage was a water stain on the living room ceiling. I brushed a light coating of grey dust from the trousers hanging in my bedroom and tucked Kurt's pocketknife under my pillow.

When Grandpa crawled into bed, he said, mostly to himself. "I wonder why Mother Nature is in such a nasty mood tonight."

I massaged my palms, chafed to near bleeding from the well rope, and fell asleep before I could answer him.

The next thing I heard was Mama rattling the porridge pot on the stove. After a hearty bowl of oatmeal, Grandpa and I discarded a waterlogged sack of flour and a box of outdated *Eureka Rundshau* newspapers from the attic. We dragged down the stairs a small wooden cabinet and an old trunk that had belonged to Grandma's mother and set them outside to dry in the sun. Grandpa picked charred sticks of thatching from the roof and tossed them onto a pile beside the house. "The framework is still good," he said, "but some of the reeds definitely need replacing. Kaspar Unruh used all the ones from the pond to fix the roof of his shop last month, so we'll have to go to Selz for some, even with all the unrest in the countryside."

A day away from home was a rare treat. Jake cantered at a steady pace, while Grandpa leaned back in the cart and lit his first pipe of the day, enjoying being the passenger as much as I did being the driver. Willows crowded the road at a steep ravine in the otherwise flat steppe, and Jake slowed to a walk only on the ascent of 'The Chasm.' The wind at our backs, three hours slipped by and we eventually paused on a hill overlooking Selz, situated on the eastern shore of Kutschurgan Liman. Two golden crosses projected high above the church roof as if keeping watch over the whitewashed houses and thick stone fences below. We descended into the town on a winding road lined with Lombardi trees and turned north on the main boulevard. In the numerous reed beds growing in the shallow lake beyond the town, frogs croaked and ducks dove for dinner; the breeze carried a scent of lily pads. My bare feet sank into the muddy bottom as I waded knee-deep in the tepid water to cut the tough, stringy stems with a pair of rusty garden snips before handing them to Grandpa.

Several hours later, the cart sagged almost to the ground from the weight of harvested reeds. "Whenever I'm in Selz, I visit my cousin's widow Salomea," Grandpa said as we secured the load with a short thick rope. "She hasn't re-married in the four years since Frederick died in the war."

Salomea was thrilled to have out-of-town visitors, and set out a raspberry-flavored drink, a nice treat on a warm afternoon. After we had chatted for a short time, Grandpa noticed me shift restlessly on my chair and suggested I explore the town. "We're leaving at three thirty to get home in daylight, so be back here in an hour, *gehl?*" he said.

I strolled among children playing tag on their way home from school, enjoying the warm sun on my face. Within a few blocks, the church Grandpa and I had seen from the hilltop loomed on my left. While I admired the stained glass windows, a lilting female voice called out, "*Guten Tag*. You're not from here, are you?"

I peeked beyond a rose bush in the tree-lined churchyard and saw a girl of my age waving from a bench. "Dooo, do you mean me?" I said.

"Of course, I mean you. I don't see anyone else." A radiant smile bowed her lips; her eyes, blue as the evening sky, sparkled below fluttering lashes.

The girls in Chornov were not so brash, nor were they as fair-skinned. "You don't look like a German, but you speak our language," was all I could think to say.

"I'm from a Swedish colony near Nikolajev. My father moved here to work at the wagon factory years ago. Do you know where

Nikolajev is?"

I felt quite ignorant. "*Nnnnaih*, I don't know that town. Is it near Chornov?"

"Chornov." She curled her lip. "Ach, that's not so far away." She patted the rough plank seat. "Come, sit down."

I sat on the extreme edge, afraid my shabby boots and the patches on the knees of my trousers would not meet with her approval. My new friend smiled and said, "My name's Ottilia. What's yours?"

"Johannes, ahhh … Hans. I'm pleased to meet you." She chatted about her family, Selz and school, while I sat and listened, enchanted by the sound of her voice.

Seemingly a short time later, four loud chimes burst from the bell towers. I sprang from the bench like a startled rabbit. "*Yesus Gott.* I'm late to meet Grampa. We want to get home before dark."

"*Ya*, our Home Guard fought off the Red Army a few weeks ago, but they might come back. Be careful."

"*Wiedersehn*," I called over my shoulder.

"Come see me next time you're here. We live on Schmier Avenue."

I arrived breathless and flushed at Salomea's house and clambered up beside Grandpa, who already sat in the cart with Jake's reins in his hands. "Sorry, Grampa. The time just flew by. Honest." I hung my head in shame; I hated to disappoint him.

"We'll still get home in daylight." He patted my back. "It's fine."

Grandpa skirted past a wagon loaded with bags of threshed grain, then urged Jake into a trot. We were almost out of the valley when an ear-shattering *boom* echoed across the *liman*. "*Lieber Gott*! Somebody's shooting a cannon into Selz! And it looks like it's the Red Army!" Grandpa said, nodding toward a regiment on horseback just beyond the crest of the hill to our right.

I knew the situation was grave when fear reflected in my grandfather's eyes, something I had never seen before.

On command, the soldiers raised their rifles and charged into

Selz. However, two riders parted ranks and galloped toward us. Grandpa slapped down my hand as I reached for the rifle under the seat. "Don't bother, Hans. They're armed better than us."

The riders guided their horses to either side of our cart. Their tunics hung loose, their hair was straggly and their beards unkempt. The one on my left came so near I could smell his musty sweat. My jaw tightened when he pointed his cocked pistol at Grandpa. "Ahhh, some Germans on the run. Should we shoot the scums right now?"

His comrade, a broad-shouldered man with fire in his eyes yelled, "Jesus no, Sasha. Ursulov wants every man alive. Take them back to town." He brusquely addressed Grandpa. "And you! Give me that rifle under the seat." The second rider slung the rifle over his shoulder, dug his heels into his horse's ribs and galloped down the hill.

Relief swept over me. They had spared our lives, but why did Ursulov—whoever he was—want us? My mouth felt dry as cotton.

Sasha grabbed Jake's reins and led us toward the rising fray. The deafening blasts of gunshots echoed between the damaged houses, the inn, and the hardware store. Two soldiers dragged a man wearing a white hat and an apron from a main street building where the sign 'Schwab's Bakery' dangled above a broken window. When one of them swung his rifle down hard on the struggling man's head, a frantic woman ran screaming from the shop, pleading for mercy. The other soldier whirled around and plunged his bayonet deep into her chest, then wiped the blade clean on the felled woman's dress. Sasha waved to him. "Good enough. That's one less *Nemetzi*," he said with a sneer.

I turned my head and retched over the side of the cart. "Keep that goddamn contraption moving, Sasha," one of them ordered. "We're going to the hall . . . and not for a dance."

Sasha tied Jake to a hitching post in front of the town hall, a stone structure with small high-set windows, and prodded us into the dimly lit room where a group of disheveled hostages cowered along one wall. Somehow, I felt relief that we were not alone. Sasha crossed the room and greeted four soldiers resting their feet on a rectangular wooden table. He tilted his head to drink from a bottle. "Those

Germans can keep their goddamn sauerkraut," he slurred, wiping his mouth on a sleeve, "but they sure make good wine."

The windows turned black when night descended several hours later. Eventually, eighty-nine of us, some wet from hiding in reed beds, others covered in chaff from straw stacks, sat cross-legged on the cool stone floor, the soldiers' ugly threats and rifle butts keeping order. When intermittent gunshots echoed from the street I wondered if a hostage recognized his wife or child's voice in the blood-curdling screams. Unable to look anyone in the face, I solemnly bowed my head.

A burly bareheaded officer wearing a grime-streaked uniform staggered into the hall sometime around midnight. Our guards scurried to their feet and saluted the officer steadying himself on the back of a chair. "I am Commander Ursulov and we, the Red Army, rep-represent Russia," he said to us, barely audible. "B-by law, you are to help drive the opposition from our country. Instead, last month you organized a Home Guard and became our enemy."

Grandpa struggled to his feet. "Excuse me, sir, but my grandson and I are only in Selz to collect reeds. We're from Chornov."

"Ch-ornov? That's close to here. You could'a been part of this Home Guard idea, too."

Grandpa's reply was calm and steady, his hand resting on my shoulder. "We weren't, and I beg you to release this boy. He's barely sixteen."

"Sixteen's old enough to use a rifle against us. Guards, m-make sure both of them stay here." The commander stormed out of the hall, stumbling on the raised threshold.

Despite feeling trapped and frightened, I wouldn't have left without Grandpa even if Ursulov had released me.

A more sober Commander Ursulov strode into the hall at first light. He crossed the floor with determined strides and fastened the top button of his spotless tunic. Raising his chin in the direction of us hostages, he announced, "For being an enemy of your country's army, each of you is guilty of treason."

All the hostages scrambled to their feet.

"You can't do this!"

"We want a trial!"

The commander drew a pistol from a black leather holster strapped around his waist. "Guards! Move them out."

Grandpa cradled my head in his quivering hands and thrust his face forward until we stood eye-to-eye. "Listen, Hans. Listen to me. If there's a chance for us on the street, I'll yell 'run.' Don't hesitate. Don't look back. Zigzag if you can, but run, and fast. Understand?" He shook me hard.

"*Ya*, Grampa, but … but what if they shoot?"

"Don't stop for nothing. If I can't keep up, you go on home anyway. *Promise* me."

There was no time to voice my opinion, so I nodded in agreement.

The zealous soldiers herded us out into the unimaginable devastation. The putrid smell of burnt flesh drifted from smoldering ashes and a pallid black cloud of smoke hung over the entire town. It seemed every building in sight had sustained shattered windows, broken doors, a scorched roof or had been reduced to a mere pile of rubble. I glanced at the grandiose church across the street and wondered if God was watching us. And if so, why did He allow such carnage and destruction? And why did He allow Grandpa and me to become hostages, afraid for our very lives?

The guards paraded us along several streets, eager to display the punishment for forming a Home Guard in opposition to the Red Army. Distraught women and children cried out from the ruins to acknowledge their husbands, fathers, and sons. The polished bayonets on the soldiers' rifles discouraged them from coming near, but in a show of defiance, they bravely followed at a distance, praying aloud. An impatient soldier yelled, "Get moving, you god-loving sonofabitch," when a priest approached and fell into step with an overwrought prisoner.

As my haggard grandfather and I trudged along hand-in-hand, he slowly nudged me toward the left edge of the tightly bunched prisoners. A few paces later, he squeezed my hand and with a tilt of his head indicated a small open field with a sprawling gray building in the distance, surrounded by tall Lombardi poplars. "Run," he whispered. He grasped my arm and with a hefty swing, launched me on my way.

The confusion in my mind cleared instantly. I crouched low and dashed through the waist-high grass in the ditch. While zigzagging around the trees, my heart pounded in my chest like the very shots pursuing me. A bullet ricocheted, peppering my face with bark before I dodged behind the building. With no other refuge in sight, I frantically grabbed a branch, swung myself into a tree and started climbing. From my high perch, I heard an exasperated soldier search the grove, cursing my soul before returning to his unit.

Over the roof of the low-slung building, I spied the overwrought women and children huddled in small groups on the hillside near a cemetery entrance. In one corner of an adjacent harvested field, the captives clustered around the priest, his cassock flapping in the breeze. With admirable courage, he held his hands high and offered blessings and encouragement. Suddenly, *rat-a-tat-tat* … Small clouds of smoke formed above two tripod-mounted machine guns and the field erupted in a cacophony of noise and confusion. Bodies pitched and fell, some rising only to fall again under the steady hail of bullets. Just as quickly as it had begun, the shooting ceased. The deathly quiet air soon filled with the haunting wails of the witnesses, three soldiers threatening to shoot anyone who dared enter the body-strewn field. My spirits soared when a man dragged himself away from the carnage. "Let it be Grampa," I prayed, until the commander pressed his pistol to the man's temple and fired.

After what seemed like hours, but was, in reality, mere minutes, the executioners' comrades rode up the hill. I was angered to see Jake among the animals herded alongside wagons filled with booty from the ruins of the town, yet felt thankful that he was alive. The two units joined ranks and disappeared down the road toward Kandel, finally allowing the distraught families to claim the bodies of their loved ones.

Wracked with anguish, I climbed down the tree on painfully stiff legs and ran back across the field to a depression in the tall grass near the road. I crept close and almost stumbled on a prostrate form on the ground, arms spread to the sides, one leg awkwardly wedged beneath the other. Recognizing the blue-checkered shirt, I fell to my knees and whispered a prayer of thanks when he turned his head and blinked sweat from his eyes. "The soldiers are gone. I'll help you up, Grampa," I said, and lifted him to a sitting position. Blood oozing from an ugly bayonet wound in the center of his back formed a red pool beneath him. My hands began to shake. 'Grampa! You *can't* die,' I thought and gently eased his limp body to the ground. He needed a doctor . . . and soon.

I dashed down the hill, relieved to see the cart beside the hall, however, our jackets, gloves, and the burlap sack were gone—everything except the water jug and the reeds. Kurt's little red pocketknife easily severed the rope and the reeds slid onto the grass. After tucking the rope under the seat, I grasped the shafts of the cart and by tugging in short spurts, wrested it back up the hill to Grandpa. I stuffed his shirttail into the seeping wound before two somber-faced boys helped me gently lift him into the rear of the cart. I gave my grandfather a drink from the jug, then lowered his head onto his folded cap before starting out, the cart in tow.

A line of mangled humanity serpentined far down the street and clogged the entrance to the hospital; immediate medical help was out of the question. I circled to the rear of the cart. Grandpa's colorless lips quivered as he spoke. "Y-you h-home."

"First, we'll go to Frau Salomea's. She'll bandage you—"

"Ap-ricot tree. Thr-ee back, two l-left," he wheezed.

My anxiety rose as I wiped a trickle of blood from his mouth with the back of my hand before raising the shafts and continuing across town. Even before entering Salomea's yard, I knew we would not find the help we dearly needed; fire had claimed the roof and the front door hung askew from the upper hinge. I searched the house for a blanket, or a coat—anything—but found only a charred piece of an apron. In a rear bedroom, Salomea's body lay face down in the ashes, the skin on her back bubbled and blistered. An involuntary scream escaped my lips as I staggered outside to the water trough, twice plunging my head into the water to flush the image from my mind.

I drew a fresh bucket of water and held the filled jug to Grandpa's lips. Decision made—I was taking him home, with or without a horse. I retrieved the rope from under the seat and tied one end to the cart's harness hitch, and slipped the crude loop at the other end around my waist. I picked up the shafts and, in that manner, managed to pull the cart around toppled trees and fences.

The road out of Selz rose on a gradual incline, and the strain soon brought me to a puffing halt. After a short rest, I tried again, concerned that my tiring legs would be unable to gain the top. On my third attempt, the cart jolted forward. I turned and saw a young woman, her swollen face smudged with soot, push at the rear of the cart. Together, we crested the hilltop, however, when I attempted to thank her, she had already started back to Selz, hot wind fanning strands of flaxen hair across her shoulders. My mind fumbled for her name. "Ottilia! Ottilia," I called. Her reply was a flick of her hand before she disappeared below the curve of the hill. I occasionally refreshed Grandpa and myself with cool water from the jug as we continued on the long journey home. When the sun left me to grapple with the darkness, and the air turned cool, I tucked my only shirt around my grandfather. I slipped the loop of the rope across my bare chest and one shoulder to alleviate the chafing on my waist. Throughout the black night, with every step taken, I left my youth further behind; there would be no turning back. As the moon dipped beyond the western horizon, I turned the cart around at the lip of The Chasm and slowly inched backward down the steep incline, my legs threatening to buckle. Upon reaching the bottom, I dropped the bloodied loop of rope from my shoulders and sat on the edge of the road to determine my next move. It would be impossible for me to pull the cart up the opposite bank of

The Chasm. My only option was to hurry home for help. Staggering to my feet to tell Grandpa my plan, I studied the line of his nose, his slackened jaw and unblinking eyes. A flood of tears dripped onto my chest; his life, like the night, had faded away. A part of me died as I brushed shut the sagging eyelids and drew my shirt over the face of the man who had loved and nurtured me for so long—the man who had just saved my life. I pressed his limp hand to my cheek and, reluctantly, said a final goodbye before dragging the little cart behind a thick patch of willows. While struggling to the ridge, my lips trembled at the reality of never again sharing a laugh with my grandfather, or smelling the sweet aroma of his pipe smoke. I turned to peer down into the valley. Unable to spot the cart, my face softened into a smile; my beloved Grandpa's body would be safe. Sheer determination drove me onward. I ordered myself to move in the morning chill. "Walk. One step at a t-time. One, two, th-three, f-f …"

Mama's face came into focus at my bedside. "Hans! You're awake. Gus found you beside the road this morning. I just finished bandaging your wounds, so be quiet and rest." She started humming a hymn, soft and low.

The porch door creaked open and Uncle Heinz, ashen and red-eyed, entered the bedroom. Mama grasped his hand. "You found your father?"

"H-he's dead …" His shoulders sagged.

My heart ached as I outlined the circumstances of Grandpa's death, but my guilty conscience prevented me from forming the words, 'It was my fault.'

"Hans," Mama said, "you were mumbling in your sleep. Something about being late and staying away from girls. What does it mean?"

Uncle Heinz and Mama quietly left the room when I turned my face to the wall and feigned sleep. Now, more than ever, I needed Kurt for emotional support.

On the day of Grandpa's funeral, Mama removed my bandages, actually strips of an old tea towel. Bare bone was visible in the 'X' worn across my chest and underarms, but the pungent smell from the lacerated flesh at my waist worried me the most.

"It's healing just fine," said Mama. "It'll sting, but let me put on a fresh layer of goose grease and some clean rags."

The finality of death brought my guilt and grief to the surface as the six pallbearers lowered Grandpa's casket into the grave. I inwardly tortured myself for my tardiness in Selz, for my lack of good character. It should be *me* in the casket covered with dirt. The wounds to my flesh would heal within a few weeks. The wounds to my soul would take longer . . . much longer.

My uncle came into my bedroom the next day after he and Gus Vetter temporarily repaired the roof and listened to my recollection of Grandpa's ramblings. "He said something about an apricot tree, three back, two left."

"*Ya-naih*, the trees are planted in rows in the orchard. Maybe we can make some sense out of that."

Within an hour, Uncle Heinz, with Mama at his heels, rushed into my room and drew closed the curtains. My thoughts immediately turned to an emergency or, God forbid, the Red Army had invaded Chornov again.

Uncle Heinz pulled an old canning jar smelling of damp soil from under his jacket. "Hans! Look what I found buried under a tree in the orchard. Obviously, your Grandpa didn't trust a bank after the Red Army raid." He twisted off the rusty lid and dumped the contents on my bed.

Mama helped sort the pile of money. "*Grosser Gott*! There's twenty-one thousand and three hundred in roubles and some old coins," she said excitedly. "This must include the money from Pius, but going to America might not happen for a while." As if in a trance, she fanned out the bills.

"*Ya*, I think we should re-bury the money," said Uncle Heinz. He rapped a knuckle on the small jar under his stump of an arm. "We'll keep it for an emergency and you should know where it is, Hans. Are you well enough to meet me in the barn at midnight?"

A harvest moon low in the southern sky kept watch as we crept toward the threshing floor. "Here," my uncle whispered to me. "Start at this point at the edge of the floor, walk straight into the orchard, cross three rows of the apricot trees, then go left to the second tree. If you scrape away a little ground, you'll find a hollow spot under the roots." He positioned the jar in the cavity and patted the soil firmly in place. "There, you can't even tell anything's been dug up. It looks so natural."

"It's perfect. Grandpa was so smart to use this spot. I-I really miss him."

"He loved you, too, Hans, very much. Old love doesn't rust; you can always count on it. Can't you just hear him saying that?" He shook his head and chuckled into his sleeve.

What would my uncle think if he knew Grandpa died because he could not count on *my* love for *him*?

12

I DON'T MAKE THE RULES

April, 1920

Kronchin, determined to solidify his control over our lives, moved into the vacant house next door to us. An assistant made himself at home with Lothar, whom I suspect extended the invitation in an attempt to elevate his status within the communist regime. Herr Klatt obeyed the administrator's order and distributed seed grain sent from the Agricultural Organ in Odessa, however, the necessary rain did not materialize and the fertile black soil of the steppe became a myriad of cracks and small crevices. The drought forced us to our knees, and the communists dug their claws in our backs by confiscating every paltry kernel to fill their export contracts.

At the same time, the administration enforced the new government-regulated quotas on eggs, beef, and vegetables in order to keep the factories supplied with healthy laborers, causing a dire situation in the farming villages. Kronchin and the assistant collected the quotas, then escorted our wagon to ensure Gus and I delivered the goods to Karpowa. The smell of rot already assaulted us a few blocks away from the rail station, where foodstuffs overflowing from a lone shed spilled onto the platform and a stray dog chewed on a side of beef in full view of two burly guards.

After the controller directed our wagon next to a pile of putrid waste, Gus jumped from the seat. "*Yop filla mut*, Kronchin. You can't be serious. Ve're not leaving good food to spoil like this shit. No goddamn vay!" he said, kicking a sack of rotten potatoes.

The administrator stared down his nose. "I don't make the rules, I'm only here to enforce them. I have orders to deliver a quota to this rail station, and it is someone else's responsibility to get it to Odessa."

I knew there would be trouble when Gus noisily sucked in his breath. "And everybody at home's hungry, 'cept you fat bastards?" he hissed.

Kronchin straightened his back. "If you haven't begun unloading the wagon in two seconds, I'll empty it myself, and have my man shoot both of you. Then I won't have to listen to your foul mouth any longer." When the comrade drew his pistol, I scampered across the load like a startled monkey and tossed carrots tied in bunches, sacks of potatoes, and heads of cabbage onto the pile, as did Gus, though not as quickly, or as quietly.

On our ride home, Gus said, "Ve're lucky there's no quota on corn. *Ya-naih*, it's only pigs' feed. But if the pigs can eat it, I guess ve can, too."

Indeed, most villagers developed a taste for corn, and soon, that supply also was exhausted. "Are you on a diet, Squeaky?" Fritz teased Herr Hoffer. "Looks like your belly button is shaking hands with your backbone."

Perhaps accepting with humor that which we could not change would get us through whatever the authorities dictated.

Shortly before winter set in, and with no advance notice, the Cheka swooped down on Chornov in four over-sized military trucks. The echo of the church bell summoned the villagers to the churchyard. "We are here to collect grain and flour from every household," Captain Shukov, a tall, wiry man with a mysterious angular face, shouted from the steps. "And I remind you that *hiding grain*, no matter how small an amount, is punishable by death."

Three members of the Cheka emptied our granary, and then together with the captain, stomped to the attic to carry away our last bag of flour, and another of oatmeal. Still not satisfied, Shukov tipped over several barrels to make sure they were empty. Relief washed over me when he ignored the tools stacked across the access hole to The Pantry and, instead, crossed to the opposite side of the chimney. He abruptly popped open the small side door and wrinkled his nose at the sight of the smoker racks. "Damned sausage-eaters. Nobody except *Nemetzis* could like that stinking stuff. Let's go!" The sausages may have disgusted *him*, but at least we would still have something to eat besides the contents of The Pantry.

In mid-afternoon, the bell rang for the second time that day. At Saint Gustav's Church, an elderly couple, Ludwig and Gertrude Reinbold, huddled on the upper step, hands tied behind their backs, fear etched into their faces. Their adult daughter, Irma, who could attain no more than Form One in school, shifted from foot to foot on the bottom step. "Mama! Papa! Come down," she cried. She wiped a sleeve under her dripping nose and pushed past a brusque sentry, who poked his rifle muzzle into her ribs and loudly ordered her into the street.

The largest of the military trucks, the timber-framed box stacked with sacks of wheat and flour, rumbled around the corner and ground to a halt in front of the church. Captain Shukov slid from the passenger seat. Exuding an authority one could almost smell, he adjusted his collar and climbed the stairs to face the Reinbolds. He raised his arm, made a fist, then uncurled two fingers and pointed to the trembling couple. "During the search, my assistants found wheat hidden under a pile of potatoes in *their* root cellar. An entire bucket filled with wheat!"

A sorrowful groan rippled through the crowd. Philomena, standing next to me, made the sign of the cross over her chest. I followed suit, mostly out of habit.

"Everyone must assist in the building of our Soviet state into a model for the world. *Your* duty is to supply grain for export to speed our country's industrialization. *My* duty is to ensure you perform your duty. Now, follow me." Shukov squared his frame and strutted down the steps.

Seven sentries, one no older than I, brushed the villagers aside with their rifles and shoved the Reinbolds in line behind the captain. We paraded toward the small earthen dam that blocked the flow from Chornov Creek, creating the pond where Kurt and I had skipped pebbles on lazy summer days. Suddenly, Irma swerved in front of the captain. She pulled on his sleeve and yelled in his face. "Where are you taking—"

It happened so quickly. The captain raised his pistol and I heard bone crack as he struck Irma on the temple. She shrieked and dropped to the ground with her arms cradling her head. Captain Shukov continued the march down the rutted dirt road, and even though the distraught woman lay in our path, no one dared stop to help her.

Two stern-faced sentries led the shackled couple onto the dam. We witnesses—victims by default—obeyed the captain's order and encircled the pond. Gertrude called out her daughter's name. Irma, blood dripping down her cheek, shoved through the crowd until Philomena grabbed her. She buried her face in Philomena's bosom, cries fading to a low moan.

Shukov strode onto the dam and glanced around, his eyes wild. "Private Toupen! Get that wire from the sluice gate," he barked.

My heart sank. Would the captain uphold the government's threat of death for hoarding a measly bucket of wheat?

"Now, tie these criminals together by the neck."

The private hesitated, perhaps in a moment of compassion. A trembling Ludwig took the opportunity to lean forward and kiss his wife's cheek. "I love you, Gertrude," he said, barely audible. His eyes searched for their daughter. "And we love you, Irma."

A sliver of sunshine broke through the high clouds, illuminating the grim scene. After receiving a glare from the captain, Toupen turned Ludwig and Gertrude back-to-back and wound the wire around their necks. A sneer twisted Captain Shukov's face as he stiffened his arms, lunged forward, and toppled the helpless couple into the water. A rush of bubbles boiled into the cool autumn air.

Women prayed aloud and covered their children's eyes with their aprons; the men could do no more than remove their caps. Irma's scream rang high and thin when she broke away from Philomena and plunged headlong into the water. Up to her chin, she groped beneath the surface for her parents before a single gunshot reverberated off the pond. Shukov, unflinching, waved his smoking pistol and spoke in an even tone. "*This* is the punishment for withholding the State's grain."

The sentries dutifully marched behind their captain and boarded the trucks. They lumbered away, leaving the shocked villagers to rescue the victims. Young Andy Boser and Herr Klatt dove into the water and surfaced with the lifeless couple, the wire dug deep into their necks. Herr Hirsch and Gus staggered from the pond and gently laid Irma's body on the shore. Blood oozed from a single bullet hole in her forehead.

Loni turned to me, her eyes overflowing with the tragedy in the pond. My distraught mother collapsed into my limp arms and rested her forehead on my chest. "*Lieber Gott*. If only we had gone with Kurt. They have it so good in America. Even if I could tell them to their faces, they wouldn't believe how bad it is here."

The callousness of the regime froze the blood in my veins. I buried my face in Mama's hair and wept unashamed at the truth of her words, at the bleakness of our future. I finally understood—we were slaves bound to Lenin's communist ideals.

PART TWO

Five years later

13

THERE'S SOMETHING YOU SHOULD KNOW

Ukrainian Soviet Socialist Republic - June, 1926

I felt a nudge on my shoulder and heard a gravelly voice. "Hey! Wake up. You told me you're getting off at Karpowa."

My bleary eyes focused on the puckered face of the old man seated next to me. "*Ya*, I'm on my way to Chornov," I replied, unable to suppress a smile. I pulled my battered rucksack from the overhead rack, my back complaining from three days of riding in the cramped rail car. As I swung myself off the iron stairs, a mangy yellow dog was leaving his calling card dripping from a rusted metal wheel of the train. 'What a welcome home from army service,' I thought.

I shook my head and glanced around the empty dilapidated rail yard. Years ago, a very serious Igor Kronchin had threatened to shoot Gus when he refused to add our load of foodstuffs to the piles of fetid beef and mice-infested sacks of potatoes. Good ol' Gus.

A dusty path led to Karpowa's co-operative store, where cobwebs hung from the lanterns, and the floor appeared covered by a slimy residue. There was no rice, no sugar, no barrels of olives or dates as there had been when the store was still a private enterprise. The surly proprietor demanded a rouble of my hard-earned army pay in exchange for a few shriveled plums. I refreshed myself at the public well situated down the street, and then set out on foot for Chornov.

An umbrella of thin cloud absorbed the sun's rays, bathing the broad flat steppe in a subdued glow. The area had seen political changes in the last few years. Following the civil war between the Reds and the Whites, the Bolsheviks quashed the Ukraine separatists' attempt to turn South Russia, a province of Russia proper, into an independent country in 1922. Consequently, South Russia, re-named the Ukrainian Soviet Socialist Republic, amalgamated with the other Socialist states, creating the Union of Soviet Socialist Republics (USSR).

Whatever the name of the area, it was a delight to be going home. I envisioned Mama and Loni bursting from the porch, laughing and crying. Though there had been no mention of Papa in the letters received from home during my service, I knew thousands of enlisted men had been classed as 'missing in action' without the disorganized Czar's Imperial Army notifying their concerned families. Regardless, I kept alive the slim hope that he would be there to greet me.

The *clink* of harness chains disrupted my rambling thoughts. A rickety wagon drawn by a scrawny team of chestnuts approached from behind me. "Hey, soldier!" The ruddy-faced driver tipped his hat, revealing a fringe of grey hair. "Hop in. The name's Viktor Lebedin."

I expressed my thanks and climbed onto the seat beside him. "I'm Hans Gerein."

"Go on! You must be Wilhelm Gerein's grandson. Years ago, my father and I went to Chornov and worked for him every harvest. Papa always said that he was the most honest German in the country."

"Did you know my father, Karl, too?"

"Strong as an ox and a hard worker, always so serious, though. Didn't laugh and joke around like your grandpa," he said, and then sighed. "My family bought land with the wages from the German farmers, and we were pretty well off 'til the revolution. Then those communist bastards arrested my father for being too rich and we never heard from him again." The man spat on the ground in disgust.

"I thought only Germans were considered *kulaks*."

"All kinds of people were on the communists' list." Viktor drew his team to a halt. "This is as far as I go. We're working over there." He waved a sinewy hand toward a threshing machine spouting dust and chaff.

I bade him farewell, proud that after all these years Viktor still held my family in such high regard.

Although Chornov was still seven miles across the steppe, the time passed quickly. I hummed a lively tune and bit into a plum, juice dripping down my chin, and recalled helping Grandpa in his orchard. Within an hour's walk of home, the cross on Saint Gustav's Church steeple became visible against the blue sky. I hadn't allowed myself to feel homesick, but tears now clouded my eyes. Upon reaching my yard, the familiarity of the surroundings calmed my nerves. I broke into a broad grin and dropped my rucksack in our porch. "Anybody here?"

Mama and Loni flew from the kitchen. "Is that you … Johannes?" Mama gasped, dropping the wooden spoon clutched in her hand. "You're home!" I swung her off her feet in a tight embrace as she rained my cheeks with kisses. How I had missed her laugh, the smell of her fresh baking, the warmth of her kitchen.

Loni threw her arms around us. "I had so many doubts about you coming back," she said, emotion cracking her voice.

"I missed you, too," I brushed stray hair back from her face. At age twenty-seven and still single, she was considered an old maid. "And Loni, have you heard from Papa?"

My sister shook her head. When I changed the subject by apologizing for being away longer than expected, she teased that I'm still worried about being late, but I'm not too late for Katie Frey.

During my years in the army, I had thought about Katie a great deal, longed for her kisses and often imagined myself lying next to her naked body, but the guilt of Grandpa's death always managed to drive any passion from my mind. "I never asked her to wait," I said, unable to admit my feelings for her. "Besides, Lothar's probably been home from the army for awhile and tried to court her."

"That misfit Degenstein? Nobody likes him, except for maybe the administrator's assistants sharing his mother's house."

"That's the same as before I left. And speaking of the communists, is Igor Kronchin still the chief administrator?"

Before anyone could answer, Aunt Monica and Uncle Heinz rushed into the kitchen. My aunt kissed me and my uncle squeezed my left bicep, remarking that he wouldn't want to meet me on a dark street. My face reflected my embarrassment. "*Ya-naih*, they worked us hard cutting trees and stuff like that. And the food got a lot better near the end of my service."

That evening, Mama and I strolled along Middle Avenue. "Doesn't Loni have a beau? I thought by now she would be married and have one or two rowdy kids of her own," I commented.

"*Ya-naih*, she's not over losing Martin. Nobody in Chornov has heard a word from him, and rumors are he died from his wounds."

A slim young woman, her shiny auburn hair drawn back in a bun, ran toward us. Freckles like spots on a lark's egg scattered across both her flushed cheeks and her nose, which turned up at the tip. She greeted Mama, and then me. Her bright hazel eyes sparkled and the small gap between her upper middle teeth peeked out as she smiled.

"Katie, it's good to see you again," I said, fighting the desire to sweep her into my arms. When she sidled closer and coyly lowered her eyes, I excused myself without regard for her feelings. Mama's glance pierced my back as I set off toward the cemetery, thankful that she hadn't questioned my rudeness.

The sight of gnarled stumps bordering the cemetery entrance shocked me. "Mama, who in hell chopped down the acacia hedge?"

"After all the native trees were cut down, we had to use the windbreaks for firewood. This coming winter better be a mild one, or the fruit trees will be next. Sometimes Goldstein Brothers Freight brings coal from the rail depot in Karpowa, but nobody can afford it, except maybe Ira Goldstein at the inn. And, of course, the administrators get the coal for free."

For the moment, I set aside my bitterness toward our political system and walked among the gravesites. 'Genoveva Gerein 1855-1914' written in molten lead on a metal plate riveted to the decorative iron cross reminded me that Grandma had been my first experience with death. When I patted the grave marker, 'Wilhelm Gerein 1852-1919' my heart burned with anguish.

Despite being happy to rest in my own bed again that night, visiting my grandfather's grave prompted horrid nightmares of a grotesque soldier lunging at Grandpa with a huge bayonet. I heard myself scream, "Run Grandpa! I'm late. It's my fault!" Upon awakening, my mother was sitting on the edge of my bed, my fingers firmly gripping her arm.

"Hans. Come, tell me. Whatever were you late for?" she asked.

I pressed her palms to my anguished face. "There's something you should know, Mama." My tardiness in Selz while spending time with Ottilia, all the dark memories and guilt, gushed from my soul.

"You're not the first boy to be distracted by a girl. Maybe you did make a mistake by being late, Hans, but you didn't do it purposely. You can't let it ruin your life," Mama said calmly.

She stole from the room and I lay awake for hours rehashing the events of that fateful day. While I sat on the floor in the town hall, filled with remorse, Grandpa had whispered to me that even if we had left Selz as planned, the assembling soldiers would still have captured us. The more I thought about it, the more the nagging ache in my mind subsided. My dear grandfather had never considered the incident my fault and it was time to end my self-imposed penance of feeling unworthy of love.

In the morning, Mama invited my uncle to take a seat at the kitchen table. After hearing of my horrid experience, he pushed back his chair and studied me for a moment. "Hans, you should have told us years ago and not lived with all that guilt." He drew a checkered handkerchief from his trouser pocket and blew his nose. "Your Grandpa wouldn't have wanted that. I'm sure of it."

Three rows back, and two rows left. Sure enough, the musty-smelling jar came into view as I clawed away the dirt beside an exposed root of the apricot tree. The rusted metal lid easily twisted off—no roubles. My family survived the lean years by prudently using the money Grandpa had stashed in the jar. My breath caught in my throat when the little red pocketknife fell into my lap. I leaned my head against the rough bark of the tree trunk. In my mind, Kurt was tossing me the knife in exchange for my slingshot. "Don't be sad, Hans. We'll join him in

America soon," Papa had assured me. Could his words, now twelve years later, come true? I re-buried the jar and confidently walked back to the house, the knife secure in my pocket.

"Mama," I called from the porch. "We're all going to *America*! I saved most of my soldier's allowance, and our names are probably still on file from Grandpa's application for passports, so to re-apply shouldn't cost much more than a hefty bribe."

She set her broom against the washstand and gave me a dubious look. "Ach, Hans, suppose you do get the passports, and then Moscow refuses to issue the visas. It'll all be a waste of money."

"If we stay here, we might be doomed for a long time, but if we join Kurt, we'd have a good life. I'm willing to risk everything I've got for that one chance."

My first move was to visit Uncle Heinz and Aunt Monica who readily agreed to my plan. Next, I surprised Loni at the communal garden. She leaned on her hoe and smiled widely. "Of course, I'll go to America, you *Dummkopf*!" she said.

On my way home, a team and a wagon approached from down the street. The driver's chunky physique and his lanky passenger looked familiar. Hubert sprang to the ground before Fritz could stop the horses and caught me in a bear hug. "Hans!" he shouted, a wide grin on his face. "Our Hans Kisser's grown up!"

Fritz chuckled. "Careful, Hubert. It looks like he could crush you like a bug." In a more serious tone, he continued, "Hubert and I were in the service four years, but it seemed like ten. Did the time drag for you, too, Hans?"

"*Ya*, and they treat you like a slave. Stoopid regime."

"You still say 'stupid' the same way." Hubert's caterpillar moustache curled at the ends when he laughed.

My friends and I crowded onto the seat and Fritz turned the wagon around. When we reached my house, we agreed to meet the following day and share our experiences of the last few years.

Darkness had nearly fallen when I asked Mama about Katie. "I guess you wouldn't know Alma Goldstein and her husband from Neufeld had twin boys, but he abandoned his family over the winter. Now Alma is busy with the babies, so Katie works the day shift at the inn." She checked the time on the Kruger clock in the living room. "But she should be home by now."

"Then I'm going to the Freys right away."

Mama's mouth fell open. "Hans! You want to marry Katie!"

"Why are you always so presumptuous?" I tried to look cross, but I was unable to suppress my grin. "You're right, and I'm going over to ask her now. It's sudden, but she'll need a passport, too."

"You can't ask her without a coupler!"

"Then *you* be my representative. But first, I'll help you with the dishes."

Mama tossed the stained dishcloth on the counter and grabbed her Sunday apron from a cupboard drawer. "To hell with the dishes." She paused by the mirror to tuck several stray hairs into her bun, placed a hand in the crook of my arm, and we strutted across the street.

Katie's younger sister, Eva, answered the door and invited us into the living room. Herr Frey's eyebrows rose as I stood before him and asked permission to marry his Katie. "You haven't been *with* her, have you?" he asked.

I shook my head, hoping Mama hadn't noticed my flushed face.

He sighed with relief. "Welcome to the family, Hans. Wait here. I'll call Philomena and Katie."

Katie inched her way into the living room. The words 'would you be my wife' had barely passed my lips when she clapped a hand over her mouth. "Hans! My God, I'd like that very much."

Our eyes locked, but with Mama, Herr Frey and Katie's stepmother in the room, I dared not kiss the girl who had been in my heart since childhood.

14

CONSIDER YOURSELF LUCKY

July, 1926

My army allowance, covered with a thick woolen blanket, my jacket and a water canteen, lay in the bottom of the rucksack. Though Mama didn't fully approve of my plan to obtain passports, she handed me a small bleached sugar sack filled with food before I set off on my thirteen-mile walk to Mannheim. I intended to stay until the passport issue was settled, one way or another.

Dusk had crept along the streets by the time I arrived at the Catholic Church of Mary, my accommodation for the night. Before finishing supper, I cut a slice of sausage for a hump-backed vagrant, then rolled out the blanket on a rear pew, my rucksack serving as a pillow; my dream of going to America would be lost without the money hidden inside.

The next morning, a black Ford's horn encouraged me to slip through the row of traffic—a mix of horse-drawn vehicles dotted by the occasional motorcar. In the twelve years since Herr Bauman drove along Chornov's dirt streets in his open Model T, the majority of upper class citizens had been executed or sent to the *konzlagers*, and now judges and officials well entrenched in the Communist Party were the persons of influence who owned motorcars.

I entered the government office at precisely nine o'clock in the morning, optimism guiding my steps. After a male clerk withdrew a file from the bottom drawer of a rickety wooden cabinet, he discreetly accepted a small bribe and escorted me to the office of Judge Rakhmitov, his superior. The judge, a portly man with darting eyes, stayed seated behind his desk and glanced through the file. "Re-application fees are twenty roubles for each person," he sniped. "And you have five people, so that's a hundred. Plus, the new applicant Katie Frey requires a four hundred rouble fee."

My lungs deflated. "Bu-but that's impossible for me."

Rakhmitov shrugged his rounded shoulders. I counted out the hundred roubles re-application fees. "You collected the full fee for my grandfather, now deceased." I added a twenty to the pile of notes. "Could you not insert the new name as a re-application?"

"I can, if I see you're making a serious inquiry."

I placed a bribe of one hundred roubles on the desk. He snatched the money and closed the file. "You will have the passports in one month."

"One month!" I blinked away the salty sting of perspiration. Only one hundred and sixty roubles remained from my army pay, but I felt compelled to present another hundred. "I need them, sir … today."

The smirking judge tugged the money from my clenched fist. "Be here at noon. Don't be late."

"Twelve o'clock sharp. You can count on it." One of his knuckles cracked under the pressure of my handshake, but really, I wanted to break all of the greedy bastard's fingers.

The clock in the outer office chimed twelve times as I arrived for my appointment. A well-dressed man, whom Rakhmitov introduced as Judge Valachenko, slouched in a swivel chair beside the desk. I suspected a trap until he explained that two signatures were required on the approval sheet for all passports. "Judge Valachenko, I'd be grateful if you signed the documents so my family can receive our passports today," I said earnestly.

"And how grateful would you be?"

My only alternative was to reach to the bottom of my rucksack and withdraw fifty roubles. He signed one of the documents, tapped his pen on the desk and waited until I reluctantly admitted there was no more to give him.

"How can you come here expecting such huge favors without

the means to show your appreciation?" he demanded.

I glared at Rakhmitov. "I showed my appreciation earlier today."

"I have the hundred and twenty for re-application fees." Rakhmitov said, struggling to keep his voice even. Although both the dishonest judge and I realized he had collected an additional two hundred roubles from me, I knew better than to point out his error.

"Show me what you have in that bag," Valachenko finally said. The blanket, my canteen, a few morsels of food and several coins fell from the overturned rucksack. "Guess you can't squeeze blood from a stone." He signed the remaining documents and huffed from the office with my fifty roubles in his pocket.

Rakhmitov tossed the documents across the desk. "Consider yourself lucky."

After putting a few blocks between me and the crooked judge, I reviewed the passports. 'Approved July 7, 1926.' A pivotal day in my life. I leapt into the air and clicked my heels, feeling like the luckiest man alive.

Excitement built as my family and the Freys gathered in our living room late that evening. Katie's brother Georg raised his glass of wine. "Hans, you did one hell'uva job. Let's celebrate!"

Aunt Monica dampened the mood. "Not so fast, Georg. We don't have exit visas yet."

Herr Frey folded himself into Grandpa's chair and drained his glass. "If the newly betrothed couple agrees to it, the little money we have can go toward the visas instead of a wedding celebration."

When Katie's eyes welled with tears, I clasped her hand and said, "It's good we both agree not to waste the money on a celebration."

Sixteen-year-old Eva tromped across the room and thrust out her chin at me. "She's crying because she won't have a wedding, not because she's happy! All girls daydream about their wedding day. The dress, the meal, the dance, all of it. With Papa promising the money for visas, Katie's dream is gone, but all you men care about is the wedding night! That's—"

Herr Frey began to admonish his youngest daughter, but Katie interrupted him. "It's all right, Papa. We need to leave Russia more than I need a wedding reception."

My face felt hot. "Katie, please accept my apology. I feel so stoopid."

She kissed me on the cheek, and then blushed at her boldness.

Mama broke the awkward silence. "We're so grateful, Franz, for your generous offer. There's still the travel expenses, but I'm sure something will work out."

We sang old German folk songs, told jokes, and discussed America. Shortly after the Freys departed, Ira Goldstein paid us a surprise visit. "Franz came to the inn and told me that you need two hundred roubles. Your grandfather and father were always good to me, Hans, so I'd like to repay their kindness with a loan. You can send back the money after you're settled in America."

"Maybe you should think about it. We might never—"

Mama pushed me aside and shook his hand as if it were a pump handle. "That is so generous of you, Herr Goldstein. We'll be forever grateful to you."

"Well, that's settled then. I'll return with the money tomorrow morning." As he tipped his hat and bade us farewell, I wondered if Grandpa would have approved of us borrowing from a friend. *Naih*, Mama had been right; he would want us to seize every opportunity to better our lives.

Two days later, I set out to clear another roadblock to America—obtaining emigration visas for my family members. After a tedious and, thankfully, uneventful three-day train trip to Moscow, I hurried from the station to the government administration offices. The old city's architecture along the wide streets captivated me. Five-story buildings painted the colors of the rainbow rubbed shoulders with one another, an array of marble columns and dark granite staircases gracing their entrances. The onion domes of the Coptic churches added flashes of color to the skyline and, in the distance, the Ivan the Great Bell Tower rose above the opulence of the Kremlin.

I elected to receive the visas in person, even though an official at the office assured me he would forward the papers by mail within seven days. I was first in line every morning to check on the approval process and, on the fourth day, an aggravated clerk handed me a large envelope. “Here, Comrade Gerein, they’re ready. Now, please go home.”

Dizzy from exhilaration, I danced down the stairs. America! We were practically there.

On the way home, I disembarked at the Karpowa train station, then visited Viktor Lebedin, with whom I had dinner before he graciously offered me a ride to Chornov. Seated in the same rickety wagon as after my return from the army, I told him about our visas and the excitement for the future. He clasped my face for a moment. “Hans, I can see the goodness of your grandfather in you.”

“You don’t know how much I appreciate the comment,” I replied. “And may you enjoy good health for many more years.”

I arrived home eager to share my news with Kurt and immediately sat at the kitchen table and penned a letter.

Kurt Gerein
Devils Flats N. D.
USA

July 19, 1926

Dear American Brother,

May the Good Lord protect you for all your days. Please read this letter with an open mind. I swear this will be the last time I ask for your assistance.

There are now six adults, including Uncle Heinz, Aunt Monica and my soon-to-be wife, Katie Frey. We already have passports and exit visas. The papers cost us all our money, plus a loan Ira Goldstein generously offered.

Our harvest should fill the government quota, but won't leave much to sell at market. Many beggars already roam the countryside, so there are no jobs available for us. If you or Uncle Pius have the means to send our ship passage, we will be eternally grateful. I beg you to do so as soon as possible, for I fear our visas may be canceled at any time. If you cannot help, we are thankful for the money you have already sent.

Your brother, Hans

I removed a small brown package from my rucksack before preparing for bed and carefully cut the string with Kurt's little red pocketknife. I had slept in an alley and fasted for three days in Moscow to save enough money to buy the delicate garment shimmering in the lantern light.

15

NOW IT'S MY TURN TO GIVE

August, 1926

August 15. By the end of the day, Katie would be my wife. As I nervously waited at the altar, my thoughts reverted to the previous week and the preparation for the wedding. Katie had excitedly displayed her trousseau stored in the wooden trunk with beautifully carved roses on the lid. Philomena and Eva commented that the embroidery along one edge of the pillowcases made from cloth sugar sacks showed an artistic touch, while Mama noted the pattern of the dainty cup and saucer set. Katie lamented that she had no decent garment to wear as a wedding dress, and let out a shrill scream when I unfolded my purchase from Moscow. She gushed over the design of the stunning white gown with narrow straps supporting the bodice. Fine darts formed a tight waist and the full skirt flared into an arc. "*Grosser Gott*, Hans!" She wrapped her arms around my neck. "It's gorgeous!" I replied that my bride deserved to look spectacular on her wedding day.

Hubert, my groomsman, nudged me back to the present, and said he could see my knees shaking, while Georg, my second attendant, eyed Genni Vetter seated in a side pew with her parents. I glanced at Mama and imagined Papa beside her, an approving smile on his lips. Although Kurt would have whispered a snide remark about me ruining my life, I still missed him on this special occasion.

The organist played the wedding march as Ivan's two young daughters scattered flower petals ahead of Eva and Loni, the bridesmaids. Katie, a long lace veil plaited through her bright auburn hair, and looking as lovely as I had imagined, proceeded slowly down the aisle with her father. The tradition-minded priest glared over his spectacles at the mid-calf hemline of the billowing white skirt and snorted his disapproval as murmurs of admiration sounded above the music. I shook Herr Frey's hand at the Communion Rail and guided his daughter to a chair beside mine. She gave Loni her bouquet of fresh daisies before I slipped her deceased mother's wedding ring onto her finger, my chest bursting with pride.

Following the ceremony, Hubert plopped a black narrow-brimmed top hat on my head. Under a beautiful sun-drenched sky, Katie and I, feeling loved and special, walked among the well-wishers in the churchyard, graciously accepting gifts and small donations of money. Frau Silbernagel presented us with two eggs from her only chicken. "You didn't need to bring a gift," I said. "Just having you here is our pleasure."

The frail old woman raised her cane in mock anger. "You and your brother and father often brought me hay and straw. Now it's my turn to give."

Her financial situation was dire; this gift was precious. I lightly touched her shoulder. "Katie and I thank you, Frau Silbernagel, from the bottom of our hearts."

Even though Herr Frey had donated the reception money for our visas, Philomena had insisted on a small celebration. The jovial guests paraded down the street to the Frey's front yard, and formed a line under the row of apricot trees where improvised tables covered with sugar-sack tablecloths held enticing plates of baked chicken, potato salad and fresh vegetables. The scene reminded me of Uncle Heinz's wedding when Kurt stuffed his mouth with cherry pie and mumbled that people should get married more often.

Tradition dictated the bridesmaids present Katie and me with morsels of bread and salt to be 'washed down' with a glass of wine. Next, Hubert stood and proposed a toast. I put a finger to my lips, afraid he would embarrass Katie with a shady joke. However, he chuckled and wished all our children to have their mother's good looks, and not to take after me!

As the women cleared the dishes from the tables, Georg opened their gate to welcome a fiddle player, an accordionist, and a man with a large harmonica. "We can't have a dance on a Sunday.

Father Heisser will excommunicate us," Herr Frey admonished his son.

Georg directed the musicians to the thoroughly swept threshing floor. "Oh, but I got his permission."

Uncle Heinz grinned. "I know our priest doesn't give in easy. What'd you have to promise him?"

"Ach, nuthin' much. Only three gallons of Mass wine." Out the side of his mouth, he added, "Any idea where I can get it?"

"Katie, come to the floor," Hubert shouted three times. He then repeated the traditional call for me.

The guests joined hands and formed a circle along the edge of the dance floor. The buzz of conversation ended as my glowing bride and I swirled to the strains of the Viennese Waltz. Franz and Philomena Frey, along with our Godparents, were the first to join us, and then Uncle Heinz and Mama. Next, the wedding attendants and the guests fell into step.

Katie later chatted with a former classmate and I shared a drink with Georg, Hubert, Fritz, and Ivan. While we discussed our army years, Hubert joked, "If Hans' grandfather were here, he would say, 'Who loves not women, wine and song remains a fool his whole life long.' That's a quote from Martin Luther."

"Well, then, I certainly won't be a fool," Fritz laughed.

Lothar joined us and tapped Fritz on his arm. "What's so funny?"

"We were just commenting that Hans never spent his money on drinking and womanizing."

Lothar scowled. "Then maybe somebody should tell him that a woman's like a necktie—you don't notice either of them 'til they're hanging around your neck."

From the corner of my eye, I saw Whiskey Wolff stagger into the yard. The uninvited guest ignored everyone and angled toward the refreshment table. He drained his first glass of brandy in one gulp and shakily poured himself another. Philomena glared with malice before adjusting the knot of her dark kerchief and stomping over to Whiskey. Hatred dripped from her words. "*Du Slabsack*. How dare a tramp like you come into my yard after shooting my son? And you have the nerve to drink our liquor?" She spun him by the shoulder to face her at the very moment he hoisted his glass.

Whiskey glanced at the brandy dripping from his fingers, and at his half-empty glass. In a motion belying his state of intoxication, he flung the remainder into her face. "You witch. I should—"

Philomena drew in her breath, then ejected a gob of spittle, which struck Whiskey's prominent nose and deflected into his right eye. He lunged toward her, but she stumbled backwards and fell on her ample posterior. "W-what the …"

It was one of the few times that I had seen her at a loss for words.

Whiskey darted back and forth like a cornered weasel, shouting profanities until Hubert and Fritz grabbed his arms and escorted him from the premises. Lothar helped his mother to her feet and brushed dried grass from her dress. The band played several more tunes, though most of the guests gathered into small groups, discussing pertinent issues such as Katie's controversial dress, and the incident with Whiskey. Even Philomena cracked a thin smile when she overheard Herr Klatt say, "If Philomena's spit is as lethal as her tongue, Whiskey's gonna be blind by morning."

Katie and I clasped hands and walked back to Mama's house as the last rays of the sun caressed the treetops. "Considering I wasn't expecting any reception at all, I will remember this day for the rest of my life, even the argument," my bride said.

For my part, our honeymoon night took priority over discussing my mother-in-law. I gazed into the eyes of the girl I had admired since we were in grade school and told her how beautiful she looked in her wedding dress. Closing the porch door, I reached behind me to drop the bolt in place, leery of our friends. I swept Katie off her feet and stumbled on the edge of the hemp rug. "Stoopid rug," I blurted, feeling the effects of the wine. Katie giggled, wound her arms around my neck, and we engaged in our first lingering kiss. "Frau Gerein, welcome to your new home. Let me show you my favorite room."

"And which might that be, Herr Gerein?"

My eyes misted over when I opened the bedroom door and saw the sheets on my grandparents' large poster bed. "T-those were Mama and Papa's sheets … before the war. She never used them again after he was taken away."

Katie lightly patted my hand. "They're very special, Hans. We'll have to thank your mother for her thoughtfulness." She glanced at the nightgown and the nightshirt on the bed. "I'll change in the living room. You can use this bedroom."

"Here. Let me help you with your veil." Katie was not surprised when I withdrew the little red pocketknife from my trouser pocket to unwind a thin strand of hair hopelessly entangled in the lace; she knew the knife was my constant companion.

My body twitched with anticipation, and I tried to embrace her, but she slipped from my arms and scooped up her nightgown. "Not so fast, my dear," she whispered over her shoulder.

We met in the center of the bedroom when Katie returned wearing her nightgown. Neither of us spoke, but our eyes and arms locked, and lastly our lips. She drew back, and massaged the tight muscles in my neck before opening the buttons of my nightshirt. The light growth of brown hair on my chest only partially covered the deep crisscrossing scars. "Does that still hurt?" she said. Feeling somewhat embarrassed, I shook my head and she traced over the lacerations with her fingertips, her touch soft as a shadow.

My clumsy fingers fumbled with the tiny buttons on her nightgown until her enticing breasts popped above the embroidered neckline. "It's good we're not newlyweds every day," she giggled as she deftly slipped out of the garment and let it fall to the floor. We dove into bed and were soon in a frenzied tangle of arms and legs.

Later, Katie rested her head on my bare shoulder. "I always knew you'd be a good lover."

I ran my finger down the small of her back. "How could I not be with you as my partner?"

We reminisced about the years we had known each other. "Remember when you told Master Blokin that Lothar kicked me and he got a strapping from the old guy?"

"Sure, I remember. Then you rescued me from him on the street. Did I ever thank you for that?"

"Why do you think my friends call me Hans Kisser?" I nuzzled her bare shoulder.

"That wasn't a kiss." She put her hand behind my head. "Come here, I'll show you a kiss!"

Her pert breasts crushing against my chest stirred the passion within me. I drew her close. The roosters were crowing before we finally fell asleep.

Bleary-eyed, I slipped on my nightshirt and answered the loud knock on the porch door. Mama, followed by Loni and Eva, pushed me aside. "Are you two still in bed? It's almost noon. We've got Katie's family and the wedding attendants coming for dinner in half an hour."

"Behave yourselves," said Loni with a lurid wink. "We've got a youngster here." She cast a glance at Eva.

Eva pouted. "I'm sixteen. I know what they did."

Mama arched her eyebrows. "*Eih*, *eih*, *eih*! What's this younger generation coming to? Even if I had known about the birds and bees when I was sixteen, I would certainly have kept it to myself." She threw my shirt to me. "Hans, get dressed. We don't have much time."

Katie hastily wound her hair into a bun, and my unbuttoned shirt collar flapped in the breeze as we finally hurried outside, but something seemed amiss. "Where's Hubert? Is that damn prankster in the house?" I raced to the porch to block the door. "Hubert, don't you dare bring that out!"

He extended his arm out the kitchen window. "You're too late. Here, Heinz, grab this."

Uncle Heinz ran between the tables with our bed sheet

fluttering behind him like a flag, the red stain clearly visible. "Uncle Heinz was so mad when somebody did that at his wedding. Now look at him," I complained to my blushing wife.

She smiled and laid her hands on mine. "Like your mother says, 'it's tradition.' Hans, let them have their fun. We've already had ours."

16

THERE WAS TRUTH IN HIS STATEMENT

November, 1926

I had written to Kurt in July with the request for ship passage tickets and expected a reply within two months. By mid-November, my family assumed we had offended our American relatives with the request for more money, or they chose to forget about us in the twelve years since they left Russia. However, I was still first in line every mail day to check for a letter. One bitterly cold morning in late December, I awoke early and decided I *had* to take action. Hubert lent me his greatcoat for my trek to the post office in Mannheim, the distribution center for mail to the Kutschurgan communities. My friend's offer was appreciated; the article with a yellow 'P' emblazoned on the left breast being his only possession from Pototski Estate.

I stomped the snow from my boots before entering the post office and waited at a counter stacked with parcels. The elderly postmaster assured me that his office held no items for Chornov.

"Could you please check the undeliverable mail?" I asked. "Maybe the address or the name was misspelled."

He refused until I threatened to lodge a complaint to his supervisor. "Judge Rakhmitov doesn't …" he began, before peering over the spectacles that clung precariously to the end of his crooked nose. "Ohhh, all right. I'll take a minute, but no more. What's the name?"

"It's Gerein. Rosina or Johannes."

He glanced at me sharply, selected a sheet of paper from a desk drawer and crossed to a window on the back wall. He laid the paper on the sill, rummaged through a large box on the floor, and returned to the counter. "*Nyet*, nothing."

Out on the street, I focused my mind on the postmaster's jumbled words. Was Judge Rakhmitov somehow involved with the disappearance of Kurt's letter? When the next customer engaged the clerk, I crept around the building and peered through the dusty window. Luck was on my side; the paper was still on the windowsill. A column of surnames followed each Kutschurgan village name. Under Chornov, I read 'Gerein.'

I stepped back from the window and leaned against the cold brick wall. Gerein? It would be impossible to return home without further investigation. I would wait for darkness in a small tavern and plot my next move.

I slogged through the snow, feeling miserable and sorry for myself. Tomorrow would be Christmas Eve and instead of helping decorate the house, I was putting myself at risk to satisfy a hunch. Near midnight, I pulled up the collar of Hubert's greatcoat and stepped out of the tavern into the brisk wind. But I wasn't alone. As a celebration of the tenth anniversary of communism, our government had recently released all prisoners, except murderers and political dissenters. Many of them wandered the streets day and night, homeless beggars looking for any shelter. I circled the block twice to ensure no one was watching me before stopping at the rear of the government building. The blade of Kurt's little red pocketknife barely fit between the window and the rotted frame. *Pop.* The lock released. I struggled to control my fear as I stood on an old crate and hoisted myself through the opening. The unlocked knob of an etched glass door labeled 'Rakhmitov' at the end of a narrow hallway turned easily in my sweaty palm.

Once inside the room, I lit a match and searched the desk drawers, but there was nothing of interest until one compartment of a side cabinet wouldn't budge. Again, the pocketknife proved useful and, within seconds, a haphazard pile of envelopes spilled out onto the floor. Kurt's handwriting! My trembling fingers slipped out a neatly folded page and a glossy black and white photograph. I brushed away tears with the back of my hand at the sight of Kurt's portrait. "*Lieber Gott*, have you ever changed," I mumbled. "We should have grown to be men together. How can we ever make up for the lost time?"

While still crouched behind the desk, I sacrificed two more

matches to study his features, and then checked the date on the letter. September?

Johannes Gerein
Chornov, Cherson
USSR

Sept. 1, 1926

Dear Mama, Loni, Hans, and Katie,

I greet all of you with a prayer that we will soon be in each other's arms as we are in the arms of the Lord.

We were so excited to get your letter and to know you are finally coming to join us. Hans, I wasn't surprised to hear you married Katie. You two were meant for each other since grade school. I recently married a girl I met in school, too, but we will have another celebration after you arrive, so please hurry. You will like Marie.

Uncle Pius and I pooled our money and with only a small loan from our bank, we were able to buy passage for all of you. I've included six tickets, which are valid for your train ride, too. So that's all you'll need to get from Karpowa to the ship and from New York to Devils Lake.

I could read no further. Feeling sick to my stomach, I frantically searched the entire file for the tickets, unwilling to believe the obvious—the bastard Rakhmitov had stolen them! Since he signed all of the passport approvals, he knew who was expecting financial aid from overseas and instructed the postmaster to intercept their letters, as the tickets would readily bring cash. The judge, although crooked as a snake's backbone, held a position of power and if I reported his thievery, the police would arrest *me* for breaking into his office. Nothing could be done except to perhaps keep the photograph. At least

I would be returning home with something. With the letters tucked back in the bundle and the cabinet closed, I eased out the window and embarked on the long journey home, the devastation of my discovery weighing heavily on my heart.

I arrived at our house mid-morning and was relieved that Katie and Loni were away visiting Alma and her boys. Mama's face twisted with anger when I related to her my discovery in the judge's office. "Now we'll never see Kurt again," she sobbed, leaning against my shoulder. "Oh, Hans. You could have at least brought his photograph home."

Her delight at Kurt's image warmed my soul. "Somehow I couldn't envision him as anything other than a boy. Except for his blond and curly hair, you two look so much the same," she said before a concerned expression wrinkled her forehead. "Is it dangerous to have this photograph?"

"The judge already took what he wanted from us. He won't look at those letters again." My misgivings evaporated in the glow of her smile.

My family exchanged simple gifts the next morning. I had used the pocketknife to whittle a comb for Katie from the burl of an apricot tree, and she, in turn, presented me with a thin envelope. After reading the artistic handmade card, I tossed it in the air and caught Katie in a tight embrace. "You are?" I whooped.

Loni retrieved the card from the floor. "I am pregnant," she read aloud.

"You're what?" Mama exploded.

Loni's face reddened. "Not *me*. Katie's gonna have a baby."

"*Ya*, in July." Katie rubbed her tummy.

Mama rushed to hug her. "This turned out to be a good Christmas after all, *gehl*?"

The news of a baby was thrilling. I had always seen myself as a family man, but it saddened me that Papa and Kurt were not there to share my excitement. And Grandpa and Grandma would surely have relished the chance to spoil a great-grandchild.

Katie closed our bedroom door in mid-afternoon and I drew her to the bed. "I can't believe we're gonna be parents! What do you want? A boy or girl?"

She looked at me with her bright hazel eyes. "Above everything, I want a healthy baby. But since you ask, a girl would be nice."

"All right, you can have your girl first, but then I get two boys in a row." We bantered back and forth until we fell asleep.

I awoke with her head on my chest; the angle of the sun coming through the window indicated late afternoon. Perhaps it was unfair to keep the news of the stolen tickets from her. Although disappointed we would not be going to America, she said we'd be fine living in Chornov, we were together and that's what mattered the most.

Uncle Heinz and Aunt Monica joined us for supper. Upon hearing of Katie's pregnancy, they raised their glasses in a toast and said we would be terrific parents.

At the end of our visit, I related the news of my discovery in Mannheim to the rest of the family. My sister listened with her mouth wide open, and then ran to her room; Aunt Monica shook her head in disbelief and grasped Mama in her arms, while Uncle Heinz sprang to his feet. "I'll strangle the crooked bastard with my one hand," he yelled. "We'll never recover from a loss like this. Never! He's condemned us all to communism."

There was truth in his statement, however, I had already accepted the pain of knowing we wouldn't get to America.

The fourth Saturday in July, I returned home from the fields and bent over the water trough to wash the sweat from my face. Loni screamed behind me, "Katie's gone into labor. Get the mid-wife and I'll call Philomena."

Torn between yelping with joy and running for help, I hurried to recruit the aged Frau Silbernagel and gently coaxed her down the street thinking, 'Come on, Frau, there's a baby waiting to be born.'

Katie settled into bed as the mid-wife barked orders. "Rosina, get some towels. Philomena, boil the water."

"Not until *he's* out of here," Mama retorted, pushing me out the porch door. "And stay away until you're called."

The realization that I would soon be a father raised some difficult questions: Would our child be happy with me as a papa? Would the baby like our world? I weeded in the garden to distract myself, and upon hearing the anguished cries of my wife, I decided never to put her through that again, though I was aware such an idea would not be realistic.

Three agonizing hours later, my sister called and I dashed to the bedroom, all the while thanking God my wife and the baby had survived the ordeal. Katie lay supported by two large pillows, her eyes closed, her auburn hair matted to her forehead. I bent to kiss her warm cheek. My heart fluttered when a tiny pink face peeked out from the fold of a tattered white towel resting on my wife's arm. Our baby!

"Meet your daughter," Katie whispered, glowing with pride. She lifted the towel to fully expose fat, round cheeks, a dimpled chin, and a head crowned with silky brown hair. "This is your papa, little one."

As if on cue, the baby stretched her mouth in a toothless yawn and fell asleep. "Guess she already thinks I'm boring." I joked, lightly stroking the infant's tiny hands. "Seriously, Katie, she is beautiful. She looks like you and definitely has your nose."

Katie gazed into my eyes. "If you agree, I'd like her to have my mother's name, Amilia. And for her second name, should we pick Lydia? It sounds so German, don't you think?"

"Amilia Lydia. I like it. July 23, 1927 will always be one of my favorite dates."

17

I COULDN'T TAKE THAT RISK

October, 1928

A year later, when Amilia was a chubby toddler, Stalin introduced his five-year plan to re-shape the Soviet Union. Before a general meeting one autumn day, a motorcar and a long, black van with barred rear windows barreled down the street and parked beside the town hall.

"Better hope it's not the new police unit from Mannheim," Fritz warned. "I've heard the GPU are damned strict."

"That's all ve need. More damn rules and regulations," Gus said. He was about to spit on the floor, but stopped himself, looking around sheepishly. "Guess that's against a rule, too."

Kronchin stood at the front of the hall, drumming his fingers on his arm. Appearing nervous, he said with authority in his voice, "Our esteemed leader Josef Stalin has a brilliant plan for our young nation. Some changes will be worked in over the long term, while others will be implemented immediately." He cleared his throat. "First, all farm land, whether allotted to you or leased, will be organized into a *kolkhoz* in each village. All decisions for the communal farms—"

His words were a punch to the stomach. My shouts mixed with those of other enraged farmers:

"How can we live if you take away our income?"

"Damned if you're going to cancel my lease!"

"You sons-of-bitches think you can do whatever you want!"

Kronchin put two fingers to his lips and whistled loudly. "Order! Furthermore, everyone—farmer, blacksmith, or shopkeeper—will become an employee of the *kolkhoz*. Wages and opportunities will be fair and equal to women as well as men. As your administrator, I will organize committees to oversee everything from land management to animal herds and the labor force."

Most of the communists' previous promises had turned sour. I glanced out the corner of my eye and the worried look on Uncle Heinz's face reflected my own thoughts. Young Andy Boser spoke first. "Tell us. Why would we be better off in your system?"

"Because we can all unite and work for the common good of our country, and for ourselves. The Agricultural Organ in Odessa promised us some machinery, maybe even a tractor, and the seed won't have to be distributed among all you small landholders, saving both time and grain."

When Ivan expressed concern about our wages, Kronchin's answer gained him considerable support. "After the communal farm's yearly quota is delivered to the rail station, we will be free to sell our excess grain and the money will be distributed according to your contribution of time worked. You'll then be able to purchase whatever you require from our co-operative store."

In a way, his statements made sense. We could probably farm more efficiently by pooling our machinery and horses, and if families loafed while others carried the workload, they would receive fewer wages. But what about personal choice? It seemed 'Uncle Joe' would have complete control over our lives.

The administrator searched our faces. "Who will be the first to assign their allotted land?"

Lothar stood to ensure everyone saw him. "I'll gladly give up my land for The Cause." It was actually smart of him to do this; he already received the privileges of an assistant administrator, and being first to assign his land would elevate his status in the Communist Party.

Whiskey Wolff swayed to his feet. "I will too."

"Me and my boys can farm our own land," said Gus, a vicious scowl doubling the furrows on his brow. "Ve don't need your commune." He nudged his sons, Albert and Josef, seated in the row ahead of him.

Albert leaned close to Josef before rising to his feet. "My brother's and my land lease is in our own names. If we don't agree with our father, can we become members without him?"

A smirk crossed Kronchin's face. "Certainly, you can."

Gus's eyes narrowed. "My sons! Vhy vould you go against me?"

"I've got a family to feed, Papa," Albert said. "I can't fight communism anymore. Besides, in the end, I don't think anybody's really gonna have a choice."

Gus kicked back his chair and stomped toward the door. "You vait and see. These bastards aren't doing you a favor."

Following his father's departure, Albert reclaimed his seat and sunk his chin onto his chest.

In slow progression, the farmers—with the exception of the Ripplingers, Gus, Mama, Uncle Heinz, and I—pledged their properties to the *kolkhoz*.

Every head in the hall turned when the door flew open and three dour-faced comrades escorted in a stocky young man, a thin folder tucked under his arm. The shuffling of feet and the chatter of the crowd faded; a sense of foreboding hung in the stale air. He briskly approached Kronchin, his pressed uniform, polished high top boots and regulation cap lending him the air of a dedicated police officer. The administrator hoisted the man's arm over his head. "This is Captain Vasily Orlenko of the GPU Police Force," he announced loudly.

The captain flashed a tight smile as Kronchin relinquished the floor to him. Without further ado, Orlenko snapped a crisp sheet of paper in his hand and said, "Religious instructions for children are henceforth deemed illegal. Wasting productive time on a God that doesn't exist is counter-revolutionary."

Father Heisser immediately rose from his chair and stabbed the air with a finger. "Are you saying we can no longer raise our children within the sacred teachings of the Catholic faith?"

"You are correct. Josef Stalin will not tolerate religious teachings by any denomination."

At a nod from the captain, two officers grabbed the indignant priest by the arms and dragged him out the door. "Furthermore," Captain Orlenko continued, "our leniency in re-instating the former *kulak* families is over." He looked around the room. "Where is Hubert, son of former Pototski Estate owner Benedict Bauman?"

No one responded. Following an angry glare from the captain, Kronchin pointed to my friend.

"Hubert's not a *kulak*," I yelled. "And he's certainly not responsible for his father's actions. You can't take him away without a trial."

The official snickered. "A trial? We will show as much mercy as the estate owners showed their servants." He signaled to his returning men, and they converged on Hubert, who grabbed his father's greatcoat from his chair and nodded to Fritz and me before they forced him out the door.

That son of a bitch Orlenko! Hubert was innocent, but protesting at this time would only result in my own arrest. I regretted that, as a family man, I couldn't take that risk.

"To ensure the system operates smoothly, my men and I will take up residence in Chornov." The captain surveyed his notes. "Fritz Ripplinger, you and your mother live in the largest property in town. Tonight, we will move into your house."

With that, Kronchin rapped firmly on the table and adjourned the meeting. The dazed crowd pushed their way outside in time to catch a glimpse of Hubert and Father Heisser locked in the rear of the black van before it roared down Church Street. "You're like a black raven, but you swoop down and pluck *people* away," Philomena yelled, waving her fist.

In the morning, Mama and I checked to see whether Orlenko had moved into the Ripplinger's house. Fritz and his mother invited us into their summer kitchen—a single room furnished with a small warped table, three mismatched chairs, and an old cabinet displaying a few chipped dishes. "I guess this room is our home now," said Fritz. "The GPU got here before we did last night and wouldn't let us take anything from the house, except the clothes they threw into the yard."

Frau Ripplinger gestured toward a pile of straw in a corner.

"That's where we slept last night."

"We'll be okay," Fritz consoled his mother. "I'm more worried about poor Hubert and sure hope he wasn't sent to a *konzlager*."

Apparently, the Communist Party intended to wipe out the former upper class, and I doubted Hubert would receive an exemption.

Later in the week, another letter arrived from America, confirming my suspicion that Rakhmitov had intercepted only the letter he expected would contain money or valuables, and had since moved on to another victim. Although not a surprise, Kurt's news was, nevertheless, devastating. Due to a meager harvest, there would be no chance of new tickets soon. We would carry on with our lives; whether to join the *kolkhoz*, the immediate issue.

That afternoon, I pushed a wheelbarrow loaded with vegetables to the communal store. Katie followed close behind me with Amilia on her hip, her skirt gathering dust from the dry roadway. The aging shopkeeper didn't make the usual funny faces for the baby. "Don't need to buy any vegetables today," Squeaky Hoffer said, his eyes studying the worn planking of the floor.

I glanced from the few wilted carrots he had in a wooden bin to the large heads of cabbage, firm turnips, and bright purple beets in my wheelbarrow. "But look at these—"

Katie silenced me. "Don't say anything more, Hans. The administrator won't let you deal with people who didn't join the *kolkhoz,* will he, Squeaky?"

"He threatened to move me to the fields if I buy anything from you. Sorry that …"

I patted his shoulder. "It's not your fault. They've got us to where we don't dare make our own decisions anymore."

After we left the store, rapid footsteps approached from behind and an unfamiliar man overtook us, blocking our path. He tipped his chin to look me in the face. "You're Hans Gerein, aren't you?" Not allowing me time to reply, he thumped a stubby finger on his chest.

"Well, I'm Luka Nikolai and I'm here to help with Kronchin's administration service. I'm living with Lothar Degenstein until a house of my own is available." When the church bell peeled an erratic chime, a sneer crossed his face as he said, "Captain Orlenko said there's no religion allowed in Russia anymore, so our men are taking out that goddamn noisy bell."

We turned toward the church at the very moment the wooden louvers in the east-facing opening of the steeple shattered into splinters. As if in slow motion, the large brass bell teetered on the sill, became air-borne, and with a deafening *clang*, landed on the steps and wedged itself against the polished stone banister. Nikolai's smirk confirmed my suspicion that he relished the repugnant aspects of his job. In that moment, I realized how heartless he could be.

Under the circumstances, I dare not lose my temper, but could at least rile him. "If there's no religion allowed, how are we going to worship your Lord Stalin?"

Nikolai shuffled like a stiff-legged bantam rooster. "Don't ever make fun of Father Stalin again." He ogled Katie from head to toe and strutted away. "What's a woman like you doing with a lug like that?" he called over his shoulder.

I ached to crush him under my heel. Instead, my wife and I trudged down the street, the still-laden wheelbarrow dragging our spirits down like an anchor.

At some point during the night, there came an incessant pounding on the door. "Be careful, Hans," Katie cautioned. Amilia stirred in her crib beside our bed, but quickly fell back to sleep.

Now wide-awake and clad only in my nightshirt, I stumbled to lift the door bolt, knowing the news wouldn't be good—not at this hour. Captain Orlenko pushed the door open and shoved me aside. "Out of the way, *Nemetzi*," he ordered.

The Bastard! "You can't barge into my house? Get out of—"

The glint of a pistol reflected in the dim light of his lantern.

"Shoot him if he says another word," he commanded one of his comrades. "And you over there! Check the other room. I'll get the bedrooms."

A groan escaped me when the comrade in the living room called out, "Hey, Captain. Look at this!"

Orlenko rushed to his comrade. "That's a young boy, not a man, you idiot!"

The sons-of-bitches were looking for Kurt's photograph! Sweat dampened my hair when the captain barged into Loni's, then Mama's bedroom, and rifled through the dresser drawers. Cursing, he stomped into the kitchen, followed closely by the women. He grabbed me by the collar. "You haven't seen the last of us. We'll be watching you," he said, his mustached upper lip coming so close that I could smell garlic on his breath. The intruders hustled away, leaving the porch door standing wide open.

My mother reached deep into the neckline of her nightgown to withdraw the photograph of Kurt. "Sometimes it helps to be buxom," she giggled.

Loni dropped into a chair and Katie ran to check on Amilia, who had blissfully slept through the ordeal. "Rakhmitov must know Kurt's picture is missing. He probably goes through those letters in his office every so often just to gloat. We have to get rid of it, and *now*," I said.

The expression on Mama's face changed to one of dismay. "You're right, Hans. But it won't be easy." She kissed Kurt's photograph. "Goodbye, my son," she said softly as she dropped the glossy image into the stove, watching the thick paper curl at the edges before it exploded into flames. She broke into sobs and slammed down the lid.

18

THE DOUBT HAUNTED ME FOR SOME TIME

December, 1928

Winter arrived with an icy blast and made its home on the southern steppe for the entire season. Most of the villagers exhausted their small stacks of manure-block fuel by the end of the month and were desperate for firewood. The first casualty, Frau Silbernagel, froze to death in her bed; the next week Frau Dreger collapsed on the church steps. We heated our house as best we could, but most nights Katie and I tucked Amilia between us, and dressed her in every piece of her clothing during the day. I blamed myself that my wife and daughter lived in such brutal conditions.

Grandpa's presence enveloped me the day I first swung an axe into the sturdy trunk of an apricot tree in the orchard. I asked for his forgiveness and prayed we would be crossing the saltwater to America before autumn.

As it happened, the cold weather was the least of our problems. One blustery day, Kronchin called the six land dissenters into his office and announced, "All persons who did not pledge their allotted land have been assessed additional taxes on the amount of property owned before the Revolution."

Gus shifted on his feet and cleared his throat.

The village administrator ignored him. "Owners like Rosina and Hans Gerein will pay a rate of thirty percent of their former assessment." He quickly waved off my protest and continued, "Rich landowners like you, Frau Ripplinger, and Fritz, and Gus Vetter, and Heinz Gerein, will pay a rate of seventy percent of the former assessment." He handed out thick sheets of paper with official seals on the front. "These are the amounts you owe."

Gus' face turned a deep shade of purple. "That's bullshit!"

The numbers on my sheet were beyond ridiculous. "Be reasonable. None of us can possibly meet that demand."

Kronchin employed his favorite excuse. "I don't make the rules. I'm only here to enforce them. Furthermore, you have one week to pay or your land and machinery go to the Chornov *kolkhoz*. I will be in Odessa, but my assistant Luka Nikolai will collect the tax. Everyone dismissed." He pushed back his chair and marched from the room.

The small group followed Mama and me to our living room. Fritz, his voice betraying his disappointment, said to Frau Ripplinger seated beside him on the sofa, "Mama, can we come up with that kind of money?"

She meekly shook her head, the knot of her black kerchief swinging below her chin like a pendulum. "I think we're finished with keeping any land."

Uncle Heinz dropped himself into Grandpa's chair. "I'd say we're *all* finished. I hate to see the communists win, but we're fighting a losing battle."

Gus' eyes blazed. "You might be, but I'm not." He stomped out of the house, letting the door slam behind him.

Minutes later, Fritz and I went to investigate a series of loud bangs coming from the Vetter yard. Gus, more enraged than I had ever seen him, raised a sledgehammer and put another dent into his grain binder. A final blow sent the twine-knotting mechanism skittering across the yard. He wiped his brow with a shirtsleeve and spat on the wrecked machine. "There," he said. "Now those sons-of-train-station-whores can have it."

We dissenters, save for Gus, entered the administrator's office at the final hour on Tuesday. Without speaking a word, we assigned our land to the *kolkhoz* and started toward the door. "Not so fast, Hans," Nikolai called. "I have a special message for you." The sly grin on his face reminded me of the day he silenced the church bell. "The head office in Odessa notified us that all emigration from Russia has been halted."

For once, I was a step ahead of Nikolai. "We've already got our exit visas, so we're okay," I said smugly.

"Except that all visas have been cancelled. You can either bring them to me, or I'll send Captain Orlenko to collect them. Either way, you won't be leaving Chornov."

Mama raised her hand to slap his face, then restrained herself and led us out the door. We were doomed. I felt totally defeated by the injustice, but Uncle Heinz had a plan. With great anticipation, we met at his house, the responsibility of being head of the extended family weighing heavily upon him. "I've been thinking," Uncle Heinz said in a slow drawl. "What if we sneak west into Romania?"

My wife stroked our child's blonde curls. "I don't know. Hiding in the countryside all day, then traveling at night on foot in the snow and the cold. What if the baby gets sick?"

Did my uncle realize what he was asking of her? Of *all* of us?

"Heinz, it is a tempting plan, no doubt," my aunt said, "but if we're caught at the border by the Soviets, we'll be banished to Siberia. And even if we get across the line, the Romanians might send us back because we don't have entry visas."

"Monica's right," Mama added. "Besides, with the reserves in The Pantry, we can survive until summer. Maybe we should just wait and see what happens."

The family meeting ended with an agreement to remain in Chornov for the time being. My uncle and I would check The Chasm for willows to use as heating fuel, while the women would scour for burien bushes in Railroad Valley, the shallow depression a mile east of our village that led up to the railway main line between Odessa and Kiev.

The next mail day, Mama hastily tore open a letter from Kurt. He assured us the crops this year were plentiful and he would be able to cover the price of new tickets by January. The sting of defeat crushed the last ounce of my spirit, since we no longer held exit visas.

My tears blurred the words explaining our situation to Kurt. I wetted the glue of the envelope and envisioned the sacrifices he and Marie had made to send us the tickets that Rakhmitov stole. Now, as Mama had warned, it had all been for nothing.

In April of 1929, my family joined the workers at the communal yard for the first time. Nikolai assigned Loni and Aunt Monica to the large communal gardens, me to the fields, and Uncle Heinz would assist the blacksmith in his shop. "And Hans. Where's that wife of yours? Go get her, and now," he ordered.

"I'm not separating her from our baby all day."

"Your old mother can look after the brat."

I threw back my shoulders. God help the little rooster if I got a good swing at him. My antagonizer backed away and yelled, "Somebody get Captain Orlenko!"

Nikolai met the policeman at the gate. "Hans Gerein refuses to bring his wife out to join the work crew. Arrest him."

"If I take him to Mannheim for leaving a woman at home, I'll get laughed out of town," Orlenko snickered. "Can't you just send somebody else to get her?"

A grin crossed Nikolai's face. "I'll get her myself. It'll give me a chance to talk to that fine-looking woman."

I blocked his path. "*I'll* go. And *you*? You stay away from her."

"Someday I'll show you who runs this town," he said, his voice no more than a growl.

Nikolai assigned Katie to the milking barn, however, the next week Loni replaced her in the barn, while Katie went to work in the gardens. That evening, my wife merely shrugged her shoulders when I asked her about the switch.

The *kolkhoz* system might have been successful were it not for the greed and inexperience of the officials. For the second year in a row, there would be very little grain left for the workers after filling the communal quota. Without a foolproof plan to escape the Soviet Union, immediate action would be required to survive another winter. Mama designed a burlap sack into a grain belt for me to wear into the field; the discreetly filled belt showed as only a slight bulge under my loose shirt. At great risk, we emptied the contents into sacks in The Pantry or into a false-bottomed manger in Uncle Heinz's barn late at night, re-establishing a modest reserve of food.

As I left our yard early one morning, Kronchin beckoned me next door to his office. "Gus Vetter didn't pay his taxes, so his land belongs to the *kolkhoz* now. But until he voluntarily joins the collective, I can't file a report that Chornov has one hundred percent membership. You know the guy, talk to him."

"*Ya*, I do know Gus. He's too stubborn to talk to." I laughed and Kronchin allowed the hint of a smile to cross his face.

Suddenly, Josef Vetter burst into the room. "Did you have my father arrested?"

The blood drained from the administrator's face. He turned his head toward the adjoining office and shouted, "Nikolai! Get in here. What do you know about this?"

Luka Nikolai nonchalantly leaned against the doorframe. "Sure, I discussed Vetter with Captain Orlenko after me and you talked about him yesterday, but I didn't *order* his arrest."

"I'll get to the bottom of this, you conniving …" Kronchin stormed out from behind his desk and grabbed his coat from the rack.

Josef and I exchanged glances. Was Kronchin actually on Gus' side, or had Gus become a pawn in the power struggle between our administrator and his obnoxious assistant?

Kronchin obviously lacked influence outside of our village. Gus did not return home, and further arrests, always in the dead of night, became more frequent. Victims were hustled away without time to gather food or extra clothing; all villagers prepared emergency bundles to grab at a moment's notice.

"Hans, I might be next for the midnight ride," Fritz said one evening in the privacy of our barn. "So many are gone. Hubert, Herr

Redekop, and now, Gus." He paused at the door and turned back to me. "We have some money hidden. In case Mama is arrested, too, I want you to have whatever's left. And if Mama's here alone, will you look in on her now and then?"

"Of course, Fritz. I would take care of her even without you asking, you know that." He nodded in appreciation, and then disclosed the location of their savings. Touched by my friend's trust and generosity, I described my family's small cache in the orchard, should fate see us arrested first.

Several weeks later, the Black Raven swallowed my boyhood friend and his mother. Georg Frey and I ignored Nikolai's threat to dock us wages for the day, and walked to Mannheim, hoping the officials would, at the least, show sympathy for Fritz's mother. We took along a bag of essential supplies for the Ripplingers, but the prison guards refused our visitation request. If I had taken money from Fritz's cache for a bribe, would the result have been different? The doubt haunted me for some time.

19

GIVE US THE STRENGTH TO HANG ON

October, 1929

To say the least, money was scarce. On one of our rare days away from work, Uncle Heinz and I offered for sale our surplus beets and cabbages at the outdoor market in Strassburg. Shortly before noon, Uncle Heinz grabbed my arm and pointed to a man selecting potatoes at the next stall. "You see that fellow over there wearing the suit? He guessed by my accent that I'm German. Claims he heard from a government official that Germany won a one-day concession from Stalin over the suspension of emigration. All German Russians who are at their consulate in Moscow on October twenty-fifth will be evacuated to Germany, then and there."

A bag of beets slipped from my fingers. "I'd really wonder if that could be true! Ach, Kronchin won't just let us go. He can't afford to lose five workers . . . but maybe we could sneak away without arousing his suspicion."

"*Ya-naih*, let's reduce the price of this stuff then get the hell home and start making plans."

That night, as a thin crescent moon glowed in the clear southern sky, I crouched low in the shadow of the stone fence surrounding the Ripplinger yard. A dim light shone from the living room window, prompting me to curse the nocturnal habits of the GPU. I crept to the moonlit side of the outdoor *Backofen* next to the summer kitchen, the odor of old smoke tickling my nostrils as I mentally repeated Fritz's instructions: *five down from the bottom door hinge, then two to the right.* I hoped, selfishly, that the Ripplingers hadn't spent all the money. When the tap of my knuckle produced a hollow sound, I wedged the blade of Kurt's pocketknife into the crack and eased out the brick. As my fingers probed the cavity, the porch door slammed suddenly. I grabbed the brick and the pocketknife and huddled behind the *Backofen*. A policeman passed close by en-route to the outdoor toilet, and after what seemed like an eternity, he hurried to the house, muttering, "My ass damn near froze to the seat."

I slunk back to the cavity in the brick structure to fish out a tightly wrapped packet and slipped it and the knife into my pocket. After replacing the brick, I crept quietly toward home and eased open the kitchen door. That afternoon the women had seemed leery when my uncle and I told them about Stalin's concession, but perhaps the Ripplingers' cache would help pique their interest.

Katie spilled the contents of the packet onto the table. "What's that?" She pointed to an old coin.

Mama picked it up and firmly bit an edge. "*Ya-naih*, it's real gold!"

Loni began counting the money. "Do you think this is enough to get us to Moscow?"

"I'm sure it is, even without the gold piece," I replied with confidence.

When the house settled into silence, Katie and I snuggled in bed and reviewed recent events. "You know," said Katie, "that man told you whoever is at the embassy will go to Germany, but did he mean they could go to America from there?"

America! The name rolled through my mind so easily, but at this point, I didn't care where the Germans sent us, as long as we escaped Russia.

October 20th arrived, five days until our opportunity for a better life, however, leaving Chornov proved more difficult and painful than we had anticipated. Mama fretted about Papa coming home and not finding us, even though she must have known in her heart that he was lost to us forever. "I'll send Ivan our address to give to Papa. And we'll write Kurt once we reach Germany," I said, trying to comfort her.

Although Katie desperately wished to let her family know about our departure, the risk was too great. When we paid the Freys a supposedly casual visit, Katie handed her wedding dress to Eva, explaining that she was un-cluttering our house. Her sister seemed confused. "Katie, you keep it. And if I ever get married, I'll ask to borrow it," she said.

Katie brushed away a tear. "No, I prefer it this way." She embraced her stepmother. "And I can't thank you enough, Philomena, for being so kind. You were a real mother to me." She surprised her father with a quick kiss on the cheek. "I tried to be a good daughter," she said softly.

Herr Frey raised his eyebrows. Her sudden show of affection left him at a loss for words.

Georg stepped back. "Please don't kiss me or thank me for anything. I'll see you again tomorrow and the next day and the next year, for that matter."

Katie, unable to control her tears, hurried from the house. Philomena winked at me and asked if my emotional wife was pregnant again.

After the GPU headquarters turned off their lights, I scrambled to Uncle Heinz's bedroom window and rapped 'meet at our gate in thirty minutes' in pre-arranged code. I rushed home to harness Herta, mentally scanning my departure list: candles, matches, twine, our few blankets, and two sacks filled with *Zwieback,* the dried bread Loni and Katie prepared that morning.

Our midnight departure contrasted sharply with those who had emigrated from our village previously. There were no public displays or laments, no sorrowful goodbyes, no wishes for good luck, no procession trailing our wagon. Only the hoot of an owl and the rhythmic squeak of a wagon wheel disturbed the still night. My uncle and I took turns walking beside the horse to help support the heavy double-yoked wagon tongue, but soon, he developed bleeding blisters on his only hand and reluctantly yielded his position to Loni and Katie. When Herta struggled to pull the overloaded wagon out of the Chornov valley, all the adults climbed down and walked until we reached the flat steppe.

Hours later, the buildings on the edge of Karpowa loomed like black hulks under the pre-dawn skies. A drowsy clerk at the rail station informed us that the next train to Moscow departed at seven o'clock. Good! There was a fair chance of getting away before the authorities missed us at home. I unhitched the exhausted Herta—more a close friend than a horse—and tethered her to a tree in Viktor Lebedin's yard a few blocks away. Not many Russians were humane to their animals, but Herta's prospects seemed better with Viktor than abandoned at the station along with the wagon. "Take care, old girl. You worked hard for us," I said, patting her damp nose.

Over the course of three days cramped in a row of rail coach seats, we entertained Amilia, watched the southern steppe give way to rolling woodlands, and slept in shifts. If hawkers had food for sale at the stations, Uncle Heinz would try to strike a bargain; if not, we dined on *Zwieback* and water.

We finally climbed from our coach upon arriving in Moscow, our sore muscles screaming. Amilia cavorted on the station platform while the adults gathered their luggage. During the long walk to the embassy, my family stood on tiptoes to marvel at the view of the Ivan the Great Bell Tower, and the onion domes of the Kremlin rising above the city. We stared in disbelief when we approached the German Embassy. The chaos, the noise, the huge crowd; the story of the amnesty must be true! Thousands of German Russians had set up camp in the overcrowded streets. Although improvised tents constructed from scraps of canvas offered only minimal protection against the elements, the occupants seemed reluctant to let the embassy's wrought iron gates out of their sight. "I bet they stay here day and night," Mama said, "but we really don't have the supplies to do that. And how could there possibly be enough visas for everybody in this mass of people?"

"*Ya-naih*, today's only the twenty-third," Uncle Heinz assured her. "We'll still get close enough tomorrow to squeeze inside the gates on the twenty-fifth. They wouldn't turn anybody away, would they?"

A light rain began to fall, and rather than risk pneumonia, we sought accommodation. We knocked on doors until Katie noticed 'Room for Rent' scrawled on a faded sheet of paper in a dirty window an hour's walk from the embassy. A withered old man wearing a stained leather apron led us to an unfurnished third-floor room and refused to leave until Uncle Heinz prepaid the forty roubles.

There was barely space in the dingy room to stack our few possessions and hang our wet clothing to dry. Mama and Loni rolled into a goose down quilt on the dirty tile near the door, while a bedspread covered Amilia, Katie, and me. Uncle Heinz and Aunt Monica lay at our feet, sharing a woolen blanket.

The night brought several hours of unsettled sleep. Uncle Heinz and I arose early and returned to the German Embassy, noting the streets were less busy than they had been the previous evening. As I gazed over the heads of a shivering couple, a soaked blanket hanging from their bony shoulders like a dead bat's wings, I could see freedom dance tantalizingly beyond the wrought iron bars of the large gate. We had settled ourselves for the long vigil when the captain of a Soviet troop patrolling the streets announced through his megaphone, "There are too many of you to be accepted by the German Embassy. Follow us, and we'll take you to the rail station for free transportation back to your homes."

A group of unsuspecting German Russians, wet clothes plastered to their bodies and water dripping from their hair, willingly accepted the offer, but others were only convinced with the tips of bayonets. A shudder rolled through my body; the promise rang false. From what I knew, the Soviet government would not pay the passage for anyone attempting to leave the country. *Siberia* was the more realistic destination.

"Uncle Heinz, let's get the hell out of here," I yelled.

We zigzagged around the advancing army patrol and entered a side street lined with dilapidated tenements where a familiar voice called, "Heinz, wait. Hans Gerein!" I turned and saw Josef Vetter standing at the end of the street. "*Yesus*, Hans," he said. "I never thought I'd meet anybody I knew." He told us of overhearing Kronchin and Orlenko discussing the amnesty in the *kolkhoz* office, then added that his brother, Albert, didn't have enough money to bring his family. "So I hopped the train in Railroad Valley and rode all the way here on top of a car. It was a hellish trip, I tell you."

"Come with us," I offered, and we set off toward our room.

Mama and Katie were as surprised as we had been when they saw Josef. As my sister embraced him, his face brightened. "Congratulations on your pregnancy, Loni. I didn't know there had been a wedding at your house. Guess I should pay more attention to the neighbors."

Loni *couldn't* be pregnant! She hadn't been with a man.

Mama snorted. "She's put on a little weight, that's true, but there was no wedding and she's certainly not pregnant."

When Loni's face reddened, Josef struggled for words. "I-I'm sorry. I feel like a fool."

We sat on the floor for a simple meal of soup before Josef left to share a room for the night with three men he met on the train.

The light of dawn shone through the tattered curtain when the incessant rain pounding on the tin roof awakened us. We moved our belongings from beneath a drip in the ceiling and packed our bedding. Uncle Heinz, always the organizer, had already devised a plan. "Monica and I will go to the gates and save a good place in line. Hans, can you and Katie get some canvas at a fabric shop? We might need it to stay dry. Loni and Rosina, you come with us."

"Maybe Loni should go with Hans and Katie," Mama intervened. "Let the youngsters do the shopping."

Loni avoided our mother's eyes and walked to the door.

Though the rain had stopped, water lapped at the entrance of the rooming house, splashing our legs as we stepped into the sodden street. "One of us will meet you in two hours under the spruce tree in front of the barber shop. You know, the one across the street from the embassy, with the red and white sign," my uncle said.

We'd seen the shop the previous day; the bright revolving colors had intrigued Amilia. Mama bent to kiss her granddaughter and waved goodbye. She walked stiffly, suffering from the damp weather and a night spent on a hard tile floor.

We moved along the street, the mud clinging to our shoes like lead weights. I realized that, with my tattered coat, threadbare trousers, and shoes held together by harness rivets and twine, I blended in perfectly with the ragged assortment of people. Even more distressing, my wife and sister appeared equally shabby. I could not remember seeing Katie in a decent dress, other than her wedding gown. I felt ashamed—ashamed of myself as a provider.

I lifted Amilia onto my shoulders and she clasped my ears with her chubby hands. We unsuccessfully inquired about canvas at several shops before struggling, filthy to our knees, to the rendezvous point. I checked for familiar faces among the press of humanity, cupped my mouth and called repeatedly for Uncle Heinz. No reply. Loni and Katie walked along the edge of the crowd, shouting for Mama and Aunt Monica. Still no reply. We asked a shopkeeper observing the turmoil from his doorway if he had noticed two women accompanied by a man with one arm. "I *do* remember him," the shopkeeper said. "They were going toward the embassy. But the army took a bunch of people that way." He pointed in the opposite direction toward a rail station.

"Were our relatives with them?" Loni asked.

"I don't know. There was so much yelling and crying and people trying to get away." He flung up his arms and walked into his shop.

"*Danke* for the information," I called after him, and shifted Amilia to my left arm. Perhaps Mama, Aunt Monica, and Uncle Heinz had maneuvered close to the embassy gate and they were afraid to separate from one another. "Here, Katie, take my hand and grab Loni's, too," I yelled. "And don't let go. No matter what!"

We shoved our way through the noisy crowd until a man built broader than a wine cask waved a fist in my face. "Hold it right there," he ordered, showing one brown tooth in his sneer. "I'll be damned if you're gettin' ahead of me."

Katie took Amelia while I stretched tall and saw Soviet soldiers herding a section of the crowd toward us. When I took a step forward and reached for Katie's hand, the broad man mistook my intentions and knocked me to the ground. We wrestled in the cold slime and mud, people tripping over us in their rush to get away from the military sweep. Eventually, I managed to subdue him and clamberd to my feet, but Katie and Loni were gone. My throat turned raw from shouting their names.

Feeling certain Katie and Loni were not at the embassy gate, I spent the next anxious hours peeking through the rusted slats of a metal fence surrounding the rail station. Darkness had almost fallen when I finally spotted Katie's blue coat among the detainees sitting alongside the rail cars. The woman next to her held a toddler. My family!

The sound of the brass bell on a locomotive billowing dark smoke from its funnel seemed amplified by the cold air. "Load the train," a man's deep voice rumbled over a megaphone. Soldiers swinging clubs and rifle butts forced the uncooperative German Russians into the cars, while those already inside tried to push their way back out. 'This could be my only chance,' I thought, hoping to take advantage of the confusion. I jumped the fence, darted to the platform, scooped Ami into my arms and motioned to my startled sister and Katie to follow me. Amilia wondered if we were playing a game, and grabbed the collar of my coat. She giggled as the crowd shoved us along to the car door, out of sight of the soldiers. We dropped to the ground, rolled under the car and clutched onto the side-ladders of a slow-moving outbound train on an adjacent track. "Give us the strength to hang on," I prayed, the frigid wind stiffening our hands.

When the train chugged beyond the station yard, we tumbled onto the wet grass, then quickly scrambled to our feet. We squeezed through a small hole in the fence and rushed down the dark street to the

German Embassy. No German Russians! No soldiers! Only a child's broken doll, scattered empty bags, and mounds of discarded canvas. I rattled the locked gates with my desperate hands. We had been so close, Lord. Why did you abandon us? Eventually, Katie pried my grip, finger-by-finger, from the black wrought iron. I fell to my knees in despair, the truth echoing inside my head: 'We are not going to America. We are not going to America!'

"C-come, Hans. Let's see if our old room is available," Katie said, tears sliding down her cheeks. She helped me to my feet and I sagged on her arm as she led me away from my shattered dream. I forced myself to believe that Mama, Uncle Heinz, and Aunt Monica had passed through the gates; the alternative was beyond contemplation.

The would-be emigrant crowd had dissipated, and our room rented for a fraction of the cost. We wrapped Amilia in a blanket for the night, while Loni, Katie, and I sat on the bare tile to discuss whether our missing family members would head back to this room if they didn't get into the embassy. "It's the only place where we could hope to meet," I said. "But we have no extra money for rent, so we'll have to go back to Chornov tomorrow."

Katie's face drooped as she spoke. "Kronchin won't welcome us with open arms, that's for sure. Who knows what punishment he'll give us."

"Couldn't we work in another *kolkhoz*?" Loni anxiously suggested. "Or go to Odessa, where there are factory jobs?"

My sister needed to know the facts. "Nobody is allowed to hire people without relocation papers and Kronchin isn't going to give any to us." She hugged her knees to her chest, pulling away when I slid beside her. "But don't worry. He's become more reasonable lately."

"He's not the problem." She stared straight ahead, as if alone in the room.

Katie and I squirmed under our blanket, but Loni paced the floor throughout the night.

In the morning, we decided to make one final attempt to locate the rest of our family. Upon seeing the double column of Soviet soldiers blocking the embassy gate, I swallowed my bitter disappointment. No tears fell, no sobs escaped my throat; every ounce of passion had drained from me. We had no choice but go back to Chornov and hope for the best.

A Jewish man in a haberdashery exchanged Fritz's gold coin for sufficient roubles to buy our train fare and, at noon, we settled ourselves into a shoddy car in the third-class section. A tantalizing odor drifted through our car at mealtime. As I handed Amilia our last piece of *Zwieback*, I pictured a communist official seated at a dining car table covered with a lace-trimmed white cloth, enjoying a hot meal with his wife and child.

By evening, a gloom as grey as the fog outside enveloped us, and soon, Moscow and our hopes faded into the distance. We spent a restless night on the creaky wooden seats. When a young couple left the train the following day, Loni and I moved across the aisle, where I wiped mist from the window and admired a stream stretched across a secluded meadow. The train gained speed after the poplar and birch wreathed hills yielded to the open southern steppe south of Kiev.

Loni, her face ashen, spoke for the first time since boarding the train. "Hans, do you think Mama and Uncle Heinz and Aunt Monica are already home?"

"*Naaaiih*, they're on their way to Germany and they'll contact us as soon as they can." Even as I spoke, I didn't believe my own words, and perhaps she didn't either.

Her eyes flooded with tears and her lower lip quivered. "And I never had a chance to say goodbye."

"We'll see them again. Things have a way of working out." I rested my head against the damp window, wondering what our reception in Chornov would be like.

"I feel bad for not being able to explain … to tell Mama."

"Tell her what?"

"That I'm *not* a slut."

I had never heard her speak such a word. "Loni, I don't—"

"You heard me. And all because of that domineering pig!" She rose from her seat, her chest heaving. "Forgive me, Hans." She ran along the narrow aisle and threw open the door to the platform between the cars.

I extended my hands, palms upward. "Katie, what's going on with her?"

My wife pushed me forward. "Go talk to her. Hurry!"

It seemed as if every eye in the car followed my movements. Before I could reach the platform, an elderly woman wearing a fur hat and thick gloves shouted, "She jumped! I saw her through the window."

The shocked conductor leaned over a seat, yanked the emergency cord and the train's brakes screeched. I grabbed a handrail on the open swaying platform and peered back at Loni crumpled on the gravel bank, her green print skirt ruffling in the breeze of the lurching cars. As the train slowed, I swung myself down, spraining a knee. I limped to her side, placed my ear on her chest and felt her neck for a pulse. Nothing. What could I do but drop to the ground and cradle her in my arms?

For the remainder of the journey, I sat on an old grease pail next to Loni's body on the splintered wooden floor of a baggage car, two empty mailbags serving as a shroud. She had seemed withdrawn lately, but I had failed to recognize her fragile mental state. Her tragic death was *my fault*. If I hadn't been so desperate to get to America, we might still be together. A better life—that was all I had wanted for us. I held my head in my hands and cursed myself for being so blind.

When we arrived at the Karpowa station, I immediately ran to Viktor Lebedin's house. He hitched his team to a wagon borrowed from the *kolkhoz* and we gently placed my sister's body inside. Herta, tethered to the rear of the wagon, followed our subdued group to Chornov.

At our once-tidy yard, potato peels and chicken bones littered the porch steps, and horse dung covered the flagstone path. Nikolai, his face purple with rage, stormed from the house. "Where in hell have you ungrateful people been? Wouldn't your miserable cousins in Moscow take you in?" Katie held Amilia aside as Viktor and I shifted Loni's body onto the wooden end gate. Nikolai grabbed me by the arm. "You're not bringing that slut here!"

I roughly caught the lapels of his coat and bellowed, "*What* did you say?" As I hoisted Nikolai off his feet, my injured knee collapsed. We toppled against the rear wheel of the wagon and his head became wedged between the spokes. The startled horses plunged forward and Nikolai's head eventually slipped from the wheel, his face mangled, his neck kinked at an unnatural angle. I felt neither pity nor delight; I only wished him to hell.

Kronchin immediately came running from his house next door and summoned Captain Orlenko to transport the injured man to the doctor in Mannheim. As the car door slammed shut, the administrator angrily turned to me. "Hans, you're in enough trouble for running off to Moscow. And now this? You'd better hope he doesn't die."

"To hell with that bastard, but it really was an accident."

Kronchin directed an assistant to move Nikolai's belongings back to Lothar's house. "He didn't need a place like this to himself, anyway," he mumbled.

The next day, Young Andy Boser's wife Helen, the village nurse and undertaker since Frau Silbernagel's death, bathed Loni and wrapped her body in a bed sheet that Mama had given me as a wedding gift. Except for a large dark bruise on her temple, my sister's face appeared peaceful. Our friends, shocked at the news of her death, joined Katie and me for a short service at the cemetery. Alma offered her sympathies and said that she would miss Loni dreadfully, but had no idea why she had been so depressed. As the men heaped the last of the dirt onto Loni's grave, I felt as if we were burying Mama, Uncle Heinz, and Aunt

Monica alongside her, without even a church bell to toll the death knell.

After we returned home, Ivan walked into the yard carrying a burlap sack and dumped seven squawking chickens into the coop. “Here. I-I took them right after you left,” he said, sounding embarrassed. “I figured I might as well get them before Nikolai does.”

His honesty didn’t surprise me. “They’re yours now, Ivan.” I said, trying to corner one of the chickens. “I’m sure he wouldn’t have brought them back.” A rooster with black tail feathers and a scrawny white hen jumped onto a pail. “Those two aren’t mine. They’re a different breed.”

“You’ve got nothing, Hans, so you better keep them. And I’ll bring milk for Amilia whenever I have extra.”

I recalled Grandpa’s proverb, ‘Receiving gracefully is only a slightly smaller virtue than giving’ and shook my friend’s hand. I knew he wanted no more than that.

A month passed before Luka Nikolai returned to Chornov, the right side of his face still crusted with healing skin, and damage to the vertebrae in his neck preventing him from standing totally erect. Kronchin decided the job of administrative assistant demanded a more fit man, but I suspect he relished the opportunity to rid himself of the arrogant Nikolai by transferring him to another *kolkhoz*. Or perhaps, he tired of Nikolai questioning why I hadn’t been charged with attempted murder. My family’s penalty for running away had been an exclusion from the profits of the year’s harvest. While relieved the punishment was so light, I worried about whether we could survive the winter on only the contents of The Pantry, the generosity of neighbors . . . and Ivan’s chickens.

Captain Orlenko arrested Herr Goldstein and Libby Epp in late November for failing to pay the exorbitant taxes levied on prior businesses. Even though I hadn’t been a businessman, Orlenko could conjure any charge, putting me in prison as well, and Katie would have to live with her family. As a precaution, Georg and I moved my grandmother's bedroom suite and a table and bench from Grandpa's house to that of the Freys. Also, we transferred some of the preserves and grain from The Pantry to a hole in a dark corner of their barn.

Sure enough, the porch door rattled two nights later, and the bolt snapped by the time I dressed and ran to the kitchen. Three GPU officers immediately surrounded me. "What's going on, Orlenko?" I angrily snapped.

"You'll find out in jail, you rotten *Nemetzi*." He prodded me to the porch with the barrel of his pistol.

There was no point resisting the arrest. "Take care of yourself and Amilia," I called to Katie, grasping the prepared emergency bag in my fist.

"God will look after you, Hans," she cried tearfully from the doorway of the bedroom.

The agony in her voice tore at my soul. "Katie, I love—" A sharp blow to the kidneys caused me to double over before the officers dragged me down the walkway and into the rear compartment of the Black Raven. The latch was about to drop when the door swung open and an officer shoved a dazed Katie onto the floor beside me. My voice rose in panic. "You stupid bastards. My wife's done nothing wrong." I braced a boot against the door and kicked my way outside. "Our baby's alone in the house, you pricks!" I knocked one officer to the ground with a swipe of my fist, then felt a sharp blow on my temple.

20

HAVE IT YOUR WAY

December, 1929

The coolness of the stone floor soothed my bruised face. I suppressed the urge to vomit, and daring to move only my eyes, glanced around the cramped, dingy cell. A range of snoring seeped into my ears from the tiered bunks lining three stone walls wet with mildew; the fourth wall supported a door of thick rusty bars. How long had I been lying here? I shook the haze from my pulsating head and staggered to my feet to relieve myself in a stinking bucket, behind which shone a rat's beady eyes. After dropping my emergency bag onto the rough wooden planks of a middle bunk that had neither sheets nor a mattress to hide the bloodstains from previous inmates, I removed Kurt's little red pocketknife from my back pocket and, for safekeeping, wrapped it inside my coat in the bag. The sudden squeak of the iron door startled me. When two guards stomped in, I grabbed one of them by the arm and demanded, "Where's my wife?"

The other guard waved a stout club in my face. "All we need—another loud-mouthed prisoner. Get in your bunk, *zek*," he commanded in Russian.

A husky voice called from a bunk behind me. "Better listen to 'im before they beat you senseless."

The guards left with an unwilling *zek* from the bunk below mine, the clank of the key in the door echoing through the cell.

Sleep did not come easily; in fact, it did not come at all.

On the first day, my cellmates seemed afraid of me, unwilling to trust the newcomer, perhaps a spy or a stool pigeon. We received our daily ration—a tin mug of water and two slices of frozen rye bread—through a slot in the door. The gauntness of each man's features revealed how long he'd spent in this cramped cell on what amounted to a starvation diet.

Sometime near midnight, the door rattled open. "You're coming with us," a guard said, prodding me with his nightstick.

As we marched down the narrow hallway, I heard a voice call out, "Name?"

The guard banged his nightstick against the bars of a murky cell. "Get back!"

"Hans. Hans Gerein," I replied, unsure of the repercussion.

Only silence.

A minute later, we entered the door on our left into a room so brightly lit that my eyes stung. The guards, appearing indifferent and bored, waited at the door. A comely woman with short dark hair rimming a police cap motioned me to sit down on the chair in front of her. She took a step forward and extended an open pack. "Cigarette?"

I shook my head. "I have to know about my wife, Katie Gerein. Was she brought here?"

"I can find out after you answer a few simple questions," the officer replied sweetly. She lit a cigarette and dropped the match to the floor. "So who helped you get to Moscow in October? Lothar Degenstein? Doesn't he believe in communism?"

I suspected a trap and chose my words carefully. "He certainly does believe in communism and he already works for The Cause."

"Then tell me the name of your accomplice, the man you left your horse with."

A fierce battle raged in my soul. One quick answer in exchange for word of Katie and Amilia, but betray a friend? No. It took great effort to shake my head.

The interrogator inhaled deeply on her cigarette and blew the smoke in my face. "Then this interview is over. My name is Elana. Call for me when you're ready to get some information on your family. Guards, take him away!"

The goddamn GPU wouldn't give up so easily. I was in trouble, and maybe, so was Viktor.

In my cell, I flopped on my bunk and fluffed up the emergency bag to use as a pillow, but didn't feel the lump. Kurt's pocketknife was gone! The theft of my prized possession infuriated me, and I dragged the nearest man from his bunk, locking my right hand around his neck. No knife in his pockets. It was then a cellmate from a top bunk held out the missing object. "This what you lookin' for? If you want to hang onto it, there's a better hidin' spot," he said in a sheepish tone.

I snatched the pocketknife from his hand and placed it back in the bag. "You thieving bastard! You'll tell me a hiding spot and then just steal the knife from there," I said, barely able to control my temper.

The sly Russian laughed and whispered in my ear. My eyebrows arched. "Are you serious?"

"Sure," he grinned. "I've put stuff there b'fore, if it's small and not too sharp. Almost nobody thinks of lookin' there, and if they do, they don't wanna be the one doin' the search."

'Not a chance,' I thought, disgusted by the idea. I climbed onto my bunk and covered myself with a blanket of despair. I had practically nothing to eat, slept on a board, and was in danger of losing Kurt's pocketknife. Worse, news of my wife and my child was available only by me betraying a friend. In order to survive, I had to put my self-pity in check and keep my wits about me.

The pocketknife thief sidled over and offered me a portion of his bread when we received our rations hours later. "I'm Anatoli Betnin," he said, showing a toothless grin.

"Hans Gerein," I replied stiffly.

"Been in here …" he counted on his fingers, "six weeks and three days. What're you in for?"

"First, what's your story?"

"Theft. What else?"

I couldn't help but laugh.

We spent the afternoon in hushed conversation. "Guess you're wondering who asked you for your name?" Anatoli said. "That's old Sergie, down in cell thirty-eight. There's only one exit past his cell, and that's into the backyard. He gets everybody's name comin' and goin' down that hall. Anybody that doesn't come back was shot. He'll call out the name to any *zeks* walkin' by and they're s'pposed to pass it around the jail so there's a chance the family'll hear about it."

I recalled the heartbreak for Mama—for all the family—when we hadn't learned the fate of my father.

In mid-afternoon, a guard shouted, "Bucket brigade."

"New man's turn," Anatoli suggested. "Grab the latrine bucket and follow the rest o' them out in the yard. You'll see where to fling it."

I grasped the handle in one hand and held my nose with the other. The smelly parade trudged down two corridors flanked by identical cells before stepping into the sunshine and frigid air of the backyard, where barbed wire topped a high stone fence surrounding the prison. After dodging the stinking contents of another inmate's bucket, the hair on my forearm bristled when I bent to empty mine. A body floated face down in the cesspool's murky depths.

On our return trip to the cells, someone behind me whispered, "Lucas Fast."

Several nights later, the guards led me to the interrogation room on the right side of the hallway. The stocky man sitting on the edge of a sagging desk ordered the guards to remain in the room. He twirled a pistol in his hand as he stood up and directed me into a sturdy metal chair bolted to the floor. The muscles in my neck clenched when he held the pistol to my forehead and cocked the hammer. "You can make this easy for yourself and give me the names of your accomplices, or you can be difficult. Actually, it'll be more enjoyable for me if you're difficult."

I winced and said in as calm a tone as possible, "If you're not prepared to first give *me* information regarding the whereabouts of my family, I have nothing to say to you."

He lowered the pistol and slapped the barrel twice into his beefy palm. "Okay. Have it your way. Kiss the floor."

I ignored the command. The two guards wrestled me, face down, on the floor, gripping my arms while the interrogator straddled my back. From the corner of my eye, I saw him remove a thick rubber truncheon from his belt. “Hold him tight so we get him dead on the nerve,” he said, prodding the lower end of my spinal column with his fingers. A second later, my brain seemed to explode and a numbing sensation coursed through my legs. I flailed, flipping the heavy bastard from my back. He swatted dust from his shirt. “Woo-hoo, he’s strong,” he said. “We’ll get him again. Then he’ll definitely settle down.”

That blow rendered me unconscious.

I regained my senses early in the morning. My legs refused to support my body, and Anatoli brought my rations to the bunk. “That’s one of their favorite tricks, whacking you on your tailbone. It hurts like hell now, but you’ll soon be up and movin’ again,” he said.

As I was about to ask whether he was talking from experience, a guard yelled through the bars of the door, “Gerein. Be ready to meet the *Troika* of judges this afternoon.”

“They must be in desper’te need for slave labor in the *konzlagers* if they put you through here that fast,” said Anatoli. “Usually, they want to work you over ’til you give them somebody else’s name. And you’d best do something with that knife if you don’t want to lose it.” He offered me a short length of the twine holding up his pants. “Here. Tie this ’round the knife so’s you can get it back out again. Unless you wanna go muckin’ for it after’ards. Spit a big gob on the end of it, then squat way down.”

The loathsome task finished, my name sounded again and Anatoli wished me good luck. “And if you don’t come back, I’ll get word to Sergie.”

Though he probably meant well, his offer was unsettling. I hobbled in front of the armed guard to the courthouse next door, feeling totally abandoned. The smirk on the face of Judge Rakhmitov, Chief Justice in the makeshift courtroom, indicated he remembered me.

"Under Article 58, you, Johannes Gerein, are charged with anti-Soviet activity," the bailiff read aloud.

Without any semblance of a trial, the three judges readily determined my guilt. "This *Troika* sentences you to five years hard labor in an Archangelsk work camp with no right to receive communication," Rakhmitov said before slamming the gavel on the desk. "Next case."

The blood drained from my head and my knees went weak. Five years away from Katie and Amilia without communication, without even being able to send them a letter! The guards grabbed my arms and unceremoniously dragged me back to the cell. I curled up on my bunk and clung to the memories of my cherished wife and child, fervently praying they were safe and that I would see them again. The thought of Katie perhaps receiving a work camp sentence flashed through my mind; she would not survive five years of heavy labor.

21

I DON'T HOLD NO GRUDGE

January, 1930

Thirty-two shivering *zeks*, myself included, were hastily assembled in the yard, methodically searched, and then confined under the ragged canvas canopy of an unheated military truck. Three armed guards in a jeep followed our transport for two hours to the Odessa rail yard. The seriousness of my situation hit home when our driver halted behind four other trucks loaded with *zeks*. The rear gate of the rail yard swung shut behind us; there was no escape. A line of dilapidated wooden freight cars stretched past the rail station, the water tower, and around a distant bend. The guards packed fifty of us elbow-to-elbow into car number seventy-one. It reeked of cattle dung—and why not? The communists treated us no differently than animals. Icicles clung to the walls and frost encircled two small barred ventilation ports set high on one side of the car. I recalled the Christmas when Papa noticed frost imprinted like tropical leaves on our living room window and had correctly predicted a wet spring. Spring would soon be arriving in Chornov, but not at our destination—the Arctic.

The door clanged shut, imprisoning us in our misery. We took turns huddling near the centrally located pot-bellied stove, the strongest staying the warmest. Before nature would expel the pocketknife for me, I crouched near the toilet—a hole re-enforced with metal in the thick wooden floor—dropped my pants and tugged on the short twine. My trouser cuff served as a buffing cloth before I buttoned the knife into my coat's inner pocket. There. Now let someone try to take it from me.

For a full week, one miserable day ran into the next, each progressively colder than the last. I gave thanks for the extra winter clothes in my emergency bag, shoddy as they were. During a brief stop, three indifferent soldiers entered the car to give each *zek* a tin mug of tepid water and a slice of moldy rye bread. One of the soldiers dragged to the open door a thin, swarthy man who had rejoined the end of the line. He put a pistol to the man's temple and pulled the trigger. After the lifeless body tumbled out onto the snow, the soldier casually holstered his pistol and kicked the extra loaf of bread onto the corpse. "One ration only," he shouted to us.

The train pulled into the crude rail yard of Arkhangelsk as two sundogs flanked the sun poised at its apex above the horizon, hardly exceeding the reach of a tall man. An unkempt guard, rifle at the ready, unlatched the door and yelled, "Move it! It's goddamn cold waiting for you bastards." We hobbled into the bitterly cold arctic afternoon, a brisk northerly breeze assaulting our senses. Three deceased traveling companions, lying stiff in a corner of the rail car, were shoveled out the door as routinely as manure.

Armed escorts marched us inside a squat log building, the deployment center filled with hundreds of other miserable *zeks*. I officially became *Zek* #42788, my labor merely another exploitable natural resource. After the captain issued us barely adequate gloves, hats, and winter boots, he pointed to a horizontal line drawn on the wall. "Whoever fits under this mark, stand to the right. You'll be working in the tunnels of the Vorkuta coal mines." About half our numbers qualified. The rest of us would build barracks along a proposed canal route eventually linking the White Sea to the Baltic Sea.

The crusty snow crunched like dry leaves underfoot as our unit of two hundred *zeks* and twenty-five guards marched beyond the boundary of Arkhangelsk. Each pair of men pulled a loaded crude sledge by a rope looped through holes in the wooden runners. The goods varied from food to tools and other essentials required for an extended stay in the wilderness. I had never before experienced such intense cold, not even during my army days near Saint Petersburg. The raw air seared my throat and clouds of my breath impaired my vision. With no break in the pace, we pushed forward throughout the brief daylight hours and into the night. High-pitched howls from a nearby wolf pack reminded me of the night Grandpa died. The memory still pained me, however, my most worrisome thoughts alternated between Katie and Amilia, and my missing relatives. Though three months had passed since the disappearance of Mama, Uncle Heinz and Aunt Monica, I hadn't given up the hope of seeing them again, in spite of my own uncertain situation.

The aurora borealis dancing across the sky in muted hues of green, yellow, and red held my attention until the commander ordered us to halt near two log buildings nestled among the fir trees. We gathered firewood from a stack in the compound and soon, the stoves radiated a welcome heat. The flicker from small bowls of burning mineral oil cast a pale light across the bare walls. We gulped our evening ration—a small chunk of frozen bread—then, footsore and still fully dressed, we retired, as such, for the night. Dreams of a ship rolling on the rough seas to America and my family nearly dying of motion sickness haunted my restless sleep. I awoke in a sweat, even though the fire in the stove had burnt itself out.

A light snowfall announced the arrival of morning. Over the course of several days, we trudged from barrack to vacant barrack, eventually arriving at an inhabited compound where the condition of the *zeks* appalled me. They were barely more than skeletons in filthy ragged clothes, eyes sunk deep into their skulls, parchment-thin skin stretched tight across fleshless faces. "How can those men still be alive, let alone do heavy labor?" I whispered to my companion helping pull the sledge.

Commander Golya, daunting in a long sheepskin coat, thick fur hat, and new felt-lined boots, his face contorted into a permanent sneer, assumed control of our troop. In order to bolster the faltering ranks of prisoners at this site, he left behind fifty of our men and a portion of the supplies. The remaining one hundred and fifty *zeks* and twenty-five guards trekked to the next site consisting of two equally sized bunkhouses on the shore of a lake. Golya and the guards claimed one unit and we *zeks* crowded into the other, sleeping side-by-side on tiered wooden platforms. Kaspar Fleck, #42742, a man so tall that his feet hung over the end railing, chose the space next to mine. The closeness of our bodies on the narrow bunks created warmth, but encouraged the rapid spread of lice. None of us had bathed since our arrest. For me, it had been seventeen days; for others, much longer.

Our Commander banged a shovel against the doorjamb before daybreak. We drowsily lined up shoulder-to-shoulder in front of the bunks. "Each unit of ten men will be given a daily work assignment and quota," he announced. "Exceeding the quota might mean extra food rations, but if you fall short, you will definitely be penalized. Shirk your duty or try to escape and the consequences will be severe." He relaxed his stance. "Now, choose your unit's leader and he'll get breakfast from the kitchen for you. Dismissed."

Through virtue of size, Kaspar was selected our leader. He returned from the kitchen and handed each of us a small metal bowl and a frozen piece of black bread. "Take care of the bowl," he warned, pouring a small amount of dark liquid from a pail. "You won't get another one." I looked at the thin soup and realized hunger would be my constant companion for the next five years. Perhaps the time would pass quickly, but the image of the men at the last camp shook my resolve.

After the allotted time for breakfast, armed guards assembled all the units into a column of five abreast, each *zek* shouldering an axe, saw, or shovel. Commander Golya stamped his feet to stay warm. "Every morning," he said, his voice tinged with animosity, "we will walk five miles ahead to build more barracks for the others coming to dig the canal. Then we will return here at night." When dissent hummed through the line, a perturbed Golya raised his rifle and knocked the nearest man to the ground then kicked him in the ribs, guaranteeing our full compliance.

An icy wind whipped our faces as we followed a trail marked

by blazes hacked into the bark of tree trunks, and arrived at the worksite some two hours later, our teeth chattering like shaken marbles. Without any consideration for the distance we had walked, the commander shouted, "You lazy criminals, get to work."

Half the force prepared a site for the barracks, while the rest of us felled trees of a sufficient size for walls and a roof. The guards sat around a bonfire for most of the day, then, as darkness settled, they tallied the day's production, called roll, and herded the units back to home camp. After a meal of fish soup and another small portion of dark bread, my stomach still growled, but the drama on the train remained etched in my mind, and I didn't ask for seconds.

Kaspar and I spent most evenings in our bunks scratching lice until our skin bled and exchanging stories about our similar heritage. He sheepishly divulged his reason for choosing me as a workmate—my physique matched his and we could easily meet our daily quota.

Observing my fellow workers confirmed my own assuredly horrid appearance. After only a month at camp, clothes hung loosely on my once-muscular body. By the end of the second month, I could feel every bone in my face. By the third, small sores refused to heal. Several men from our original crew had already died, and if our rations remained meager, the tally might soon include me. To justify antagonizing Judge Rakhmitov by taking Kurt's photograph I convinced myself that Orlenko could have concocted any number of reasons to have me arrested.

Upon the completion of two buildings, the commander halted work on the 'forward camp' and concentrated on expanding our own compound for the men that would eventually dig the canal. Winter gradually receded and our workday lengthened in accordance with the hours of daylight. The intensity of the sun increased, tiny rivulets of meltwater turned into torrents and patches of the forest floor became visible again.

One sunny afternoon, Kaspar noticed a black object protruding from a melting snow bank at the eastern limits of the camp. The crew encircled the site and watched as he repeatedly drove his shovel into the slush.

"Stop! Don't dig anymore." I fell to my knees and scooped snow with my bare hands, ignoring the pain of sharp ice crystals under my fingernails. Upon recognizing the faded yellow 'P' stamped into the coarse fabric, I moaned. "It's my friend's coat. Out of my way!" I grabbed Kaspar's shovel, scraped away more of the crusty snow, and made the sign of the cross over Hubert Bauman's emaciated frozen body. Why was it the fate of this good person to suffer such a cruel death, alone, thousands of miles from home?

"You better look out. Here comes the big guy with a dog," warned another *zek*. Now that the snow was melting, Golya had brought trained dogs into the camp to discourage any escape plans.

The Commander stomped to the hole in the snow, glanced down and rubbed his chin. "That's a nice coat —if a lousy *zek* hadn't died in it." He tapped me on the shoulder with the barrel of his rifle. "Back to your crew, Seven-eighty-eight."

I tested Golya's determination by refusing to move. "I need to bury my friend."

Without giving me a second chance, he whistled to a large dog. "Get 'im, Laika! Get 'im."

My foot caught on a stump when I turned to run. The growling canine leapt forward and shredded the back of my coat; cotton stuffing floated on the wind like snow. I rolled over and kicked hard. Laika growled deep in his throat and sank sharp fangs into my left calf. "Get him away from me! He's gonna break my leg!" I screamed, the surge of pain knocking the fight out of me.

Golya called off the dog. "Now are you ready to get back to work, Seven-eighty-eight?" he mocked as Laika, lips drawn back, anxiously awaited the next command.

His cold gaze and sarcastic laugh grated my nerves. I wanted to say, "Go to hell, you whore-monger," but, instead, sweating, and unable to bear weight on my injured leg, I dragged myself upright against a tree. My coat and pants were in tatters and blood trickled into my boot.

The surly official patted his dog and turned to Kaspar's wide-eyed crew. "Should I set my friend here loose on you, too? He's developing a taste for German blood."

After Golya left, balls of snow staunched the blood flowing from the gashes on my calf. The sheer depth of one of the puncture wounds caused me to waver with dizziness. I steadied myself and, after a few minutes, managed to cover Hubert's body with dead branches, the best that I could do under the circumstances.

I felt no animosity toward my workmates when they shunned me for 'wasting time over a rotting body.' After all, our crew hadn't filled the daily quota and Golya had reduced our already-meager rations.

We worked in the same vicinity for a few weeks. Kaspar assigned me to chopping limbs from felled trees, a task requiring limited movement. Hubert's body, clothed with two shirts, one barely covering the holes of the other, and two pairs of equally tattered trousers under the greatcoat, escaped its icy bed one particularly warm day. When I dragged the corpse to dry ground, Kaspar pushed his way in front of me and rolled Hubert out of the muddy greatcoat. I would need to stake my claim to the garment immediately; the dog had ruined mine, and my survival the next winter hinged on finding a replacement.

Kaspar glanced at my extended hand, and in a swift, determined motion, swung the greatcoat behind his back. "I found it. It's mine," he said, grabbing me in a headlock. "And if you wanna fight, I'll kick your goddamn ass."

I flipped him to the ground with my last bit of strength and reached into my pocket for Kurt's pocketknife. "So help me Christ, I'll use it!" I hissed through clenched teeth, pressing the open blade to his throat.

The disgruntled man waved his arms in the air. "Get off me.

The damn coat's yours."

I snatched the greatcoat and slowly backed away. "And I'm taking a pair of pants. You can have what's left."

Fearing Kaspar would report me for having a weapon, I waited until our guard fell asleep in the sun, then crept behind a thick bush. Memories of home flooded back to me as I dug in the damp earth and tucked the pocketknife under a gnarled root. The money in the jar buried in the orchard had saved my family from starvation during my army years. Perhaps this little red pocketknife someday would be *my* salvation.

As spring progressed, nature offered some variety to our diet: spruce buds substituted for vegetables, bird eggs provided protein, and wild blueberries growing near the water were a terrific source of vitamin C.

Commander Golya kicked open our barracks door one warm evening after work. "The lake's open now and you're all gonna get rid of those godforsaken lice," he barked. The job of barber—actually chopping hair with dull scissors—fell to two of my bunkmates, as no guard would touch a 'filthy *zek*.' The freshly groomed waif-thin men stumbled to the muddy bank and stripped for a much-anticipated bath. Kivil, a Ukrainian watchmaker from Odessa, noticed the ugly red and blue lines radiating from the dog bite on my leg. "You've got a big problem there. My mother always said that if veins get infected all the way up to your heart, you're a goner. So you gotta clean that wound up, if it isn't too late already. Better put maggots on it."

I held back my laughter. "Maggots? You're kidding!"

"You've already got a fresh source in the woods." He winked and picked up his clothes from the pile on shore.

With each passing day, the smell of decay grew stronger near Hubert's body, however, Golya wouldn't allow me the time to bury him. As I held my nose while piling thick branches and rejected logs around my friend's body, a log rolled against him and several maggots wriggled out from his armpit. Kivil had been right! I bent over and placed three squirming larvae into the blackened folds of my wound, and thanked Hubert before completely covering his corpse. "Ach, my friend, you deserve better. Forgive me," I said, and hummed a tune we had learned in Form Two. Never could I have imagined burying him under refuse, a childish tune serving as the funeral dirge.

The scavengers going about their business tickled annoyingly, but perhaps, the cleansing would save my leg, and my life. Two weeks later, duty done, they morphed into flies, leaving healthy pink tissue in the ugly scar as a reminder of my close brush with death. Kaspar leaned his saw on a tree stump and pointed to my leg. "How's it coming along?"

Though we were bunkmates, we had not spoken since our fight. However, to his credit, he had neither reported my pocketknife to Golya nor attempted to reclaim the greatcoat. "Good," I curtly replied.

He bent low and whispered, "I-I'm sorry for the disagreement. I don't hold no grudge." His massive shoulders slouched as he walked away.

At the dimmest hour of the northern night, Kaspar slid from the bunk and whispered, "It was nice knowing you, Hans."

Grosser Gott! He intended to escape. There was no point trying to change his mind. We were already staring death in the face on a daily basis. All I could think to do was nod and mouth, "God be with you."

He gathered his extra clothing into a bundle, and as the door clicked shut, I prayed for his safety. In spite of our dispute, I admired his resolve to escape, something I lacked the nerve to do.

The morning roll call revealed Kaspar's absence. "Take four men and two good dogs and bring the sonuvabitch back!" Commander Golya shouted to the lieutenant so loudly his voice turned hoarse.

All units received orders to assemble in the compound after work late that afternoon. "I bet they got the big guy," the man behind me murmured.

The beaming commander stepped onto an overturned crate minutes later and addressed us. "When we arrived here last winter, I told you that obedience was mandatory and attempting to escape would not be tolerated. All eyes on the prisoner."

A guard swung open the door on the small windowless storage shed and Kaspar's mutilated body tumbled to the ground. I had fully expected a wound on his arm or leg, however, it was much worse. Several teeth protruded from what remained of his cheek, and ripped clothing revealed a gaping hole below his ribs. Bloody stumps of fingers dangled from one hand. I grimaced as suddenly the poor man's arm quivered. Could he possibly be alive? Golya stepped forward and growled, "Give *me* the honor." Kaspar's head snapped violently backward with each bullet fired into his mangled face. The ruthless commander waved his smoking pistol at the assembly. "That's a lesson for the rest of you. And you're all on half rations until further notice."

The decomposing body hung from a tree in front of our bunkhouse as a reminder of the punishment we could expect for an attempted escape. By the fourth day, the smell permeated the camp and Commander Golya ordered the fly-infested corpse dumped in the forest.

Our workday shrank as autumn approached. With more free time after dark, I lay on my bunk, hands under my head, and imagined Katie and Amilia picking wildflowers in the west pasture. My heart ached when I recalled how my image of Papa blurred after he had been away for several years; in time, my own daughter would no longer remember me. I often dwelled on Loni's death, on what compelled her to take her own life. Somehow, I felt responsible in the same way as I did for the disappearance of my dear mother, uncle, and aunt. While revisiting my litany of regrets my thoughts often turned to Kurt and, in my mind, I framed a letter to him, resentment festering my imagination:

Dear American Brother,
Do you know how lucky you were that Mama and Papa chose you to go to America? I thought it should have been

me. Was it because you were the oldest, or just that Papa liked you better? Now you have a privileged life and mine is filled with hardships you can't even imagine. If it gets much worse . . .

I soon realized a grudge would drive a wedge between my brother and me, and quickly tore up the imaginary letter and slid, with both feet, into a bottomless pit of despair.

The day of the first snowfall of the season, I pulled Hubert's extra pants over my own two pair. Once the severe cold was upon us, his greatcoat would be a blessing. I set aside my summer shoes, actually, strips of birch bark, and insulated my worn winter boots with dried moss. The soles showed extensive wear and seams were opening in places, but there was no alternative to using them.

As winter wore on, I knew it was late December and asked if anyone in the barracks could tell me the exact date. A man across from the stove checked the underside of his bunk, where he had used a sharp pebble to scratch a crude calendar. "The twenty-third," he announced.

"Tomorrow's Christmas Eve. We should do something. I'm sure the Good Lord won't mind how we celebrate."

"What the hell have we got to celebrate?" said a gruff voice. Following a long pause, a willowy man stepped into the aisle. "No God would let this happen. I don't believe in God."

"Well, that's your choice. But considering our situation, you might want to stay on His good side."

The majority of men cheered and a childlike excitement swept the room.

The next day passed the same as any other. That evening, we hung Christmas decorations—small spruce boughs smuggled in a coat sleeve or down a pant leg—from the roof trusses. In the glow of the stove, a sorry lot of ragged men shook hands and wished one another better days ahead. We drank bowls of hot water and shouted down the lone person who suggested brewing the spruce boughs for tea. An old man who resembled my grandfather approached the stove, and winced as he eased off his tattered birch bark shoes. The remaining three toes on his left foot were a swelled mass of blackened flesh. My stomach churned when I tilted his shoe to add some of my extra moss and the two missing toes rolled out. "Why didn't you ask for help before it came to this?" I admonished.

He shrugged his shoulders. "Everybody's got th-their own problems."

Kivil glanced over the edge of the bunk and noticed the old man's dire situation. "This is how they treat us?" He gritted his teeth. "I don't give a damn if Golya cuts my rations. The Lord takes care of bastards like him in His own way." He cursed the commander again, then arose and reached for the door latch. "Let's go outside and sing a Christmas song."

A roar of support echoed to the rafters as the men flocked to the yard. "Over there! That's the Star of the East," Kivil shouted with boyish enthusiasm.

Though the old man was adamant he should not wear them, I slipped my winter boots onto his swollen feet and said, "Come, let's join the others outside."

He leaned on my shoulder for support and hobbled out the door. A hush fell over the snow-encrusted compound when, in surprisingly strong voice, he began:

"Silent night, Holy night,
All is calm, all is bright."

Emboldened by his lead, the rest of the men joined him. Through our breath rising on the frosty air, I noticed a procession from the guards' bunkhouse, but a silhouette, surely that of Commander Golya, remained in the doorway. When our song ended, a youthful voice rang from the cluster of guards. "*Pozdrevlyayu s prazdnikom Rozhdestva i s novim godom*. Merry Christmas."

The air was heavy with silence as we solemnly filed indoors. "Please accept my appreciation for h-helping me in my final struggle," the old man said to me. He placed my winter boots under my bunk before crawling into his own space.

In the gray light of dawn, the old man failed to answer the wake-up call; the merciful Lord had freed him from his hell. The disposal crew stripped off his clothes and carried his stiffened body into the snowy woods. I wondered then, why Hubert was clothed when Kaspar found him buried in the snow. Perhaps he tried to escape during a storm and lost his way.

22

NOTHING COULD STOP ME NOW

May, 1931

A rumor circulated that before dogs were brought to the camp, one prisoner, a former athlete, had escaped by simply running into the forest. Whether he survived, I did not know, but that man became my idol. From that moment on, escaping wasn't just what I thought about, it was *all* I thought about. Four more years in the camp would kill me—one way or another. Dying from exposure in a bid for freedom seemed a better ending than going mad or starving to death.

Shortly after the much-anticipated arrival of spring, fishing duties became my next assignment, no less taxing than felling trees. I spent miserably long days on the lake reeling in heavy wet fishnets alongside my foreman, Stephan, a feisty Hungarian sporting a bright red beard. The buffeting winds stung exposed flesh, my hands blistered and the joints swelled until my knuckles broke through the skin. I would never again complain about working the fields with Herta, if ever that opportunity arose. When I wondered aloud about an end to this damn hard job, Stephan shook his head. "Only gonna end when we quit eating. And now, they're putting up a supply of salted fish for all the guys coming in to dig the canal. A goddamn canal. And all the way to the Baltic, too."

I cautiously questioned a young surveyor of a civilian crew marking the construction line for the canal near our launching area. "The Baltic Sea is at least a couple of weeks' walk westward from here," he said. "But there's some awfully rough country in between."

Interesting. The idea that the Baltic route could be my best chance of escape intrigued me. According to Headmaster Blokin's geography lessons, Saint Petersburg stood on the southeast shore of the Baltic Sea. From there, I could hop a train to Moscow, and then to Odessa, jumping off at Railroad Valley. Only one problem seemed insurmountable: the tracking dogs at the camp—Kaspar's downfall.

Early one morning, while Stephan and I paddled our fishing raft away from the launching area, I noticed three large fir trees on a nearby promontory flooded from the spring runoff. One of the trees grew behind the other two, making it visible only from the lake. By the time we reached our destination, I had formulated an escape plan.

That evening, Commander Golya rewarded Laika with chunks of fish. Perhaps the guard dog's appetite could be of use to me. I removed two bits of fish floating in my supper bowl to tuck into my pocket—the one without holes. When the owls began to hoot in the dead of night, I crawled from my bunk and quietly rolled my extra clothes into a tight ball. After one last look around the room at the sleeping *zeks,* decent men sharing so much misery, I tiptoed from the bunkhouse, a glance at the tree in front of the window causing my heart to miss several beats. With a sharp eye on the guards' quarters, I surveyed the dogs encircling the camp and approached Laika, chained under a small spruce, his neck hair on end, his lips curled. He relaxed his ears at the smell of the fish extended on my fingertips. I crouched down to give him the morsels, stroked his head, and slunk past him into the forest, beads of fear dripping down the small of my back.

Kurt's little red pocketknife retrieved from the soft soil beneath the bush easily fit through a tear in the lining of my coat. My one regret was not risking a farewell visit to Hubert's grave. With my heart hammering against my ribs, I scampered toward the fishing launch, ever aware of any sound coming from the camp. I tied my extra clothes and birch bark shoes together with the wire shoelaces, and then slung the ungainly bundle over my shoulder. At the edge of the water, I bent low to take a long drink before wading to the promontory. The tree that extended farthest into the lake appeared the most suitable to hide in for one, possibly two days.

Several hours after settling among the thickest foliage, shouts from the barracks summoned the *zeks* for roll call. Baying hounds soon raced toward the shoreline, running in frenzied circles at the fishing launch. Commander Golya's voice reverberated with rage. "You,

Feodorin," he yelled to his assistant, "get in there and find Seven-eighty-eight's tracks."

"I'm looking, but I can't tell which are his," Feodorin shouted to the commander. "There's too many tracks from the fishing guys always coming and going." I felt goose bumps rise on my arms when Laika waded through the shallow water to the base of my tree, but breathed easier when Feodorin shouted, "You stupid mutt! There's no time for a swim."

"Take your men and two of those dogs that way around the lake." Golya waved his arm toward the northern shoreline. "I'll take the other two this way. Seven-eighty-eight's gotta come out of the water sometime. We'll see how smart he is when I get my hands on him."

The search parties moved quickly, ducking under branches, sinking to their ankles in the marshy areas. When the baying of the hounds eventually faded, my body shook so violently my feet nearly slipped from my perch. If Feodorin had looked up … if he had followed Laika's lead, this would all be over.

Though my fishing mates seemed trustworthy, I remained silent on my perch when they arrived at the launching area for the workday. "I kind of wondered about Hans, always lookin' around the lake, but running is suicide," Stephan said. "If the dogs don't get 'im, the bugs and wild country will."

His new partner pushed their raft into the water and started paddling. "I'd like to get the hell outta here, too, but I wouldn't take the chance. Not with that sadist Golya in charge."

By late afternoon, the sun beating down relentlessly, my tongue thickened from thirst and my back muscles throbbed. As a safeguard, I tied myself to the tree trunk with the shoelaces when my head began to nod. My brief dreams were not of Katie, Amilia, or even Kurt and America, but of dogs sinking their fangs into my throat.

The sound of barking grew louder as the sun swung low, and I surmised the search parties had returned to the camp. Within minutes, the fishing raft bumped against the shore and Stephan's partner said to him, “Remember on the other side of the lake when we heard Golya tell Feodorin that the dogs never found footprints leavin’ the water? Do you think they gave up the search?”

“Yeah, for sure they quit lookin’ for him. I’d say he tried to swim across the lake and drowned.” Stephan called across the water before heading to the barracks. “Goodbye, my friend!”

Regretfully, I dare not acknowledge his sentiments.

Although lingering doubts eroded the confidence in my escape plan, the time seemed right to begin my odyssey; I was hesitant to proceed, but could hardly go back. Near midnight, I left the safety of the tree, red-hot pins flowing through my legs as my circulation increased. Numerous handfuls of water scooped to my mouth eventually relieved my cracked lips and parched throat. After wading two miles, I felt secure enough to leave the water and slip on my birch bark shoes. Reaching Saint Petersburg seemed impossible, but with certain death behind me, and the prospect of reuniting with my family ahead, I set off across the inhospitable taiga. One of Grandpa’s astronomy lessons helped me determine that if Saint Petersburg lay to the southwest, I would need to travel directly opposite the point of the rising sun.

The torturous days eventually blurred together. I endured slogging through bogs, insect bites and scratches from thorns swelling my arms. The rough forest floor shredded my birch bark shoes, leaving my feet a bloodied mess. When hunger gnawed a hole in my stomach, delicate petals of wildflowers tasted every bit as good as had Grandma’s homemade *Kuchen*. Meandering streams provided welcome water, and low-hanging branches sheltered my weary body at rest. Each night, I prayed to awaken the next morning.

On perhaps the tenth day, I cornered three ducklings against a partially submerged log in a shallow pond. Barely taking time to pluck the feathers, I devoured their carcasses raw, blood dripping from my beard, and felt every bit the wild man I was. However, the decision to eat raw meat on an empty stomach wreaked vengeance on my digestive tract. I spent the following morning doubled over in agony, and the two deer bounding away from behind a bush didn't seem like a missed meal.

One sweltering afternoon, while considering whether I could possibly continue on, my pulse quickened at the sight of an expanse of pale blue stretching to the horizon beyond a break in the trees. I shuffled to the water's edge and wet my fingers. *Fresh water*? Not in the Baltic Sea. Where in hell was I? My drained body buckled to the coarse sand, and spread flat on the shore. The thought of the waves sucking me into the water's depths seemed strangely calming.

After resting to gain strength, I crawled into the hollow of a driftwood pile and soon dreamed of Amilia giggling while Katie tickled her ear. A smile crinkled my face until I realized the sounds were outside my head. I cautiously stretched my neck, peering out from the shelter. Two elderly swarthy men and a younger woman sat on the sand, while brightly clothed children played near the water's edge. Hunger surpassing my fear, I crawled from the pile of logs and laboriously raised my arm, my lips too stiff to shout. One man hesitantly came near, my hideousness clear from the expression on his face.

I collapsed in a heap. Someone carried me down a short path to a broad meadow dotted with mud-plastered willow huts, where a matronly woman bathed my face and chest with warm water. Given the state of my health, I had no choice but to depend on the goodness of the rescuers for my survival. My heart sank when I learned of my diversion from the intended route; this was Lake Ladoga, not the Baltic Sea. However, the gypsy band's leader, Petrov, explained in broken Russian that it was my good fortune his group had found me, since this area was only their temporary home, and they would soon move south for the winter.

The kindness of the gypsies stood in stark contrast to Papa's poor view of "those damn *Zigeuner*," as he would say. Three weeks of recuperation, plus a haircut, a shave, and a gypsy remedy that rid me of lice made me feel human. Even though my bones still threatened to poke through my skin, the vibrant colors of my donated trousers and shirt renewed my spirit.

I admired my hosts' simplistic lifestyle. The older men often relaxed and conversed around the jagged soot-blackened stones that formed a communal fire pit in the center of the camp. Petrov enjoyed telling stories about his youth. "Me and a few friends went to the city once long ago, when we were young," he said one day. "We found some loose women and had a hell of a time, but we ran out of money. I got caught stealing my supper, and ended up in jail for a month. When the buggers finally let me out, I headed for home and never went back again." He laughed until his belly jiggled. "It was an adventure, but nothing like what *you've* told me, Hans."

Time passed and my health improved. I earned my keep by building an elevated platform of interwoven branches on a grassy area between the huts and the forest. One unusually warm afternoon, Petrov's young attractive daughter eyed me as she placed paper-thin slices of venison on the platform to cure in the sun. Petrov winked at me. "She likes you," he said. "She'd make a good wife."

"Petrov, I have the highest regard for you and everybody here," I said, as kindly as possible, "But I *have* to go home." The last weeks I had felt particularly anxious about Katie, whether she had returned to Chornov. And my arms yearned to hold our daughter.

His smile faded. "I know what you mean. Family is important."

Pleased he understood my rejection of his daughter's feelings, and wishing to leave on good terms, I gratefully accepted a pair of deerskin shoes and a pouch of dried meat from the people who had rescued me. The children offered a small trinket made from acorns and twigs as a parting gift, and the adults took turns saying goodbye. "How can I express my gratitude with more than a heartfelt thank you? I have nothing else to offer," I said.

"Having you here was no bother at all and you owe us nothing more," Petrov said. "We would like you to stay with us, but if you must go, that is the way to Saint Pete." He motioned toward the water. "Follow this shoreline south for three days, then just past a sharp hill, there's a trail to the right. Go through the village and keep on that road. You'll find the way." He patted my back, "We'll miss you, Hans and the best of luck getting home."

On the third day of my journey, I followed the trail that led to the village and ignored my conscience when trading my clothing for a less conspicuous set on a clothesline. After hitching rides and walking for a week, I finally crawled under the rusty metal fence at Saint Petersburg's main rail station, six days by train to Chornov. Home! Nothing could stop me now.

23

I HUNG MY HEAD IN SHAME

July, 1931

Rail car rooftops provided transportation for tramps and vagrants of varying ages, most appearing as if they had plucked their wardrobe from a ragbag. The wind whistled in our ears and the locomotive's smoke left us stained with soot. To pass the time, the other men exchanged hard luck stories, but I dared not tell my own. We jumped from the train before reaching the various stations, then re-boarded at the outskirts of the towns, thus avoiding the security guards. At protracted stops, water from the village well quenched our thirst and scavenged food eased our hunger.

In Railroad Valley, thick burien bushes crept up the hillside and young willows in low areas displayed their leaves in the pink hue of the setting sun. When the locomotive slowed considerably during its climb out of the valley, I released my grip from the ladder on the side of the car and hit the ground running. As the train clattered into the distance, I took stock of my situation. At twenty-eight years of age I could have passed for forty, my hollow cheeks were splotched dark from scurvy, my hair showed patches of grey. Though doubtful anyone would recognize me, my plan began with hiding behind a bush until nightfall. I thought no farther ahead, and didn't even consider how to explain my return to the villagers.

Near midnight, I inched along River Street, keeping to the black shadows cast by the stone fences. Despite the warm July air, my arms felt chilly and my knees weak. Please let Katie and Amilia be here and, God-willing, Mama, Uncle Heinz, and Aunt Monica, too. At Grandpa's property, I peeked in through the kitchen window and saw three unfamiliar men passing a large bottle of vodka around grandmother's old table. Certainly, my family was not here. A dog's bark followed me across the street to the Frey's darkened house, where

I tapped on the rear bedroom window. A shadow loomed behind the glass before the groggy voice of a woman answered.

"Philomena, it's me, Hans. Hans Gerein."

"*Lieber Gott*, Johannes! Go around and I'll lift the bolt." She swung open the door, grasped me by the shoulders and pulled me inside. "I can't believe it's you!"

We engaged in a tight embrace. "You don't know how good it is to see a friendly face, Philomena. And Katie and Amilia, are they all right?"

"Amilia's here with us, but we haven't seen Katie since the two of you were arrested."

Deep wracking sobs immediately escaped me—sobs of relief that my daughter was safe, and sobs of sadness at Katie's unknown fate. Philomena placed a hand on my arm. "I know how you feel, Hans, but I'm sure your wife will come home soon." She lit a lantern and walked toward the nearest bedroom door.

Katie's sister Eva sat up in bed. "Who is it?" She rubbed her eyes. "Hans! Is Katie with you?"

Before I could answer, my sleeping three-year-old daughter briefly opened her eyes, and then curled into a tight ball. Her angelic face felt soft to my touch; I had carried this moment in my heart for almost two years.

"Ach, the darling's been no trouble at all," Philomena said. "Let her sleep, and we'll sit at the table so we can talk." She dimmed the lantern as we entered the kitchen. "We found Amilia crying in her crib when you and Katie didn't come to work that day. Franz and Georg tried to visit you in jail, but they weren't allowed in."

"I am so grateful …" I hugged the two women who had harbored Amelia, and wondered if it would ever be possible to re-pay their kindness.

Georg, followed by Gus Vetter's daughter, Genni, rushed from a bedroom at the rear of the house. He pulled me into a bear hug. "Didn't they feed you in that godforsaken place?"

"Apparently not enough."

Georg put his arm around Genni's waist and drew her near. "We got married last summer. Best damn thing I ever did."

I expressed my sincere congratulations to both of them, teasing that they would probably have seven or eight children. "By the way," I said, turning to Philomena. "Did Lothar marry?"

She rolled her eyes. "I don't think he ever will. He's my son, but I'll admit he sure has some strange ideas."

Hesitant to agree and risk hurting her feelings, I forced a respectful smile.

"It's not what you want to hear, Hans, but things are probably worse than when you left," Georg said. "And the GPU spy on us day and night."

Eva sighed. "It's work, work, every day, even Sundays. I'm in the milking barn. I hate it."

"The granaries are nearly full, but the government won't give us our share of the grain," Georg grumbled. "They want to sell it for money to build factories and ammunition plants. And the food situation is bad. We get only a measly dumpling for dinner from the *kolkhoz*."

Ashamed to have forgotten about Herr Frey, I inquired of his whereabouts. Philomena's reply rang with melancholy. "The GPU arrested him last year on charges of being a *kulak* and we haven't heard from him since. So many people have disappeared since your and Katie's arrest. Genni hasn't heard from her father either."

I felt she should know of Gus' demise. "Sorry to be the one to tell you, Genni, but the word circulated in the Mannheim prison that he was executed."

"It's what we suspected. Papa wouldn't bow to any authority. But my brother Josef wrote to me from Canada. He mentioned meeting you in Moscow and wondered if you got to America."

"Too bad it didn't work for you, Hans," said Georg. "You always wanted to join Kurt."

Thankfully, the near-darkness masked my overwhelming remorse that Katie hadn't returned and that my family had been cheated of the opportunity to immigrate to America. "You know what? It's good to be home, but I'm exhausted," I said, yawning widely.

"Why don't you sleep in the living room?" Philomena offered.

The softness of the sofa made the bare plank bunks at the work camp seem like a bad dream. The lingering aches in my body, however, reminded me of the truth: I was an escaped convict.

The morning sun cast shafts of light across the floor as the bedroom door opened. Amilia, wearing a threadbare nightgown sewn from an old dress, pattered into the kitchen. "Beakfas'," she squealed before noticing a stranger at the table.

"*Guten morgen,* Amilia," I said, trying to envelope her in my arms.

She pulled away and ran to Philomena. "Amilia, don't be scared. This is your Papa. Amilia's Papa," she said.

"Not my Papa! Papa an' Mama wit' *Yesus*."

Her grandmother seemed embarrassed. "But Papa came back from visiting *Yesus*."

"Amen," my daughter responded proudly, remembering her prayers. I chuckled at her innocence and thanked the Lord for my good fortune in seeing her again.

"The others are already gone for the day," Philomena said. "Frau Vetter and I baby-sit at the care center for the mothers working at the *kolkhoz*. Amilia likes to play with her friends, don't you, my dear?" Philomena removed the child's nightgown and slipped a tattered sleeveless dress over her head. "We'll be home late because everybody works 'til dark. It's probably best if you stay away from the windows, Hans. Maybe it was a mistake to tell Amilia her father is home."

Philomena pulled me aside that evening. "We have a problem. Amilia wouldn't stop talking about you and my boss asked her questions. She's a Russian woman sent here from Odessa and she might report you."

"Then I won't stay here and put you in danger. I've been planning all day on how to find Katie. That will take me out of Chornov for a while. The thought of leaving my daughter stabs a hole in my heart, but it's best if I leave soon. Tonight."

I had almost finished packing a makeshift rucksack when a knock rattled the porch door. Georg held a finger to his lips. Another knock, and then a loud voice. "It's Igor Kronchin, not the police. I know Johannes Gerein is in there, and I've come to speak with him. Now! Or there will be grave consequences."

I apprehensively opened the door, half expecting a pair of handcuffs. Kronchin's mouth flattened into a thin smile. The familiar black intensity still burned in his eyes, but his hair had developed a shade of grey, and a small bulge protruded over his belt. He clasped my extended hand and glanced behind me. "We need to talk in private."

Philomena swung Amilia into her arms and motioned to Georg, Genni, and Eva. "You two stay in here, Hans. We'll go to the barn," she said.

The village administrator seated himself across from me at the table. "I'll come straight to the point. I can tell the local police and the villagers that you served your sentence. But for my part, I'm quite sure you've escaped from the *konzlager*."

My face flushed; my guilty look verified his suspicion.

"There's a possibility I can keep you from being arrested again. And I trust you will be honest, or there could be repercussions for all concerned, including me." He cleared his throat. "Are the authorities from your work camp still looking for you?"

I briefly described my escape, and concluded by saying, "The search party thought I drowned because they didn't find my tracks leading away from the lake. So, they probably do consider me dead."

"That's good news. If they thought you were alive, they'd send a report to our local police to watch out for you. But when someone is listed as dead, the file is closed."

My attention heightened as he detailed his plan. "We are behind with our harvest and short of workers, so I'm offering you a way out of your predicament. But above all, you must always live in Chornov, since I can't give relocation papers to a dead man."

His words hit a raw nerve. How could I immigrate to America? And I had given Kurt my word.

"Your wife was sentenced to a coal mine in Donetsk for two years, so she should be home soon. If you give an honest effort here, when she returns you'll already have membership in our commune and the community store."

"A coal mine has to be the worst work for a woman. I'll go look for Katie, then start work with the commune in two weeks."

"You'll start tomorrow, or you won't start at all. Be ready to work in the morning and I'll keep secret your escape. Disappoint me, and you and your family will rot in the gulag system."

Although angry words surged to the tip of my tongue, my reply was, "Your proposal is gratefully accepted."

He slammed the door behind him as he left the house. I had forgotten that, first and foremost, the *kolkhoz* chief administrator was a communist who only tolerated a tenuous situation if it benefited The Cause. The government expected him to deliver a set quota each year and he meant to do just that. I could only hope that Katie would find her way back to us without my help. Igor Kronchin had ignored personal risk by not reporting me to the police, but he had effectively chained me to Chornov forever, crushing my American dream. And without money for postage, I couldn't even let Kurt know I was still alive.

Black clouds threatened rain the next morning as Lothar, my immediate supervisor, assigned me to a crew gathering sheaves for the threshing machine. Though our relationship had never been cordial, I was determined to tolerate him for the sake of my freedom. In the barns, Herta whickered a greeting and sniffed my pockets for treats. Her mane had thinned and a distinct sag had crept along her back over the past two years. She showed her age, as I did mine.

The sound of footsteps attracted my attention. It was Ivan! "It's so good to see you again, you old devil," he said, hoisting me off my feet. “I better do this now before our gourmet diet puts the weight back on you.”

I tugged his neatly manicured beard. “And where did this come from? A dead gopher?”

“If a gopher could grow hair like this, it’d be handsome like me!”

I realized, with Fritz and Hubert gone, Ivan was my only close friend.

Harvest stretched far into October. There had been better crops, but there had also been worse. The administrators, self-serving as they were, diverted the government’s quota to the communal granaries only after their personal sheds overflowed. In addition, the majority of the communal animals were sold at market due to the shortage of fodder, further escalating poverty among the villagers. The Freys had forfeited their cow the previous winter, and now only a small flock of skinny chickens scratched for seeds among the tree stumps in the orchard.

The best meal since my return had been a thin gruel of corn meal, carrots, and potatoes. I worried that our food supply would not see us through the winter. To offset the inevitable, Georg, Genni, and I wore grain belts similar to the one used in the earlier lean years. We buried the pilfered grain in the garden late at night or re-filled the false-bottom drawer in the kitchen cupboard. Since Orlenko hadn’t arrested me for hoarding grain, I assumed The Pantry in Grandpa’s house remained a secret.

By early December, we still had not received wages. Kronchin refused to discuss the subject, leaning on his favorite excuse that he didn’t make the rulings, he only enforced them. The temperature inside the unheated house often dropped below freezing, and hoarfrost coated the windows so thickly that our propaganda newspaper curtains froze to the glass. Although coal was unaffordable and firewood nonexistent,

Kronchin insisted the *kolkhoz* manure was field fertilizer, not heating fuel. Ivan, Georg, and I spent moonlit nights in the frigid air, scouring harvested cornfields for overlooked stalks, a crime punishable with imprisonment. When not in a drunken stupor, Lothar occasionally pilfered for us a chunk of coal from the administrators' storage. Philomena would beg him to stay and visit, but he replied that officials shouldn't fraternize with the workers, which was fine with me.

Christmas arrived on a sunny, but cold day. That evening after work, Georg stoked the fire in the *Backofen*, a warm house a most welcome gift. The Freys, Amilia, and I knelt in the kitchen and recited the rosary for Katie's safe return. Philomena sat Amilia on her lap, and with elaborate hand gestures, she told my daughter about the birth of Christ in Bethlehem and the arrival of the Three Wise Men. It was well after midnight when I donned my coat and stood on the porch step to observe the Star of the East shining as bright as a sapphire in the clear sky. I wondered if Katie was singing Christmas carols as we had done at *Konzlager* 127. While mentally sending her my love and prayers, I blew a kiss to the heavens.

We finally received a portion of our wages in mid-January 1932. I carefully selected a page of the only writing paper stocked in the communal store. In my first letter to Kurt in more than two years, I asked whether Mama, Uncle Heinz, or Aunt Monica had contacted him. Fearful of the censors destroying the letter, I did not mention the misery of our dire situation. The letter I had imagined while in the work camp came to mind, and I hung my head in shame. My brother could not be blamed for choices that were not his own.

24

HER WORDS CUT ME TO THE BONE

February, 1932

"Hans, there's somebody here asking for you," Ivan said, as he stepped into the stall where I brushed nettles from Herta's tail. "Better be careful out there."

I wiped my hands on my patched trousers and peered around the barn door. A young man too shabbily dressed to be a police officer climbed from an unfamiliar wagon on Church Street. "I'm Pavel Lebedin from Karpowa. Viktor's son," he said, showing a gap-toothed smile.

"Of course, Pavel. You were much younger when I left my horse with your father. Tell me, how is he?"

"He died suddenly last year. We think it was his heart or something."

"I'm sorry to hear that. He was a fine man and hard worker."

"We sure miss him in the field," his son said. "But the reason for my trip is I brought somebody who wants to see you." He removed the wagon's end gate.

I eagerly jumped inside the box and pulled back the rumpled blanket. A thin figure lay shivering on a bed of straw. Freckles dotted her pale face and the tip of her nose swooped upward. Katie! With my heart in my throat, I gently caressed her cold cheek. She opened her eyes, vacant and empty, and tried to speak, but managed only a gurgling wheeze. I stood up and shouted toward the barn. "Georg! Show Pavel to our house. Katie's come home!"

As the wagon rumbled along the frozen road, I cradled my wife's head on my lap and stroked her matted hair, the love for her in my heart now stronger than ever.

Eva rushed to our yard, flushed and panting. She climbed onto a wheel of the wagon and peered inside, "Is she … *alive*?"

Pavel drew on the reins to steady the horses. "She knocked on our door this morning, shaking like a leaf. Said she was the wife of Hans Gerein and wanted to go home. I had to sneak the horses and wagon out of the *kolkhoz*. I don't know any more than that."

"Thank you, Pavel, for bringing her here. I had almost given up hope of ever seeing her again." When I scooped Katie in my arms, blanket and all, she felt as light as a child. Georg held the door open and I eased my wife onto Eva's bed.

"Katie, we missed you so much. We'll take care of you," her sister said. "And Amilia will be home soon." She kissed Katie's forehead, then looked up at me. "Her skin is so cold, Hans. How will she get warm in this unheated house?" With the administrators also feeling the scarcity of commodities, Lothar could no longer smuggle coal for us.

Recalling the hypothermia emergency procedure used by the army, I slipped off Katie's tattered clothing and mismatched shoes, then stripped to my under shorts before snuggling against her emaciated body, her heartbeat faint against my chest. Eva covered us with woollen blankets and Katie soon fell into a deep state of relaxed sleep.

Several hours later, her skin no longer cold, I cocooned her with the blankets, got dressed and happily hugged Philomena and Amilia when they arrived home from daycare. I roused Katie and sat beside the bed with Amilia on my lap. "This is your Mama," I said to her.

Tears welled in my wife's eyes as she feebly reached for Amilia's hand, but the child recoiled and buried her face in the nape of my neck. Philomena gently brushed a tear from Katie's cheek. "Don't worry, my dear. Your daughter's just shy," she consoled. "It's so good to have you home. You'll feel better after Eva and I give you a bath."

That evening, Eva moved her meager belongings to Philomena's bedroom, and I abandoned the sofa to crawl into bed beside my daughter and my wife. Katie coughed incessantly through the night; something drastic had to be done or she wouldn't survive the week.

Igor Kronchin appeared startled when I barged into his office the next morning. "My wife came home yesterday a very sick woman. She's going to need help to recover, so I'm taking time off work to nurse her back to health."

He rose to his feet. "Calm down, Hans. I'm happy she has returned, and I'll talk to Lothar about giving you time off."

"And we need coal from the storage shed, because if she spends another hour inside a freezing house, she will most certainly die."

"You know coal is for sale to everyone."

"Except at those ridiculous prices, nobody can afford it." I planted my fists on his desk. "I'm going down to the storage shed right now, with or without your permission, and if I have to knock somebody down to get coal, I will." I turned toward the door.

"Here. I'll give you a note," he muttered, scribbling on a scrap of paper. "Why don't you make it easy on yourself and join The Party? Do you have to be so stubborn?"

Igor's words rolled through my mind on the way to the coal shed. Perhaps under different circumstances we could have been friends—he believed in his convictions as much as I did in mine.

Though still despondent, Katie sat propped up with pillows for a longer period each day. I told myself to be patient, that she would eventually forget the horrors of the coal mine. Her spirits rose when a large package arrived from our generous relatives in America. Our daughter sat on the bed next to her mother and, together, we carefully removed the brown paper for re-use. A tightly wrapped pair of men's trousers protected a photograph, a letter, a ten-dollar bill and an assortment of clothes. "Is it for me?" Amilia squealed when she saw the head of a doll peeking out from a felt-lined boot. She jumped to the floor and raced in circles while clutching the treasure to her cheek. "Dolly's name is Groetel. Groetel."

Desperate to learn the fate of my relatives, I unfolded the letter with a mixture of dread and enthusiasm.

Johannes Gerein
Chornov, Cherson
USSR

Jan. 16, 1932

Dear brother Hans, Katie, and Amilia,

We greet you in the name of the Lord and hope that this letter finds you together again as a family should always be. We were so happy to hear from you. I can't tell you about Mother, Uncle Heinz, or Aunt Monica because we haven't heard from them, either. Did you know most Germans kidnapped on Moscow's streets that day were sent directly to Siberia? Our German-American newspapers reported that many starved or froze to death the first year, and those who survived are considered prisoners without the right to communicate. We must hope that our relatives are alive but simply can't get word to us.

On a brighter note, Marie and I now have two boys. They remind me of us, Hans. It's no wonder we got so many lickings if we were like these two scamps, and I'm sure we were.

Uncle Pius co-signed with me to borrow money from the bank and now I have two quarters of land, about 120 dessiatin in Russian measure. The crops have been poor and with the grain prices down since 1929, I'm hoping I can keep up the land payments. But we still have enough to eat. I know you didn't ask for any help, Hans, but we sent some things for you, Katie, and the little one. I'm sorry that they are used, but it's all we can afford in these tough times.

Katie spread a flowered dress on the bedcovers. “Look, there’s not even one patch. Write him back and tell them that these are like royal robes to us.” A bitter expression suddenly passed over her face as she tossed the garment to the floor. “What must they be wearing when they send us their old stuff and it’s better than anything we’ve ever had?” She fell into a fit of coughing and I wiped black phlegm from her chin with my handkerchief.

For a moment, I was caught up in her lament, but quickly chastised myself for dwelling on regrets: if the communists hadn’t won the civil war, if we had all gone to America, if, if, if … “You’re not being fair to them. They made some big sacrifices to send us this parcel. For my part, I’d send this money back to them.” I tossed the crisp bill on the dress. “I don’t like to accept charity any more than you, but we have no choice. And how will we raise our future children if we can’t even manage with the three of us.”

Katie answered in a calm, steady voice. “There won’t be any more to worry about.” Her unfocused gaze rested on the bill. “In the Donetsk coal pits, I vowed not to have any more children.”

“You have to give yourself time. Things will get better, and then we’ll want a brother for Amilia and—”

“I was pregnant before going to the mines.”

The words were like a punch to the face. “What are you saying? What happened to the baby?”

Her eyes glazed over. “I was at the mine for about six months and was working underground when the labor pains started. Another worker took our only lantern and ran to get the overseer. Everything happened so fast. When they came back, I was holding the baby in my arms, but he wasn’t crying or anything.”

A son? We had a son? I studied her expressionless face and attempted to control my racing emotions.

“When that witch of an overseer saw that the baby was dead, she cut the cord with her shovel and grabbed him from me.”

Vomit rose in my throat. "What did she do with him?"

"She put him on a loaded coal trolley and sent it to the surface. The other workers were afraid to interfere." Katie continued in the same monotone. "I lay there all day with no strength or desire to get up. When our shift ended, I felt stronger and searched the coal pile around the tipple for his body until a guard chased me away. You know, with all the people who must've died at that camp, I didn't find even one graveyard."

I tried to tell her how sorry I was. I tried to put my arms around her. I tried to ask her what I could do to ease her pain, but she pushed me away and ordered me out of the room. Couldn't she see *I* suffered the loss of our son, as well?

Herr Hoffer had only a small amount of foodstuffs in stock at the Chornov co-op store. "When the *kolkhoz* didn't pay all our wages in January, I knew it didn't matter if there was nothing on the shelves," he said. "Nobody has money anyway. Never did I think we would be living so poor in Chornov." I placed the ten-dollar bill on the same counter where, years ago, Lothar had slammed down crows' feet in exchange for candy. Squeaky looked up at me. "*Ya-naih*, Hans, what do you think this is? Sears Roebuck? I can't take American money. The new Torgsin store in Mannheim was opened for people just like you with foreign money."

Upon my return from Mannheim, my first stop was the Goldstein Inn, confiscated by the government following Ira's arrest and re-named the Chornov Inn. Alma acted as manager and lived in the rear of the building, along with her mother and her young twin boys. Her eyes widened when I placed a small bag of rice on the kitchen table. "You are so kind to share your goods with us."

I waved off her thanks. "Your father gave me a loan. Please consider this as a payment."

At the communal yard the next morning, my fellow workers chided me about my rich American relatives. "It's nobody's goddamn business," I retorted, feeling somewhat self-conscious wearing the decent clothes sent by Kurt.

To my dismay, Igor *did* believe it to be his business. "I'm disappointed to hear rumors that you are accepting bribes," he said to me in his office. "Josef Stalin already knows some of you German Russians are spies for your Fatherland. I'd hate to think you're doing the same for America."

I tried to explain the parcel was an unsolicited gift, not a bribe, but he insisted The Party would consider me a traitor if any further foreign correspondence arrived for my family.

My mood was somber that evening as I penned a letter to Kurt. I thanked him profusely for the parcel, and then asked that he not write to us until we contacted him again; the danger had simply become too great. Writing that our son had died in the coal mine proved to be one of the hardest things I ever had to do.

As we sat at the supper table, Georg and I bantered about the rooster imitation Nikolai unwittingly performed whenever he was agitated. Philomena snickered and Genni light-heartedly chided her husband for demeaning an authoritative figure. Katie ignored us and, as usual, spooned Amilia extra sauerkraut soup from her own bowl. Without warning, there was a pounding on the porch door. Were the requisitioners searching for hidden grain? Last week, Igor had informed us that Chornov fell short of its quota. Officially, there was not to be a kernel in the entire village.

Philomena's eyes darted from Georg to me. While cooking the soup, she had abandoned her customary caution and added the last kernels of wheat from the false-bottomed drawer in the kitchen. "*Schnell*! Eat quick," Georg whispered.

The second knock ended with the bolt snapping from its mount. Two burly officers, one brandishing a sledgehammer, stepped aside for Captain Orlenko. He snatched the bowl from my hands, the contents splashing across the front of my shirt. "What's the hurry to finish supper?" he scowled, holding the bowl near the lantern. "I know you're hiding something and we're gonna find it. Comrades, search the kitchen."

While his men pulled our few dishes from the cupboard and dumped out the contents of the drawers, Eva stared at me and lightly tapped her chest. I covertly popped into my mouth a kernel that had been stuck to one of my shirt buttons. We both slowly exhaled.

Captain Orlenko banged his nightstick against the kitchen walls. When an area sounded hollow, a possible hiding spot for grain, his smirking comrade smashed the plaster with the sledgehammer.

"Be damned if I'm gonna watch you wreck my father's house," Georg yelled, trying to grab the sledgehammer from the officer. When a blow from the handle knocked Georg senseless Genni sprang from her chair, but the captain ordered everyone to remain seated.

The intruders stepped over my brother-in-law to scour the rest of the house and the attic before heading to the barn. Georg leaned on my shoulder and limped to bed.

"We're lucky this was empty," I whispered to Philomena while replacing the false-bottomed drawer. "They'd have felt the extra weight."

"*Ya*, it's good we buried the rest in the garden."

In mid-summer 1932, Kronchin's own food supply suffered the effect of the communist's recent increased quotas, and he transferred several of his assistants back to Odessa. I gratefully accepted when he offered me Uncle Heinz's now-vacant house. Georg helped carry Grandma's bedroom suite and the table and bench I had moved to the Frey's before my arrest. Though Katie's temperament seemed to improve, she still rejected my attempts at intimacy. I didn't feel at fault, and apparently, she didn't either. Twice, I attempted to discuss our son, but she refused to acknowledge him.

One evening Katie struggled to lift Amilia onto the bench. She fed our daughter a bowl of the dandelion soup, and then dipped the spoon into her own bowl, as well.

"Katie, you've got to eat some soup yourself," I gently cautioned her. "You won't be able to take care of Amilia if you get much weaker."

Her words cut me to the bone. "If you loved your daughter, you'd go to Kronchin and demand flour so I could bake some bread. How is she supposed to grow into a strong young woman when you don't even have the backbone to provide her with a decent meal?"

I bristled with indignation, but held my tongue and walked outside into the cool evening air. The fiery glow of the sinking sun reflected my emotions. It hurt me to the core that I couldn't provide my family with the basic necessities for survival, and even worse, there was no end to our misery in the foreseeable future.

After entering the house, I opened the bedroom door and approached the bed where the two people I loved most huddled under a thin blanket. My wife, in a voice as cold as ice, told me I was no longer welcome in her bed.

Her rejection felt like a kick in the stomach and the hardness of the floor in the second bedroom went unnoticed. I began to regard my wife in a new light. A warm, loving woman was taken from me; only the shell had been returned.

"Some bastard stole our last chicken!" announced Georg as a small group chatted for a few minutes the next morning before work. "I sure hope the *kolkhoz* keeps serving us that dumpling for dinner, because that's all we're gonna have to live on 'til harvest time."

"And they don't even send out propaganda newspapers anymore. Guess we'll have to start using corncobs for toilet paper," Ivan joked.

"Everybody's ass will get a little tender, especially since the cobs are so dried out this late in the year," I said, then chuckled.

The animals also suffered from a lack of food. Herta, little more than a bag of bones, drooped her head and rubbed her nose against my arm as she stumbled across the low threshold while leaving the barn. "Didn't you get any sleep last night either, old girl?" I said. "You feel just like me this morning." When I laid the harness on her back, she dropped to her bony knees before rolling onto her side. I sank to the ground and wriggled her head onto my lap. A tremor ran through her body, then she lay still. My mind went numb, my arms slack.

In a flash, two *kolkhoz* workers shoved to the front of the gathering crowd and dragged the harness aside. One of them reached into his work pouch for a knife, thrust it into my horse's haunch and cut away a chunk of flesh. I sprang to my feet. "For Christ's sake! This is *Herta*."

He waved the dripping blade under my nose. "The damn horse is dead and my family needs food, Hans. Now, get back before Kronchin comes and claims it!"

Spurred by his lead, three more workers plunged their knives into choice sections of Herta's body. The smell of hot blood made me sick to my stomach, but I was at a loss of how to stop the butchery. I felt a tug on my sleeve and heard Katie yell, "Don't stand there and let them rob you. Do something; she's *your* horse!"

She was right. With my jaw clenched and my hands shaking, I opened Kurt's little red pocketknife and stabbed into Herta's neck. Unable to look at her face, I hacked to the bone, whipping the knife faster and faster, images of my starving family playing through my mind. 'God forgive me,' I prayed, hoping that someday I could forgive myself.

All that remained after only a few minutes were entrails and a dark patch of blood-soaked earth where I had said goodbye to my faithful horse.

25

GOD WILLING, THAT WILL BE ENOUGH

April, 1933

The villagers had eaten their vegetable seed stock to keep from starving during the intense winter; therefore, no one could plant gardens in the spring. To make matters worse, the government's continued practice of exporting grain caused the feared shortage in the *kolkhoz* granaries, prompting the administrator to eliminate our daily dumpling. As the spring weather encouraged new growth, we gathered tender grass sprouts from around the pond and budding weeds from along the creek. What would Grandpa think if he saw us foraging in the pasture like animals?

While Amilia's condition concerned me, Katie's was the more worrisome. Her once-attractive freckles had turned to ugly black dots, and while her abdomen protruded like an inflated balloon, her arms and legs resembled leafless twigs. I sat upright when my wife, the light of a full moon silhouetting her emaciated form, knelt beside me in my dank corner shortly after I retired one night. "We're in the most serious trouble since the labor camps," she rasped. "I'm so tired all the time I can hardly get out of bed." When she brushed a hand through her lifeless hair loose strands fell to the floor. "But if we can make some kind of pact between us, I'll breathe easier in my final days."

"W-what're you talking about? We're going to come out of this soon and—"

"Shhh, just listen." In hushed tones, she laid out her plan.

She could have as well torn out my heart. "What did you say? You can't be serious!"

She grasped my arm. "Do it for Amilia. Please, Hans. I'll never rest easy in my grave if she dies, too."

"But it—"

She clapped her hand over my mouth. "Promise me. You *have*

to promise." An ugly expression contorted her gaunt features—her conviction was real.

"*Naih*!" I pried her hand away and bolted from the room, unsure which was more disgusting—Katie's request, or the deliberate starvation tactics of the communist regime. Damn you, Stalin, for doing this to her … to us. Damn you to hell.

Several evenings later, Katie motioned me to her bedroom and slid our sleeping child to the back of the bed. She urged me to lie beside her, and then kissed me for the first time since her return from Donetsk. Though I had envisioned this moment for three years, my starved body denied me any desire and I drew her close only out of pity. "You were a really pretty girl already in Form One. I was crazy about you, but didn't want my friends to know. And it was good you liked me, too, because here we are with a beautiful daughter."

Perhaps in a moment of vanity, Katie gloated that Luka Nikolai had also once found her attractive. I detested how he had leered at her, and the very mention of his name curdled the blood in my veins. "What reason do you have to say that?" I asked, anxious to know the truth.

"He cornered me in the milk barn the first day I went to work in the *kolkhoz*. And he tried to kiss me. When I wouldn't let him, he said he would have you arrested."

"The sonuvabitch. How many times did he bother you?"

"Only a few times, because Loni came into the barn when Nikolai was after me. She thought she could handle him with a little kissing and hugging, so after that, she took my place in the barn, and I guess she got pregnant."

I lay still, waiting for the room to stop spinning. Now Loni's suicide made sense to me. "*Lieber Gott*, Katie! Why didn't you tell me about her situation?"

"Loni and I agreed not to because we knew you would kill him, then spend the rest of your life in jail."

Pure hatred for Nikolai burned my throat and my words came

out as a hiss. "He murdered my poor sister, the same as putting a gun to her head. And I never had the chance to thank her for the sacrifice."

Katie flung her arm across my chest, dissuading me from rising out of bed. "I-I know it's hard to accept that you might have prevented Loni's death if you had known the facts. My request is different, but in a way, it's the same thing. If Amilia dies, could you go through life knowing you had a chance to save her and didn't take it?" She turned toward me. "Please, Hans, if you ever loved me, grant me this favor." Katie's voice rose, as if in panic. "At least promise me you'll think about it. I have to know that much!"

I simply stared at the ceiling until she fell asleep, then left the room.

In early summer, the food shortage progressed from a hardship to a death sentence. Whiskey Wolff collapsed on the path near his house the same day that Frau Goldstein passed away in her rocking chair. Three of us men met at the cemetery to prepare burial plots. Georg wiped his brow after we had dug the first grave. "Do you guys have the energy to dig another one? I don't."

Balzar Boser, Young Andy's son, rested an elbow on his shovel. "I hate to say it, but what if we put both bodies in this hole?"

"*Ya*, that's a good idea," said Georg. "Hans, since you know Alma best, you should break the news to her."

I walked the two blocks to the Chornov Inn, apprehensive about Alma's response to the request. She argued that her mother deserved her own plot, but finally accepted the reasoning behind my friend's suggestion. Herr Wolff and Frau Goldstein would rest side-by-side, without the benefit of coffins or the dignity of burial garments, even ragged clothes deemed too precious for the deceased.

Katie planned a special surprise for Amilia's sixth birthday in mid-July. I arrived home from work and, with some difficulty, swung my excited daughter into the air. "How's my birthday girl today?" I asked.

She tipped her sallow face to me. "I'm good, but Mama's sleeping in bed. Swing me again, Papa."

I lacked the strength to hoist her a second time and suggested we go to the pond to allow Katie some time to rest before supper. Our daughter had become fond of the outdoors, a trait I liked to think she inherited from me. We walked out the front gate and across the road. Amilia ran across the footbridge spanning Chornov Creek, and then slowed, her energy spent. She squatted at the edge of the pond to watch a water beetle, but lost her balance and dirtied the hem of her only dress. I swished off the mud without admonishing her, recalling Papa's anger when he saw my soiled school clothing. We held hands on the way home, where she ran into the bedroom yelling, "Mama! I saw a really big bug."

Upon entering the room, I fought to remain calm. Katie lay on her back, mouth agape, glazed eyes staring at the ceiling. Choking back my emotions, I felt her neck for a pulse and placed an ear on her parted lips. With great effort, my trembling hand forever closed her once-bright hazel eyes. How they had captivated me on our first day of school when she turned in her desk and smiled. How those eyes shone years later when she cradled our infant daughter.

My vision blurred. "Come, Amilia. Sit with Papa on the bed." I couldn't expect her to share or understand my grief, but I needed her beside me.

"But Papa, it's my birthday and Mama said she'd have a surprise for me."

How could the finality of death be explained to a child? "Mama can't wake up anymore. Her soul has gone to heaven to be with *Yesus*. We'll say our night prayers with her and then have supper." I bowed my head and began: "Now I lay me down to s-sleep …"

"On the Good Mother's lap. She tucks me in and makes the sign of the cross over me," Amilia said, "and we should tuck Mama in so she doesn't get cold in heaven." My daughter grasped the edge of the thin blanket, her hand brushing against Katie's pocket. "Look at this, Papa!" She proudly held up a large slice of cheese that Katie must have stolen from the *kolkhoz* storeroom. "Mama bringed me a birthday present! *Danke*, Mama!" My heart warmed when she smacked a kiss on Katie's cheek before scampering to the kitchen table.

This is what you would want, my dear Katie. When Amilia is older, she will remember you as a kind, loving mother. God willing, that will be enough.

That evening after supper, we broke the sad news to the Freys. The distraught women accompanied me home to prepare Katie's body for burial and to keep a night vigil. Eva wailed that she would miss her sister forever, while Philomena knelt on the floor to comb her stepdaughter's hair. "Life wasn't always kind to you, was it, my child?" she said. "But now, you can rest easy." She kissed Katie's folded hands.

Our friends paid their condolences before work the next day, and we reminisced about our youth. "She liked you since I can remember, and Hans, it was obvious you liked her, too," Ivan said, the familiar smirk on his face. "Made for each other, I'd say."

Georg nodded. "My sister was a good-looking girl, but most of all, she had a kind heart. I remember when Frau Silbernagel was sick a few years ago, Katie took her hot soup every day."

Fortune gave me a good wife, but was I a good husband? Upon her return from the coal mine had I tried to lessen her pain, or had I only been concerned about my own desires? After some soul searching, I decided I had done my best, but the guilt of not agreeing to her final request still haunted me. Perhaps it wasn't my place to judge whether Katie, or I, was wrong—the matter was between God and Katie.

Philomena and Eva planned to hold another vigil the next night, that it was the decent thing to do, however, I convinced them to let me spend time alone with my wife and our daughter. Katie's body reposed on a blanket on the living room floor, the candle next to her casting a warm glow across her face. After Amilia recited her night prayers, her chin trembled and she began to cry. "Why won't Mama take me along?" she said. "I'm going to miss her." My heart ached when she stooped to kiss her mother goodbye for the final time.

I tucked my daughter into bed and she crushed her doll to her chest. "My Mama is going away, Groetel, but Papa will take good care of us," she said.

Katie had been right—Amilia's welfare depended entirely on me. Not allowing time to second-guess my decision, I barred the bedroom door with a bench, shuttered the kitchen window and locked the porch door. I wrapped my quivering arms around my wife's body and sorrowfully carried her to the kitchen table.

Grim task complete, I asked God's forgiveness for honoring Katie's last request. Feeling nauseated and dizzy, I stumbled up the attic stairs, and, steeling myself, opened the door to the smoker rack in the chimney.

The sun had not yet breeched the horizon when I pushed Katie's body along a secluded path in a borrowed wheelbarrow, the grating of the iron wheel the only sound. With Kurt's little red pocketknife, I cut shoots from the old hedge stumps at the cemetery entrance to arrange on the damp floor of the grave dug the previous day by my friends. "These will soften your sleep, my dear," I mumbled, the words distorted by the lump in my throat. I eased my wife's body into the hole, then gently arranged more foliage over her, all the while grieving for the relationship cut short the night of our arrest. Pity for my wife's lost years overwhelmed me. She would not see our daughter's first day of school, her transformation to an adult, her wedding day, or the birth of our grandchildren.

On the way back to my house with the empty wheelbarrow, the red hue of a poppy peeking between blades of grass caught my eye. As I leaned over and cut the stem, a warm breeze caressed my face and a peace settled deep within me; Katie's soul was finally at rest.

The Freys arrived at my door before work hours and were angry that Amilia was already at the daycare. Eva's features tightened. "Hans, how could you keep her from seeing her mother to the grave?"

"That's a horrible last image for a child. And I already took Katie to the cemetery."

Georg clenched his fists. "I had a right to help you. I'm her *brother*!"

The eyes of Katie's family burrowed into my back as I quickly walked away from the house. God help me if their friendship had died along with my wife.

I jumped into the hole at the graveside to place the poppy in Katie's folded hands. "Here's something for you. You truly deserve much more. Rest well in Heaven, my love."

Georg glared down at me. "Why is she still wearing her dress? Nobody gets buried anymore with clothes on. My wife's dress is worse than that. Take it off Katie and give it to Genni."

Under no circumstances could I allow anyone to remove the dress from Katie's body. Thankfully, Genni cried, "Stop it, Georg. If Hans wants to bury her with a dress, then let him. That old rag isn't worth hard feelings."

Ivan extended his hand and helped me to the surface. After he, Georg, and Balzar methodically filled the grave with soil, I sprinkled weed seeds over the compacted mound, while Ivan sang a traditional Russian verse:

> "All birds big and small, welcome.
> Speak kindly to this dear departed soul
> So she will fly away with you."

Amilia gradually adjusted to life without Katie and asked about her mother less frequently, but it broke my heart to tuck her into bed every night knowing she was hungry. Finally, a Torgsin store supplier agreed to exchange a small sack of corn and a bag of rice for Grandma's prized bedroom suite. After the loaded wagon left our yard, I took inventory inside the house: a crude kitchen table and bench, and a thin corn straw mattress that Amilia and I would share. Nothing left to barter.

After we depleted our food supply within a few weeks, I competed with other villagers picking potato skins from the scrap heap behind the *kolkhoz* kitchen until Kronchin's newly appointed bodyguard threatened to shoot anyone 'stealing food' from the property. Thank goodness, the administrator once again ignored our scavenging of the harvested fields for cornstalks that substituted for firewood, and leaf tips that were mashed into a broth of sorts.

One evening before sunset, I noticed a mouse scurry around the field, always returning to the same pile of stalks. I flung them aside, unearthing a small hoard of seeds. The kernels, precious as gold nuggets, could be ground and added to our grass soup. "This is the best porridge I've ever eaten," Amilia exclaimed. "The best in the whole world. I'll just hold it in my mouth until it's all mushy." She puffed out her sunken cheeks.

I wondered if Kurt's children in America considered grass porridge a treat.

Subsequent searches occasionally resulted in the discovery of more seed caches, and after snow covered the fields, fresh dung on the street from travelers' horses became a valuable commodity. Amilia pinched her nose while I picked assorted grains from the putrid feces, but it meant we had cheated death for another day. I cursed Stalin's quota system and the food it took from the mouths of innocent citizens, whether German, or Russian.

The day my daughter lacked the energy to rise from bed without my help, I knew the time had come to complete the loathsome task Katie had entrusted to me. I bolted the porch door and climbed the attic stairs to the smoker rack, my conscience protesting my every step. With great trepidation, I returned to the kitchen and prepared supper for Amilia.

By November, no one had the strength to dig a grave. When the stench from bodies stored in the old blacksmith shop became unbearable, Igor Kronchin requested a bulldozer from the military base in Elsass to excavate a large hole for a mass grave. If something wasn't done soon, by spring there wouldn't be anyone left in our village.

One especially cold afternoon, Kronchin, still relatively healthy from having access to the communal granaries, held a meeting to announce he had received permission to distribute a minimal amount of grain. When a loud cheer rose from the crowd, one disgruntled citizen wasn't so quick to forgive. "What took so damn long? We've been starving for a year!"

The administrator's voice remained calm, yet forceful. "This is the third time I've sent a request to the head office, but it was always denied. Now, get a pail and I'll meet you at the granary."

The villagers were certain the decision to release the grain was not Stalin's alone, and they were grateful that others in authority had come to their senses.

26

GUILTY AS CHARGED

March, 1934

Our fortunes reversed when plentiful spring rains encouraged an abundant crop, albeit an ample supply for export and a small amount for the villagers. As an added bonus, we received sufficient seeds to plant our personal garden plots, and the improved diet eventually gave my daughter back her energy. On her first day of school in September, Ami smiled broadly, exposing a small gap between her new front teeth. Except for the light-colored hair and lack of freckles, she was my Katie from so many years ago. We set off, proud as could be. Alma's boys dashed across the street, puffs of dust rising from under their boots. Recalling the discipline meted out to Kurt, Lothar, Fritz, and myself, I hoped the twins didn't have our devil-may-care attitude.

At assembly, an aged and stooped Headmaster Blokin peered down his crooked nose as Ami lined up with the other first graders. How times had changed; communism provided everyone with equal opportunities. The Russian parents were now encouraged to send their children to school. Perhaps there were some good aspects to the Bolshevik system, after all.

That evening, my daughter announced in a decisive voice, "Amilia is a baby name and I'm a big girl. Call me 'Ami' from now on, Papa."

"*Ya-naih*, that sounds nice." I shook my daughter's hand and said, "*Hallo*, Ami."

She giggled and accused me of being silly. "And Semion, do you like my new name?" she asked. Ivan's son, a thoughtful boy of her age, often played games with Ami in our yard. A grin crossed her face when he shyly nodded his head.

Kronchin stood on the hitch of a plough and waited as the villagers gathered at Pototski Field after the Red Harvest Day parade in October. "The Soviet Union is entering a phase of unparalleled growth. With the help of these machines, production this year has risen." He patted the fender of a newly imported John Deere tractor, the green paint shimmering in the bright sunshine. "We have surplus grain to distribute this afternoon. And thanks to our agricultural minister Kirov, and our great leader Father Stalin, there should be a cash payment early next year."

We had suffered years of starvation diets and were elated by this turn of events. Lothar, though, had something else on his mind. He sidled up next to me and said, "Hans, the other day Captain Orlenko asked me if you still want to immigrate to Germany. And from his other questions, it seems he thinks you and me are together in something. Probably has to do with my mother marrying Katie's father. I suppose that does make us sort of related."

Related? I shuddered at the thought. Before he could continue speaking, a worker called to him and we parted company. Why would Orlenko be trying to connect me to Lothar?

Late the following Thursday night, Police Captain Orlenko yelled for me to open the door or he would force his way in. Still half asleep, I drew back the bolt. He shoved me onto the kitchen bench, then hunched over me while his comrade shone a flashlight beam into my eyes. "For how long have you and your brother-in-law been communicating with Germany?" said Orlenko.

I shielded my eyes with my hand. "What are you talking about? Georg and—"

"I mean Lothar Degenstein. Here's a letter you wrote for him to the German embassy in Moscow in November 1929." The captain's coarse mustache worked back and forth beneath his ample nose like a maid's scrub brush.

"It had nothing to do with Lothar. It was an inquiry asking if there was a record of my family entering Germany on the amnesty day, but I never got an answer."

"That's because our Investigative Organ intercepted the letter to decipher your code." He held a piece of paper under the beam of light, and moved so close we bumped foreheads. "It was only a ruse that you were inquiring about your family, wasn't it?"

It felt as if a bomb exploded in my gut—Orlenko was framing me. Terrified of him arresting me and leaving Ami abandoned again, I mumbled, "It wasn't a code. I'm not guilty of anything. I don't even associate with Lothar."

"I don't believe you," he retorted. "And the Troika won't believe you, either. But if you co-operate with me, I can save your miserable ass. There's going to be a trial soon and you *will* testify for me." He slapped me in the face with the letter, and then huffed from the house, his comrade at his heels.

Tap, tap sounded on the bedroom window as I settled back into bed. "Hans, let me in," a voice whispered.

Lothar! "Go to the porch door," I replied apprehensively.

He slid a rifle from beneath his overcoat. "You gotta hide this for me in case Orlenko searches my house. I need a few days, then I'll come back for it and get the hell out of Chornov." The fear of the devil showed in his face. "They're after me; I know it, and now you know it, too."

"And . . . and what if the police search *my* house?"

Lothar brushed off my concern and took a small roll of thin wire from his coat pocket. "If you hang the rifle from the smoker rack in your chimney, it'll cover with soot and nobody will know it's there."

"And what should I do with the bullet? Hide it in the *Backofen*?"

The sarcasm escaped him and he clutched my nightshirt. "Please, Hans. Help me, for old time's sake."

I owed Lothar no favors, but honored his request as payment for Philomena's kindness toward Ami. After he left, I slid the bullet he had handed me into a niche behind the kitchen cupboard, then climbed the attic stairs to hide the rifle until he returned for it. Unfortunately, the Black Raven swooped down for Lothar the next night.

Despite my protests, Captain Orlenko demanded I testify at Lothar's trial in Mannheim the following week. To my great relief, Rakhmitov was not one of the three presiding judges. Lothar entered the courtroom, his leg iron clinking on the stone floor as he shuffled toward the prisoner's box. Though he stared at the floor, the extensive bruising on his face still showed. I felt sorry for him but feared that, to save himself, he would testify we were, indeed, accomplices.

The bailiff shoved him forward. "Lothar Degenstein," he read in a detached tone, "You are hereby charged with espionage."

One of the judges yawned. "What evidence is there to support the charges?" he said.

My breath turned shallow when I recognized the envelope Captain Orlenko waved above his head. "I hold the letter that Comrade Degenstein compelled his brother-in-law to write to the German Embassy in Moscow. It provides information on the ethnic Germans' movements within the Soviet Union," he announced. "The simple peasant you see seated here didn't understand what he was writing."

I ignored the slight to my intelligence and indicated to Lothar with a shake of my head that Orlenko's statement was misleading, but for all I could tell he may have fallen asleep.

The Chief Justice supported his chin with a gnarled hand. "What makes you think he forced the witness?" he asked.

"His superior, Igor Kronchin, signed an affidavit that Mister Degenstein used his position as assistant administrator of the Chornov *kolkhoz* to spy on the Communist Party. In addition, my officers reported that the accused delivered coal to the home of my witness on numerous occasions." He pointed at me and said, "Is that not so, Johannes Gerein?"

"He brought coal to our house, but his—"

Captain Orlenko interrupted me. "That was how he manipulated Comrade Gerein. By controlling his essentials of life."

Then he shouted at me so loudly that a dozing judge rose slightly from his chair. "You sent this letter to the Moscow Embassy, did you not?"

"I sent a letter, but it was—"

Orlenko threw the paper on the table. "There you have it, Your Honors. This prisoner is guilty of supplying confidential information to a foreign power. In other words, espionage."

Angered beyond reason, I stood up and clutched the rail. "Let me finish! I didn't say what you are insinuating!"

The judge pounded his gavel on the table. "This is a court of law and I will not accept interruptions. If you make another disturbance, you will join the prisoner in the dock. Do you understand?"

I fell back in my chair and nodded. What choice did I have?

He turned to his associates. "How do you find the accused?" After receiving two guilty verdicts, he removed his glasses and squinted at Lothar. "Guilty as charged. I hereby sentence you to twenty years in any northern *konzlager* that requires your services. Bailiff, remove the prisoner!"

My breath caught in my throat. He should have given Lothar the death penalty; twenty years in the gulag system would be worse than a bullet in the back of the head. Lothar faced me as a guard led him from the room. "Hans, tell Mama I love her and you t—"

The guard slammed a nightstick into his face. I grimaced at the crunch of shattering teeth.

Kronchin arched his eyebrows at my question that afternoon, verifying Orlenko had falsified the affidavit. After assuring himself that no one was in the adjoining office, the administrator confided in me. "Adolph Hitler is steadily increasing the size of his army and may become a threat to the Soviet Union. No one will ever make it official, but Father Stalin doesn't want any of you Germans in positions of power and that's the reason Lothar was arrested."

"Are you saying Josef Stalin has the right to persecute us just because we're of German descent?"

"Whatever furthers The Cause is justifiable."

27

BECAUSE OF THE ROSE

January, 1935

The year began on a high note with Kronchin fulfilling his promise to give increased wages to *kolkhoz* members. I carefully counted my roubles before purchasing lumber to build a bed for Ami, and another for myself; sleeping on a cornhusk mattress on the floor was for dogs.

Two other welcomed changes were the end to the rationing of potatoes, meat, and sugar, and the resumption of milling wheat into flour. One Sunday morning Ami and I enjoyed freshly baked bread in the Freys' kitchen. Ami, who could not remember having eaten bread, smacked her lips after her first bite. "Gramma, this is so good. And I have something for *you*. An announcement!" She wriggled in her chair. "I belong to a club. We sing songs and learn to march in the yard."

"Now that she's in Form Two, I let her join the communist's Young Pioneers League," I explained.

Philomena took a sip of dried dandelion tea. "Ami, do you mean the town hall yard or the church yard?"

Ami became agitated. "You old people still call it a church, but there is no such thing in the Soviet Union. Comrade said to forget about God and churches. *Father Stalin* is our leader."

Philomena's eyes narrowed. "Is that what they're teaching you in that … that club?"

"Ami, if you forget about God and all your prayers, you can't go to any more of those meetings."

"B-but, Papa, Comrade said if we're good students, she'll take us to visit Moscow and Comrade Lenin's Maso … masone … his grave."

"You mean Lenin's Mausoleum," I prompted.

"Papa, never say his name without using Comrade first. Semion did that and she whacked him on the bum with her baton so hard that he cried."

Apparently, communism hadn't advanced the methods of training children. Anyone who dared strap my child would have to deal with me. "*Ya-naih*, Ami. You can go to the meetings, but don't forget about *Yesus*. That's our secret, okay?"

"I won't ever forget because Mama's with Him," she announced, swinging her braids from side to side.

Although Philomena chided me for allowing Ami to attend the meetings, I decided my daughter should have every opportunity to succeed under whatever system she must live. I began volunteering within the League, and was present at a meeting where Kronchin's well-prepared speech exalted Russia's huge advances since the revolution. After stepping down from the podium, he said, "So, Hans, you finally see the benefits of our system. Welcome to our ranks, Comrade."

I glanced around to ensure no one overheard our conversation. "Don't celebrate too much. I still believe in God, not Uncle Joe. Ami loves the singing and the camaraderie, so for now, for her sake, I tolerate communism. Because of the rose, one must also provide water for the thorns."

Kronchin furrowed his brow. "Are you foolish enough to think communism in Russia will ever collapse?"

"The people's desire for freedom will eventually win out. Maybe I won't see it, but I fervently hope my daughter will. In the Soviet state, the rungs of the ladder are made out of human suffering. To rise in the ranks means stepping on your fellow man."

"You're wrong, Hans. Your daughter will grow to appreciate communism, if you don't poison her mind first." He swaggered away and left me standing at the door.

Josef Stalin eventually feared a revolt within his hierarchy. Although there were no reports in the communist newspapers, word of mouth circulated that he eliminated most of the former administration by execution or a life sentence in a *konzlager*. In the autumn of 1936, the communists flicked Igor Kronchin from his rung on the human ladder; seemingly, the administrator's total dedication to The Cause made no difference. I recalled Igor once telling me, 'Communism is thriving because our leaders aren't afraid to make tough decisions—if toes happen to be stepped on, so be it.' Now that *his* toes were under the boot, had his faith in the system perhaps wavered?

In a sense, Kronchin's arrest freed me; now, no local authority knew of my escape from the labor camp. However, my reprieve had come at his misfortune and the liberty was bittersweet. Even though he had been a dedicated communist, the harsh treatment of the villagers seemed, at times, to disagree with his personal ideals.

On a blustery morning shortly after Igor's arrest, I stood at the fringe of the crowd of *kolkhoz* workers gathered in the town hall yard to meet our new chief administrator. He was a small man, but not one easily dismissed. A full-length coat and fur hat set him apart from the villagers. As he marched onto the front step, the peculiar tilt of his head and the large purplish scar covering his right cheek spurred an instant fury in me. *Yop filla mut*—Luka Nikolai! That lecherous bastard had raped my innocent sister.

My headlong dash carried me the length of River Street, through our barn, and up the attic stairs, two at a time. I unwound the wire from the smoker rack and pulled up Lothar's rifle, slamming shut the door with such force the chimney shook. My frenzied hands peeled layers of soot from the weapon, but in my mind, I was brushing the dirt from Loni's face as she lay crumpled beside the train track. When I yanked aside the kitchen cupboard to retrieve the hidden bullet, the front sight of the rifle slammed against the doorframe and skittered across the floor. *Yesus*!

I crept along the cemetery path to the rear of the communal granary, pleased to see the *kolkhoz* membership still assembled across the street; Luka Nikolai was not only arrogant, but long-winded, as well. Despite the cool day, I wiped the sweat from my face, shimmied up an old wagon tongue braced against the eaves of the granary and scrambled across the roof on my hands and knees. Flopping onto my belly, I chambered the bullet at the moment Nikolai ended his speech and disappeared inside the hall. Damn it! Moments later, I heard the door creak open and inched my head above the ridgeline. When Nikolai paused on the step to don his hat, my finger caressed the trigger. *Baaang*. The ferocity of the report and the puff of gun smoke made me giddy with revenge. Nikolai fell to his knees, glanced at the splintered hole near the top of the door, then in the direction of the shot. He leapt to his feet and ducked behind the hall.

I clambered to the rear of the building, dropped to the ground and ran to a clump of bushes near the Goldstein's backyard. Alma's sons were in school and barring a daytime guest, the inn would be a safe refuge until the excitement subsided. The dry hinges of the back door protested both the opening and closing. I crossed the kitchen and paused, mid-step, relieved that the image glaring at me was my sooty reflection in the office mirror. "Alma … Alma, it's me, Hans," I said, when she hurried into the room. "Quick! Do you have something that'll clean this black off?" I briefly explained the situation as she led me to the back porch, where I doused a rag with kerosene and scrubbed the soot from my face and hands.

"You'll need a clean shirt, too. One of Papa's is still in the closet over there."

"*Danke*, Alma." I wrapped the rifle inside my soiled shirt, dropped the bundle into the Goldstein's well and walked casually onto Church Street.

Ivan, exiting the co-operative store, asked, "Who do *you* think tried to shoot Nikolai? Heard it was somebody in disguise."

"I wouldn't even try to guess," I replied, barely controlling the edge in my voice.

Ivan stood on his toes to peer at me more closely. "*You* have some black marks around your eyes and …" He broke off, a sudden display of enlightenment creeping across his face.

"If the sight on my gun hadn't broken off, the little rooster would be in hell right now, exactly where he belongs," I said with a scowl.

Ivan shook his head. "Nobody likes him, but to take a shot. Isn't that a little much?"

I trusted my friend, but thought it best not to divulge the reason for my hatred of the man.

Although the Agricultural Organ in Odessa grudgingly accepted Luka Nikolai in an office position, the concern remained for some time that he suspected I fired the shot and would request an in-depth investigation by the Mannheim GPU.

28

NOT EVEN AFTER I DIE

June, 1941

Hitler breached his non-aggression treaty with Josef Stalin, and the German Army invaded the Soviet Union on June 22, 1941. My fellow villagers and I cheered wildly as jeeps towing artillery guns led a disciplined line of infantry down Church Street, combat tanks with steel tracks pulverizing the road. The power of the *Wehrmacht* pushing south seemed endless, their boots pounding in unison, turtle helmets pulled low on their heads. Young female admirers stepped forward and handed freshly picked flowers to our liberators. My facial muscles ached from grinning as repeated shouts of "Heil Hitler" echoed along the street. This could be our chance to cast off the communists' shackles, for while I *felt* Hitler was trustworthy, I *knew* Stalin was not.

An open jeep at the rear of the military unit halted near the church and a stocky captain in full regimental gear leaned over the windshield to yell into a megaphone. "*Achtung*! Gather around for an important announcement."

The euphoria on the street subsided. Was this a repeat of what we knew so well? Restrictions and arrests?

When the young captain pumped his fist in the air and shouted, "Communism is dead!" a thunderous cheer rose from the relieved crowd. The captain, pleased with the response, called for quiet. "The first thing we need is a liaison between our army and the people of Chornov. In effect, we need a trusted person to dismantle the commune. Does anyone have a suggestion?"

"Hans Gerein! Hans Gerein!" Ivan chanted. The crowd soon joined him.

I reluctantly stepped forward, humbled by their confidence.

"Are there any objections to Herr Gerein being your *Bürgermeister*?" the captain asked, moving up beside me.

No protests. He turned to me and pushed back his hat, revealing short blond hair and a long scar on his forehead. "Meet me in the town hall in fifteen minutes, *Bürgermeister* Gerein."

I stood in the vacant room and speculated on the demise of the former administrators until the officer entered and extended his hand. "I'm Captain Schmidt, the re-settlement officer for the Kutschurgan colonies. Our control base is in Elsass, but you will answer directly to me."

"I'll give the new posting a try and see what happens," I said, a bit unsure of my duties.

"Good enough. Proceed as you see fit and I'll check in with you next week. And, by the way, are the former police still in town or did they get advance warning from their compatriots that we're coming? The last ones we caught, the ones who were too slow or complacent, are still dangling from the windmill in Karpowa."

His laugh left me feeling nauseated. Perhaps my enthusiasm had been premature. Such actions—a disregard for one's rights, a barbaric presumption of justice—seemed no different from the Soviet Troika's swift verdicts.

After I assured him there were no GPU agents remaining in Chornov, the captain called back to me before passing through the doorway. "Pick a few trusted men to help you plan the return of all property to private ownership. There will be some dissenters, of course, but don't worry about them. If they become a problem, give me their names."

'No one in this village will be turned over to Captain Schmidt,' I thought as the jeep bumped across the rickety Chornov Creek Bridge.

My newly-assigned assistants Balzar—married to Eva shortly after Katie's death—Young Andy Boser, and Ivan, followed me to the administrator's former office. Balzar and Ivan would determine a fair distribution of the *kolkhoz* animals to the families in Chornov, and Young Andy would be in charge of the weekly grain distribution from the communal storage.

"What a mess!" Balzar remarked. Desk drawers and papers lay scattered over the floor. "And we couldn't get enough paper to write a goddamn letter."

Ivan removed a charred piece of paper from the stove. "They probably burned some important stuff, too."

A noisy crowd in the street attracted our attention. "Sounds like everybody's in the mood to have fun. Doing business can wait," I said, anxious to celebrate the events of the day.

Ivan hung back, appearing concerned. "Are you against private ownership?" I asked.

"*Nyet*, but what if Hitler decides there is no room for Russians in Chornov."

"Whoa, Ivan. This village is your home as much as ours. Since Hitler has the support of his people, he must be a reasonable man. Germans aren't fools, you know. Now, go enjoy the day with your family."

The atmosphere reminded me that it had been years since we had a reason for a celebration. I chanced upon Ami mixing with the partiers on the street. "Most people long ago traded their instruments for food, so now they use whatever's available," I said to her above the slightly off-key music floating from Boser's yard. Squeaky Hoffer sat on an upturned pail at the edge of the threshing floor, coaxing a tune from a dilapidated accordion. Young Andy tapped his toes while strumming a washboard and Ignatz Hirsch clacked a large set of metal spoons against his leg, emulating the sound of cymbals.

"Polka," Georg shouted from amidst the revelers. "Come on, Squeaky, can you play a polka on that old thing?"

"Sure can, but do you remember how to dance? Or are you as slow on your feet as you are in the head?"

Alma stood to one side with a friend. I bowed and asked her to dance, then we joined others swirling on the floor until another man requested a waltz with her.

"Papa, teach me to dance like that," Ami said. My daughter

and I swept in wide circles, me avoiding her toes.

Semion approached us when we paused for a rest. He stared down at his shoes and said, "Mister Gerein, can I have permission to dance with Ami?"

The teenagers gazed into each other's eyes, seemingly unaware of their bumping knees. Eva paused beside me, a toddler balanced on her hip. "Ami and Semion remind me of you and Katie at that age," she said. "They like each other, but are too shy to admit it."

"Come on, Hans!" Balzar said, already affected by a quart or two of wine. "Let's go to the table and have a drink. Remember, you didn't want your Papa always watching you either."

When the festivities ended, Ami and I returned home and sat on the bench with our sore feet propped on a stool. I leaned back and loosened my shirt collar. "Ami, now that the communists aren't living in Grandpa's house anymore, should *we* move there? The house and barn are bigger, and besides, the place is full of good memories for me."

A mischievous grin played at the corners of her mouth. "Are you thinking about getting married? You danced with Frau Goldstein. I think she likes you."

"We're only good friends." I patted her knee. "Now, you go to bed while I write a letter to Uncle Kurt. It's been almost eight years since we were allowed to communicate with foreigners. There's so much to tell him I won't know where to start."

The following day, Ami and I moved our belongings and settled into the spacious house, Grandma's large table backed by a row of cupboards along the rear wall still dominating the kitchen. Overcome with emotion, I sank into my grandfather's worn, over-stuffed chair and drew Ami in beside me. "I remember your great-grandfather sitting here after supper. A big blue cloud of smoke would rise from his pipe to the ceiling." I threw my arms in the air. "My grandma would say, 'Wilhelm, when are you going to quit that filthy habit?' 'Not even after

I die, Genoveva, so pack my pipe in the coffin with me,' he'd always answer." I laughed, but my eyes turned misty.

"Papa, you take after him. That sounds like some of the funny things you say."

Tomorrow I would show Ami the secret pantry and tell her about a certain special kiss.

On his next visit to my office, Captain Schmidt reviewed my proposal for dividing the *kolkhoz* land—half shared by all citizens, including the Russians, and the balance divided among the families of former landowners.

"We're here to stamp out communism and you want to re-introduce it?" he balked, thumbing through a pile of papers.

"The original village land grant was held in common for all German settlers. Individual farmers got ownership only by buying land from the Russian Counts in the area. True, a few Russians had bought land around Karpowa, but all private owners in Chornov were German. I feel that everybody, including the Russians who didn't have a share, helped build the community and should now be considered citizens."

"Ha! I'll bet most of your neighbors won't agree with you."

"Then those that don't like it can vote for a different *Bürgermeister* when the election comes around."

The captain raised his eyes from the papers. "What election?"

"I was only assigned by you as a temporary *Bürgermeister*. Surely we'll have elections soon. We aren't just jumping from one dictatorship to the next, are we?"

He shrugged and rose from his chair. "I can't be bothered with political shit, Hans. About the land issue, put your foot down and make a decision. I grant you absolute power."

Could an army captain bestow such authority on a civilian? "Don't make me totally responsible for the land division. I-I can't be the judge," I said. "For Christ's sake, I'm no Rakhmitov."

"Do you mean the judge from Mannheim? How do you know

him?"

I detailed my devastation upon learning about our stolen ship tickets. "And besides me and Katie, he had others arrested on false charges. Gus Vetter, the Ripplingers, Ira Goldstein and—"

Captain Schmidt halted me in mid-sentence. "Goldstein. Is that a Jewish name?"

"It is, but Alma and her boys go to our Catholic church now that an army chaplain is holding Mass." A wry smile crossed his face when I said, "So they wouldn't be considered Jewish anymore."

The captain changed the subject. "About Rakhmitov. We caught him hiding under the altar in the church at Mannheim. He tried to bribe us, but we arrested him and had a few good parties with his unbelievable amount of money." He slapped me on the back. "When you give this testimony at his military trial, he'll be *kaput*."

With the sweetness of revenge so strong, I could taste it on my lips, I pledged to attend the trial whenever and wherever it would be held.

Captain Schmidt brought his battered jeep to a jolting halt in the laneway several days later and we were soon on the road to Mannheim. The trial was conducted in the same courtroom where Rakhmitov had often presided as judge, except now he sat in the prisoner's box, hunch-backed, nervously tangling his shaggy beard with his fingers. A door at the front of the room opened and two aides escorted in the district's commanding officer, a row of medals clinking on his chest. He stood erect with his heels together. When he called for verification of the prisoner's identity, no fewer than ten men in the packed courtroom disdainfully shouted out the judge's name. The military prosecutor read a list of charges, however, the testimony during the trial consisted mostly of unconvincing hearsay until I took the stand. The prosecutor asked me to detail my involvement with the prisoner. "I-I went directly to Judge Rakhmitov for my family's passports so there wouldn't be a long delay, which was common at the time," I began, then coughed nervously. "In the end, he demanded most of my army pay as a bribe before agreeing to have the paperwork completed."

"Is that the only time you did business with him?"

I recounted the theft of the ship tickets from Kurt's letter, and related the false charges levied against the scores of people he had sent to their deaths in the *konzlagers*.

Rakhmitov jumped to his feet. "I challenge the witness! He's only seeking revenge for my lawfully—"

The prosecutor ignored him. "Is there anyone here who can vouch for this witness's character?"

My superior stood tall in the back row. "Sir, I am Captain Schmidt, re-settlement officer for the Kutschurgan colonies. I work closely with Herr Gerein and have found him to be honest to a fault. He was the villagers' unanimous choice for *Bürgermeister*."

The general slammed his gavel on the table. "Case closed."

Later that day on the way back to Chornov, Captain Schmidt veered his jeep around a sharp corner at the Mannheim flourmill. A sudden gust of wind turned a bearded corpse swinging from a noose tied to an upper railing. Judge Rakhmitov! I lowered my eyes, knowing my testimony had been crucial in sending him to the gallows. Revenge was mine, but strangely, I felt no pleasure.

29

WHAT A DRUNKEN MAN SAID

April, 1942

The land division disputes were well behind me by the spring thaw. After collecting the mail one pleasant day in mid-April, I sat at my desk staring at an envelope marked with Kurt's return address. Almost nine years had passed since his last letter. A renewed connection sprang up as I kissed the paper touched by his hands. The first paragraph detailed Kurt's relief upon finally hearing from me. The second paragraph, however, stunned me—the United States had declared war on Germany. Worst of all, Kurt had been called to duty. I read his closing words aloud: "*This effectively places you and me on opposing sides. How did this happen? I hate the idea of war, even if it would stop that maniac Adolph Hitler.*"

Maniac? He wasn't aware of how much Hitler had improved our lives the past year. And if the Allies defeated Germany, perhaps we would even come under American jurisdiction. Excited by this new prospect, I answered his letter immediately.

I was about to leave for the day when Captain Schmidt strode into my office and demanded a large quantity of flour for his army unit. "That'll mean Andy Boser will have to lower the weekly distribution of grain to the villagers," I informed him.

"The German Army has to eat, too, and while you're at it, add twenty bushels of potatoes to the order. Speaking of the army, draw up a list of Chornov men eligible for conscription. We have troops stalled all over the Soviet Union waiting for reinforcements. We need more men, and don't be mad at me," he said, noting my obvious disdain. "I don't make the rules."

His words chilled me; I had heard them before—from the communist Igor Kronchin.

With a number of my young workers lost to conscription, the job of delivering grain to Karpowa fell to me. One day, after unloading the wagons at the grain brokers, I went in search of Pavel Lebedin. At a weather-beaten house cowering among straggly willows, a frightfully thin child with the stick-straight black hair of his grandfather Viktor pointed to a low-slung building down the street. As I opened the battered door to the tavern, the stench of stale tobacco smoke and alcohol assaulted me. Four grubby men at a sagging table shared a bottle of vodka; Pavel's sharp nose and sloping forehead were immediately recognizable. He peered at me through bloodshot eyes, a hand-rolled cigarette dangling from a corner of his mouth. "It's you! I took your wife home a few years ago. Come have a wodka," he said in a drunken slur, pushing a full glass across the table. I sat down, ignored the greasy fingerprints, and drained the glass. Over the next hour, he and his friends related the benefits of the recent land division in Karpowa. They had sold their newly acquired plots and, apparently, intended to dispose of the windfall as fast as their inebriated brains could absorb alcohol. Pavel gulped the remainder of his drink. "Your German cousins are g-gonna be real good for this country. We've them to thank for gettin' rid of the lazy communist administrators, don't we?" His friends raised their arms in a cheer, elevating the odor of unwashed bodies. "And when they finish with those bloodsuckin' Jews, this'll be the best country in the world."

"Finish? What are they doing with them?" I asked, surprised at the news.

"Don't know, but the SS took them all away from here." When Pavel shook the empty vodka bottle, I handed him a few roubles to buy another drink and, eager to draw fresh air into my lungs, excused myself.

On my journey home, both the popping of the tractor's engine and my thoughts settled into a steady rhythm. Why did German Secret Service troops arrest the Karpowa Jews? Perhaps there was a connection between Captain Schmidt's interest in Jewish families in

Chornov and Pavel's account.

Upon arriving home, I surprised Alma with a visit and repeated Pavel's observations. "What are you suggesting?" she asked, drying the last of the dishes stacked on a tray. "After all those years of suffering under the Soviets, do you expect me to hide in a hole because of what a drunken man said? Business is good now and lots of officers spend their Reich marks here."

"Maybe he was drunk, but I'm still worried about you."

Her dark brown eyes searched my face. "You have been a good friend to warn me, but my father built this inn to support his family, and I intend to run it the same way. Now, if you'll excuse me, there's work to do."

She hurried to the dining room, a bright green scarf flapping against her back, while I stood in the hallway with an uneasy feeling in my gut.

On Tuesday, August 17, 1943, a shaft of sunlight from the small bedroom window highlighted Ami's blonde hair as she packed her clothes in my old army rucksack. It saddened me that Katie wasn't here to share the experience of our sixteen-year-old leaving for secondary school in Selz. I sat on the edge of the bed and cautioned Ami not to go on the streets alone at night and to choose her friends wisely. "But you don't have to study all the time. Do some fun things, too."

"I have lots of good friends here, especially Semion."

"Semion? Who in hell is Semion?" I said with a grin.

"*Ya*, Papa, he reminds me of you—always teasing."

Ivan was aware of our children's fondness for one another and he approved of their friendship, as well. "Finish packing so we're not late. Grandma's coming over to say goodbye and Captain Schmidt will be here soon," I said.

The captain, with a business meeting scheduled in Selz, had offered us a ride. At precisely three o'clock, we heard a horn outside the gate. Semion, his shoulders slumped, waved to Ami from the last corner in Chornov.

My daughter and I stepped down from the jeep at the home where an acquaintance of mine, the *Bürgermeister* of Selz, had arranged for Ami to live. "I'll come back for you in two hours," Captain Schmidt called over the rumble of the motor as he drove off, stirring a cloud of fine dust.

Before I could knock on the weathered porch door, a petite woman with vivid blue eyes and a wide smile waved us inside. "You must be Hans Gerein and Ami," she greeted. "I'm Ottilia Erickson."

Her fingers felt thin and fragile in my calloused hand. "It is nice to meet you," I said, then placed a large sack of flour in the kitchen. "I'll pay for Ami's keep with all the flour your family needs while she attends school here."

"*Ya-naih*, that is very generous of you. My husband died in the famine ten years ago. Now tailoring is my only income, but I manage," she said, as two young boys, either shy or instructed to stay out from underfoot, peeked from a doorway at the opposite end of the room. She took Ami by the arm. "Enough about me. Come, sit to the table and we'll talk."

When Ottilia poured hot water from a small samovar into ornate china cups, I studied the woman with whom I would entrust my daughter. Her long hair, prematurely streaked with gray, hung straight to her shoulders, and the trials of a difficult life creased her brow. As she turned toward the cupboard, her profile caused me to gasp—the tilt of her head, the manner in which she swept the hair from her face. "A-are you of Swedish decent, Frau Erickson?" I asked, almost afraid to hear the answer.

She turned to face me. "*Ya*. I sure am. But I was raised here in Selz."

I chose my words carefully. "Do you remember the Red Army raid in the summer of 1919? W-when all the people were killed?"

"Of course. My father was a victim. How could I ever forget?" She closed her eyes for a moment and made the sign of the cross over her breast.

"Did you help a teenage boy get a cart up the hill at the edge of town?"

"How would you know …" She turned pale, her mouth agape. "Are you *serious*?"

I jumped to my feet as Ottilia rushed around the table to meet me in an embrace of sorrow and regret at all that had transpired that day: the destruction, the looting, the murders …

She held me at arm's length. "Oh, Hans. I remember your grandpa was badly wounded, and you wanted to take him home. I thought of you many times over the years and wondered what happened."

Ami rose from her chair and gushed, "He pulled the cart all the way to The Chasm. Show her the scars, Papa," she said, then began to apologize for her forward behavior.

Ottilia interrupted her. "It's good to be proud of your father." She clasped Ami by the shoulders. "And you and I are going to be such good friends, aren't we?"

The huge grin on my daughter's face reassured me that she could not be in a better home.

On the return trip to Chornov, I took stock of the situation. More than a decade had passed since Katie's death. Gradually my sad thoughts had disappeared and, instead, I remembered the good times we shared: our wedding day, our first Christmas together, the birth of our child. She would forever be my beautiful Katie, but I wished to move on with my life. I was forty years old and didn't relish spending my later years alone. Ami would probably never live at home with me again. Her ambition was to be a teacher in Selz, unless we could immigrate to America and live my dream held since Kurt left Chornov twenty-nine years ago. Twenty-nine years! At times, it seemed like only yesterday, yet half a lifetime had passed.

30

NOBODY KNEW MUCH ABOUT IT

December, 1943

The morning of December 23, I groomed Star, the horse received from the disbursement of the *kolkhoz* animals. I would travel to Selz the next day, and watch Ami perform in the holiday pageant before we attended Christmas Eve Mass. Suddenly, the barn door flew open and Philomena rushed in, nearly tripping on the hem of her dress. She gasped for breath, then managed to utter a few words. "*Eih*, *eih*, Hans. They're arrested. Do something."

I dropped the pitchfork and reached to steady her. "Slow down, Philomena. Who's been arrested?"

"Alma! Alma Goldstein and her boys. Some soldiers took them away in the back of their truck!"

I hastily bridled Star and set off at a gallop for Captain Schmidt's headquarters in Elsass, only to find the office door locked. Following another half hour's hard ride, I drew my lathered horse to a halt in front of the army headquarters in Mannheim. To my surprise, Schmidt sat in the waiting area, calmly making entries in a notebook. "What did they do with the Goldsteins?" I barked, ignoring his greeting.

His eyes darted around the room. "Wait a minute, Hans. Come with me." I followed him outside, where he opened the door to his jeep and we slid onto the front seat. "We're not going anywhere. I just want to talk to you in private." The captain tugged on my coat sleeve. "Don't shout all over town that you're a friend of Jews."

"Why not? Alma *is* a friend of mine. I've known her since childhood."

"Hans, listen to what I'm saying! Unless you want to get arrested, too, shut your damn mouth. You can't help her. Nobody can. And—and I can't be seen associating with a Jew-lover."

"Then I'll find her myself."

As I reached for the door handle Schmidt leaned across the seat to pull away my hand. "Hans, be reasonable. Believe me." His mouth twisted in a menacing scowl. "Jews are all the same, every last one of them. The Führer's right—the world will be better off without them."

I rested my head against the door. Captain Schmidt had just described Adolph Hitler as a devil, not the savior that I imagined him. I turned to his implacable face. "Are you telling me Herr Hitler *knows* about these types of arrests? That he's allowing this kind of thing to happen?"

"I'm saying that he *ordered* these arrests. Now, use your head and stay on the right side."

As he attempted to explain the Jewish situation, I recognized Schmidt for what he was—a demented Nazi. Just then, four SS jeeps escorting two canvas-covered army trucks rumbled past our vehicle. Crammed in the confined space, men, women, and children with fear shining in their eyes peeked from beneath the canopies, the tip of a bright green scarf fluttering from a corner. I lurched forward. "Follow those trucks!"

"Hans! Use your head. You don't want to get involved in this."

"Dammit, I already am!" I jumped from his jeep and yanked free Star's reins. I galloped after the convoy until the trucks turned onto a dirt trail leading into the Baraboi Valley and parked near a willow and reed hut in a cutbank of the river. Riding closer, I saw smoke rising above the hut, but it was not coming from the chimney. Anguished screams rose above the crackle of the blaze. My soul froze. 'Please, God,' I thought, 'wake me from this nightmare.'

I flung myself from Star and dashed down the bank. Sweat dripped into my eyes as I dodged the nonchalant soldiers gathered in a semi-circle. The *Hauptman* shouted an order to stop, but I surged toward the barricaded door, screaming Alma's name. I dropped to the ground and crawled forward until the skin on my face blistered from the intense heat of the fire. The wails of anguish subsided when the roof collapsed, sending a shower of embers billowing into the winter air. Incredibly, a child, engulfed like a torch, staggered out of the inferno and toppled to the ground. As I inched toward the burning figure, a strong grip encircled my ankles.

Upon regaining consciousness, the captain was splashing water from his canteen on my scorched face. "What the hell were you doing?" he yelled.

The sound of his voice sickened me. I slapped the canteen from his hand and dragged myself to Star. Rising to my feet, I wept into her mane.

Before I reached Chornov, the first snow of the season began to fall. Star plodded along in the eerie calm, the flakes accumulating on her haunches. My conscience gouged a hole in my soul. If only I had asked Captain Schmidt why he wondered whether Alma Goldstein was Jewish; if only I had insisted Alma and her boys leave Chornov.

Late in the afternoon, slumped in Grandpa's chair, the screams still echoed in my head. Tomorrow the congregation at Midnight Mass would sing carols honoring the birth of *Yesus*. However, I wished to be in a bubble—alone, isolated from the pain I had witnessed.

An overnight gale howled across the steppe and by morning, the snowdrifts were deep, visibility near zero. Though feeling somewhat guilty, I was pleased not to be going to Selz where I would have to feign happiness. Surely, Ottilia would do her best to comfort Ami on her first Christmas away from home. I entertained the idea of writing a letter to the South Dakota *Eureka Rundschau* to notify America, and indeed, the world, of the recent atrocities. Or might the German authorities censor the mail and exterminate *me* for what I knew? For Ami's sake, I decided the risk was too great, and eased my conscience by reasoning that one voice would make no difference anyway.

The storm abated by evening. I shoveled a path to our gate and followed sleigh tracks to Saint Gustav's Church for Midnight Mass. Philomena, bundled head to toe, approached me on the steps and asked what happened to Alma and the boys. I couldn't bring myself to tell her the truth, nor worry her about something she couldn't control. "I'm not sure. Nobody knew much about it," I answered her.

She stood on tiptoes, examining my scorched eyebrows and blistered face. I held open the church door for her and said, "Ach, the forge flared up at the blacksmith's when I had one of Star's shoes repaired in Mannheim."

Weeks passed before Captain Schmidt visited my office. I resisted the urge to spit in his face, and we avoided the topic of the Jews; the pain was too raw. "You haven't told me lately about the gains of the Führer's army," I said sarcastically.

Schmidt seemed relieved with the nature of my inquiry. "There haven't been any gains, only strategic retreats. We're holding the Soviets at the Dnieper River east from here, and our Western Front in France and Belgium is secure." A smile crossed his face. "Come spring, the Red Threat in Russia will be finished for good."

"So, I shouldn't worry about my future? My family will enjoy peace here?"

"If you've got one hundred percent German blood, you belong to Hitler's Master Race. And if your family line remains pure, they will all enjoy full benefits of the Nazi Party. But there's room for all kinds, you know, so long as they're Aryan." I pulled back when he reached out to shake my hand. "Besides, you're a ranking German, and the Führer loves your type, Hans."

Captain Schmidt had unwittingly revealed the true extent of my dilemma; in Hitler's eyes, I was a member of the Master Race, while in Stalin's, I was the Jew.

31

NOTHING NEEDED TO BE SAID

March, 1944

Ami's voice came to me as if in a dream. I staggered bleary-eyed from the bedroom and found Captain Schmidt standing in the living room, my trembling daughter by his side. She ran to me and threw her arms around my neck. "Why did you send for me, Papa?"

I angrily faced the captain. "What's going on? You have no right to take my daughter from Selz without my permission!"

"Hold on, Hans. I knew there'd be no way to reason with you unless she was here." He removed his hat. "There's bad news. The Soviet Army broke through our lines a few days ago, and I've got orders to evacuate all the Germans from the Kutschurgan Colonies."

"*Evacuate* us?"

"We're not sure what in hell is keeping the new troops, but they haven't shown up, so we are forced to retreat. If the Soviets get their hands on you German Russians, that'll be the end of you."

"And exactly where are you taking us?" I asked.

"West. Ahead of our retreating forces. Maybe as far as Poland."

His statement seemed absurd. "You come here and upset our lives and don't even explain *why*?"

"The Führer wants loyal farmers in the countries surrounding Germany." He smirked and continued, "And who better than you discontented German Russians?"

"I *won't* do it! Besides, everyone would need more time—"

The captain snapped to attention. "Hans Gerein, as *Bürgermeister* you will organize all persons of German descent to evacuate Chornov tomorrow morning at eight o'clock sharp. Not you or anyone else has a choice. And that's final!" He leaned in close, his breath hot on my face. "I'd hate to do it, but my orders are to shoot any

German who isn't ready to leave at the designated time." He spun on his heel and marched from the house. Moments later, his jeep careened from the yard.

Ami sank onto the sofa beside me. "Papa, I want to start at the Teachers Institute in the autumn, and all my friends—"

"Ami! I know the captain and he meant every word. This seems so stoopid, but there's nothing we can do." While pacing the floor, I envisioned a time long ago when Grandpa sent me to warn the villagers about Igor Kronchin and his dangerous comrades after they raided Pototski Estate. I drew my daughter to her feet. "Listen to me. I'll do the houses on Church Street and you go down River Street. Tell everybody, and I mean *everybody,* to meet at the hall immediately." A gentle shove encouraged her toward the door. "*Schnell*!"

I dressed quickly, turned up the collar of my coat against the chill, and knocked on doors. One groggy face after another greeted me, many questioning the agenda of the meeting. Ivan was already in the yard tending to his chores. "Come to the meeting, my friend. You're staying in Chornov, but you should know what's happening," I said.

A short time later, I pushed to the front of the overcrowded hall and Ivan put his fingers between his lips to whistle for silence. The vague information from Captain Schmidt created a storm of protest. Georg, for one, was clearly against the evacuation order. "How can the bastards expect us to be ready in one day? And leave everything we've got?"

"I won't go, either," another shouted from the back row.

Balzar whipped around to face them. "You can stay if you want, but damn right I'm going. If the communists were rough on us before, just imagine what they'll do now since we sided with the Führer. We're leaving a lot behind, but is it worth your *life*?"

My message carried across the hall, loud and strong. "Captain Schmidt was absolutely serious when he said any German who stays behind will be a *dead* German. Now listen to what I'm saying. Load your wagons with clothes and enough food to last at least a month. And include some grain for the horses, too. Take along a cow for milk, especially those of you with small children."

"But we don't even have a wagon," Frau Hirsch said.

"Then you'll be put with somebody who does." I raised my voice. "And make a canopy for your wagons because you'll be sleeping in them. Now get busy. Twenty-four hours isn't a long time."

Philomena tugged at my arm, her face haggard. "How's Lothar gonna find me when he comes back? I'm staying here. The communists won't do anything to an old woman."

"You *must* leave." I lightly touched her cheek.

"I don't like this one bit, Hans." She shuffled away, her pain evident.

I watched Ami listlessly sort her clothing and felt compelled to pull the drawers from the dresser and dump the contents on the floor. "Ami, pick out what you need most and leave the rest. Put our pictures and addresses in something to keep them dry. And don't forget warm clothes, too."

She threw herself on the bed. "Papa, I can't leave my friends in Selz without even saying goodbye." She looked up at me, her eyes begging. "Can Semion at least come with us? If he stays here, the Soviets will conscript him into their army."

Oh, to be in love. Selz had become my destination whenever possible. Ottilia and I enjoyed long walks along the *liman*, reveling in each other's company. I taught her shy boys to play stickball, surprising them that someone my age could still run! "Believe me," I said to Ami. "I know how you feel, but Captain Schmidt said only Germans can go, and if he disobeys an order at a time like this, he'll face the firing squad. This is hard to do, but at least we're together as a family. You can write later and tell him where we are."

She rose and folded into my arms. "But what if I never see him again, Papa?"

There was no time for explanations. "Go pack. Then you and Gramma make all the *Zwieback* you can."

Ivan and I butchered a few chickens and a young pig, then packed small chunks of the meat into canning jars and poured molten lard on top to seal out the air. I thought about our long friendship, and said the first thing that came to mind. "Ivan, I'd be honored if you'd take over my house. And there's a cow, last year's calf, and the rest of the pigs and chickens. The root cellar is still half-full, too. I'd really like your family to have all of it." For certain, the Russian families would fight each other over the abandoned properties.

"Your house is so big and beautiful compared to mine, and I really appreciate the offer." Ivan rubbed his chin. "But to make it a bit more fair, let's do a trade. You have only one horse for the trip. I'll give you one of mine and a set of harness in exchange for whatever you leave behind."

Considering he could have had it all for the taking, I replied, "That's the best deal I've ever made." I told him about The Pantry in Grandpa's house, and the rifle in the Goldsteins well. "The gun will be rusty as hell, but just having it will make anybody who wants to kick you off the property think twice." I swallowed the lump in my throat. "Ivan, I'll always think of you as my closest friend."

He smiled and shook my hand. Nothing needed to be said.

Ivan, Ami, and I stuffed several bags of flour, numerous jars of meat, a crock of sauerkraut, two sacks of potatoes, and an assortment of tools and kitchen utensils into the four-foot by twelve-foot wagon box. There was barely room left for a trunk of personal belongings and three thin straw-filled mattresses. A barrel of water, a small cask of wine, and a sack of horse feed hung on the outside of the wagon. Ami turned up her nose in disgust when I constructed a canopy by throwing tanned cowhides over a framework of long poles taken from the pigsty, but we had no other lumber.

I rested my back against the load, feeling nostalgic and, at the same time, dreading the days ahead. '*Ya-naih* Papa,' I thought. 'I hope your old wagon lasts the trip. If only you and the rest of the family were here to go with us.'

At first light, Ami accompanied me to the cemetery where the iron crosses stretched their decorative arms as if in prayer. My heart ached that my deceased infant son did not have a site at which I could mourn. We knelt at the graves of my grandparents, then at Loni's. Next, we stooped beside Katie's grave, where I kissed the headstone bearing her name and sent a silent message: 'Katie, if only I could have changed the path of your life. Goodbye, my love.' Would I ever share with another person as many traumatic experiences as I had with Katie?

As my daughter and I walked out the cemetery gate, Andy Boser and Squeaky Hoffer, long-faced and heads bent low, arrived to pay respects to their departed loved ones. Their presence reminded me that many of the people I had known either rested in this cemetery, or had suffered an undignified death in a *konzlager*.

A few minutes before the designated hour, I harnessed the horses and stood on the seat of the wagon. Shading my eyes with my hand, I studied the yard, and pictured Kurt and me helping Grandma catch chickens, Grandpa's pipe smoke drifting on the breeze, Uncle Heinz announcing his intention to marry Monica. I envisioned Mama and Loni picking peas in the garden, and Ami finding a locust, believing a baby bird had fallen from its nest. The tightness in my throat near choked me.

Philomena shut the door to her house and leaned heavily on Ami's arm. I felt more sorrow for her than for Ami or myself. She was too old to embark on such a difficult journey, one with an uncertain destination; her words confirmed she felt the same way. "Hans, my life will end if I leave this village," she said, bracing herself against a wheel of the wagon. "I've made up my mind. I'm not going with you."

"Philomena," I said, climbing down to face her. "You —"

She held up a hand. "Hans, I'm *not* going! I've already talked to Ivan, and he'll tell the Soviet Army that I'm his mother."

I could do no more than wrap my arms around her and pour out my gratitude for her many acts of kindness. Philomena hugged Ami for the last time, kissed her cheeks, and tottered toward Ivan's house. My daughter drew close to me, sharing her pain.

In front of the town hall, twenty-seven wagons formed a line behind mine, some passengers clearly showing their frustration. Andy Boser's wife wailed that she would never see her home again, while Albert Vetter's young son insisted on taking along his favorite puppy. I divided the wagons into support groups of five, leaving Eva, Balzar, their two children, and the Georg Frey family to join me. But where was Georg? Trouble already.

Captain Schmidt and three of his soldiers careened around the corner in his jeep. He pulled his watch from his pocket. "Is everybody ready to move out?"

"All except for one family. Georg and Genni Frey."

"Where do they live?"

I hesitantly pointed toward River Street. "First house on your right after the corner."

Two soldiers marched to the Freys' yard. Seconds later, a gunshot! I feared for my brother-in-law's life, only sighing with relief when his two-horse wagon, drawn by a single steed, burst onto the street. At least Georg was in the driver's seat and not lying in a pool of his own blood. Schmidt rested a boot on the bumper of his jeep and motioned to his left. "Proceed through Elsass to the Tiraspol road. Wait for me there. And *don't* get in the way of the military traffic." He and his three companions sped over the Chornov Creek Bridge and disappeared beyond the west pasture.

The horses jerked the wagon into motion when the reins slapped across their rumps. For one last time, I gazed down Church Street, at Saint Gustav's steeple, Hoffer's Store, Epp's Blacksmith, and the Chornov Inn. We waved to the Russian families gathered on the church steps. Ivan wildly shouted a farewell from atop the stone fence in front of my property, rusty rifle in hand. I realized the magnitude of our undertaking when he started singing the funeral dirge:

"No one is exempt from his fate.
Death rules over scepter and crown."

I saluted, hoping I had been as good a friend to him as he had been to me.

As we headed westward from the village, Ami leaned out the side of the wagon to hold hands with Semion. When he could no longer keep pace, she lowered her head onto my shoulder. It would be hypocritical to tell her to be strong while feeling so unsure myself. I had ached for an opportunity—a chance to get out of Russia—but being *forced* to leave was an ironic twist to my long-held dream.

In time, we passed near the creek in which I had muddied my school clothes, prompting Papa to strap me. A few miles later, I gazed upon the spot where he had confiscated Kurt's little red pocketknife following the slingshot incident. He had been overly stern with me at times, but I had forgiven him long ago.

All went well until we reached the steep incline leading out of The Chasm. The loaded wagons were heavier than most of the horses could manage, forcing all able-bodied travelers to walk up the dirt road. At the top, I unhitched my panting team and returned to Georg and Genni, who struggled with their lone horse.

"My Russian neighbors laughed at me this morning when I wanted to trade them my steer and two pigs for an extra horse," he said. "And it took time to convert the wagon pole to a single pull."

"Maybe you shouldn't have left everything to the last minute," I retorted.

He kicked a wagon wheel. "Nobody believed it would come to this. And then that damn soldier shoots so close over my head, my ear's still ringing."

It seemed Georg had no appreciation of how fortunate he was to be alive.

Soon we approached the turmoil in Elsass, where the German Russians were preparing for the journey, as we had yesterday. "See you along the way," an elderly man yelled as our caravan rolled by the northern edge of town.

We waited at our rendezvous point all afternoon for Captain Schmidt. A wolf's eerie howl echoed across the expanse of open steppe as the sun paused on the horizon, and still no sign of the captain. I had hoped he would arrive early, affording me the opportunity to ride to Selz, only an hour away, to say good-bye to Ottilia. Worried that Schmidt had misinformed me about our meeting point, I ordered camp be set up, and paced our site for most of the night; we couldn't turn back as the non-Germans from the surrounding villages would have already claimed our houses, our machinery, and our livestock.

My concerned fellow villagers crowded around my wagon the next morning and made their irritation obvious. "Hans, you got us in this mess, now get us the hell out of it," one of them shouted.

"You had no right to make us leave home," another added.

I had begun formulating an alternate plan when, finally, Captain Schmidt drove into camp. "My superiors took so long to decide whether you should use the Tiraspol land route or go along the Owidiopol road and cross the Dniester *liman*. They chose the water route, but if there's congestion at the ferries, preference goes to the army vehicles."

"Certainly, it would have been closer to go straight south through Mannheim," I said, hesitant to offer him advice.

Captain Schmidt cast me a hard look. "Hans, if this is the only unnecessary detour you make on this trip, I'll take forty lashes. Now, bypass Friedenstal and continue to Owidiopol. The other Kutschurgan wagon trains will meet you there. I sent the Mannheimers off this morning, and the Selzers will leave in a few days."

I motioned him aside. "If you have time, could you give a message to Ottilia Erickson? Tell her that I had planned to ask her to marry me."

So far, unseasonably good weather, decent road conditions, and no breakdowns had blessed our journey, but the wait became endless at the lake crossing. Convoy after convoy of army vehicles usurped the overtaxed ferries, and the ever-arriving groups of wagons soon sprawled along the shore. On the eighth morning, Soviet artillery rumbled in the distance. Balzar climbed from under the canopy of his wagon, followed by Eva's harried voice. "*Lieber Gott*, Hans. We're really worried," he said, his face ashen. "Are we just going to sit here and let the Soviets blow us into eternity?"

His concern was valid. We finally convinced the captain to present our case to the ferry operator. However, by the time we boarded the decrepit ferries in late afternoon, a brisk wind pitched our vessels on the waves, frightening both the passengers and the horses. After a perilous landing we pushed onward another two hours in darkness until heavy wet snow blew inside the open ends of the wagons. Ami and I strung blankets as shields and huddled on the soggy mattresses, the gale keeping us from sleep most of the night.

When the storm ended at dawn, the sun flexed its muscles and soon water flowed along the ruts in miniature torrents. Our wagon train dodged seemingly bottomless potholes, the wheels clogged with heavy clay doubling the strain on the struggling horses. "Everybody get out and walk again," I shouted to the driver behind us, as did he to the driver behind him. The message traveled down the line like an echo.

We stopped for the night earlier than usual, allowing the men time to clean the hooves of each horse to ensure the iron shoes were still in place. Before dark, Ami lit a small cooking fire inside a ring of rocks, and formed flour, milk and our last egg into a loaf to bake on a cutting board under a pyramid of hot rocks. "Balzar, bring down that cask and we'll have wine with our supper," I suggested, hoping to boost the mood at the camp. A wagon train from Baden joined us in the field and a lively harmonica tune bolstered by an accordion and a fiddle soon wafted into the clear evening sky. We, stateless Germans, enjoyed music and camaraderie under the sparkling stars far into the night. "I remember my grandfather saying, 'Worry makes you old before your time,' so let's make the best of it tonight," I said, taking a sip of wine.

"At this rate, I'll be a hundred years old next week!" Squeaky Hoffer giggled.

Our motley entourage straggled into the Romanian border town of Vulkaneschti at noon the next day. An angry Schmidt greeted us with bad news. "They want bribes before they'll issue our visas," he complained. Over the next three days, the customs officers coerced us into handing over most of our cows and a good portion of our money. "Time means nothing to these sons-of-bitches," Schmidt said, pacing back and forth between his jeep and my wagon, while giving me instructions for the next leg of our journey.

I bit my tongue. It seemed time meant nothing to the German Army either, as we had expected by now to be much closer to our destination, far ahead of the Soviet Army.

Once on the road, we trekked rain or shine for nearly two months, a testament to human endurance. At Weiskirchen, Hungary, the captain directed our caravan to a series of weather-beaten clapboard buildings, one with a sign 'Shower Hall.' After the ordeal of the past months, no one seemed concerned about modesty when we were crowded, nude, into common showers, men to one side, women and children to the other. Feeling clean and refreshed, we chose used clothes and footwear from a pile in the next room, not questioning their origin. And the wholesome food served in the dining room renewed my hope that Germany would treat us with respect. Even Georg admitted he had been wrong in criticizing me.

The much-needed respite ended three weeks later when our group boarded the freight cars of a northbound train one drizzly morning. The limited space allowed room for only the healthiest of livestock and the best equipment, and the locals happily accepted our old wagon and the horse Ivan had given us. Ami and I huddled on a crate of our belongings, a nervous Star nearby. Memories of traveling home with Loni's body so many years ago clouded my mind.

Four days later, the train whistle announced our arrival in the Wartegau, a section of Western Poland. The German authorities studied our facial features and measured each person's skull. They questioned family backgrounds to ensure pure German blood before issuing citizenship papers. After the interrogation, Ami and I anxiously waited in front of an ink-stained desk where an indifferent officer flicked through a few pages in a well-used binder. We grinned when he slammed the stamp on a form and said, "*Ya*, you and your daughter are approved."

In an adjoining room, a clerk assigned us to a farm. "Better than the one you had in Russia," he said sarcastically. "You'll be sharing with another family. Anybody you prefer?"

"My in-laws, Balzar and Eva Boser at the back of this line."

"Send them here for approval. One of the drivers in the yard will take you to the property." Without even glancing up, he handed me an official-looking paper.

After an hour's ride through the rolling countryside, our driver veered off the main road and continued another mile down a rutted lane before turning left into a yard enclosed by mature fruit trees. We slid from the rear of the military truck, and untied Balzar's horse and Star from the bumper. "This is almost like an estate," Eva said, while lifting their boys to the ground.

The trim hedge and freshly painted house and farm buildings indicated someone lived here until a few days ago. It seemed unfair to simply *take* another farmer's property. "Did Herr Hitler buy farms just for us?" I said to the driver.

"The Führer confiscated them from the Poles to distribute to people like you. Isn't this beautiful place good enough for you arrogant *Russlanders*?"

"We're German, not Russian!"

"Ach, a Roosian is a Roosian. You should show better appreciation to Herr Hitler for saving your hides from the communists."

My fists clenched inside my pockets. True, we were grateful the army saved us from the communists, but we seemed to have gone from one ruthless regime to another. I thought it best to remain silent and unload our meager belongings.

32

THAT'LL STOP THOSE BASTARDS

September, 1944

The majority of former Chornov residents, though homesick, were optimistic about the future. As was the custom, we offered each other moral and physical support during the re-settlement. Unfortunately, I had occasion to accept their generosity. Harvest had barely begun when a nasty farm accident cut my calf muscle to the bone. Balzar wrapped his shirt around the gushing wound and helped me onto the rough floor of the wagon. As we bounced across the rutted field, I worried that the remaining fieldwork was too much for him, Eva, and Ami. However, early the next morning, Georg led two of our neighbors with their equipment onto our fields, while Genni dragged a bag of potatoes from their wagon. The inherent goodness of people made life worth living.

I limped behind Balzar as he answered an abrupt pounding on the porch door one sunny morning. Two German Army officers strutted in, jackets buttoned to their throats, hats pulled low on their heads. "Both of you get ready to leave, and now!" they demanded.

Balzar confronted the nearest officer. "You can't just barge in here and order us around."

"You're damn right we can! We're rounding up thousands of guys like you to fight those Russian bastards," he barked.

I hobbled to a kitchen chair and removed the bandage from my fresh wound. The officer grimaced. "You're no good to us," he said, then nodded to Balzar. "But *you* be outside the door and ready to go in fifteen minutes."

I braced myself against a wall in the bedroom while Balzar packed his rucksack. "I sure don't feel right that you're going to war and I'm not," I said.

“Maybe you were hurt for a reason. This way there’s a man here. Who knows what might happen yet.” He gripped my shoulders. “Please, Hans. Take care of my family.”

I laid my hands on top of his. “I promise, my friend.”

I shed a few tears of my own as Eva, his young sons, and Ami smothered Balzar with kisses. He wiped his eyes on a sleeve, softly closed the door, and walked away.

Early in 1945, convoys of German Army vehicles passed our property, then turned west at a nearby corner—west toward Germany. Captain Schmidt brought his jeep to a halt in front of the barn, the morning air thick with fog, January’s rains coating the countryside in layers of ice. He greeted me with a curt nod. “My men are alerting all German Russians that the Soviets are closing in, but I wanted to personally warn you. Get the hell out of here, and head for Germany. The trip shouldn’t take more than a few weeks.”

His surprise news required an explanation. “You forced us from Russia, and now you won’t protect us? And what about our men you conscripted last autumn? We haven’t heard from them even once, and how will—”

He tugged down the visor of his cap. “Our army’s in trouble and I regret to say that you are on your own.” He leaned in close. “If I were you, Hans, I’d get on the road *now*.”

Schmidt had gone out of his way to give me the warning and there was no sense arguing with him—he had no control over the matter. Sincerity shone in his eyes as I grasped his hand and he returned my grip. He saluted, and then drove away into the fog.

I immediately instructed Ami and Eva how to prepare for the journey. Eva swayed on her feet as if she were about to faint. “I’m not going without my husband. Besides, with most of the Poles gone, they’ll need farmers here, won’t they?”

“Eva, think about it. You don’t want to be here when the communists come. And I promised Balzar that I’d take care of his family."

Eva placed her hands on her hips. "Hans, I have a right to make my own decisions, and only God knows the outcome."

I reluctantly acknowledged her reasoning; an argument would only cause hard feelings, and I didn't want to part on bad terms, even though I felt sure we would never meet again.

Within the hour, Ami and I squeezed minimal clothing, blankets, and food into a small, uncovered cart, leaving the wagon and second horse for Eva. As I urged Star through the gate, not even Ami's tearful pleas could change her mind.

Our neighbors' overloaded wagons already clogged the ice-encrusted roads. Occasionally, an army vehicle's horn blaring from behind spooked the horses and caused serious accidents. I purposely reined Star into the ditch, seemingly a safer place to travel, but she often slipped to her knees. In this chaotic manner, my daughter and I, along with our fellow countrymen, fled toward safety.

Darkness rendered the icy road even more dangerous. I tied Star to a willow bush in the ditch and tended to her knee. Ami shivered under our blankets in the back of the cart while I lay awake and prayed Balzar would forgive me for leaving his family behind.

Before the sun rose, we nibbled on frozen *Zwieback,* while Star munched on grain from a sack. As I urged her back onto the road, a drop in temperature added another layer of frost to the already treacherous conditions. The sound of curses and the snap of whips carried sharply on the frigid air. A ragged woman with a young boy in tow ran out from the haphazard line of refugees tramping along the road. "Please, sir," she begged. "Can we just sit on the back of your cart?" Asking God's forgiveness, I shook my head. Star already had both knees scraped to the bone and she couldn't manage to pull another ounce.

The woman grabbed onto the side of the cart and dragged the boy along. "Get off or I'll use this," I ordered, raising the whip.

The boy lost his grip and his mother let go of the cart.

Ami stared from me to them, speechless. I knew the guilt of my actions would haunt me, but compassion was impossible in our dire situation.

Late in the miserably long day, a German lieutenant leading a cavalcade of vehicles in the opposite direction frantically waved to us from his jeep. "Turn around! The Soviets are blockading the bridge ahead," he yelled. "Detour north about thirty miles then bear west until you reach the next bridge. But *schnell*! When all our army vehicles are across, we're blowing it up. That'll stop those bastards." He saluted and sped off.

Now it was every man for himself. I attempted to turn Star and the cart around on the narrow road, but other drivers doing the same impeded us. Finally, Ami pointed to a gap between two wagons and I maneuvered into the tight space. For three days, a cold wind battered our rag-tag procession as we crossed small creeks and crawled over hills wreathed with leafless poplar. The terrain sloping toward the Oder River still two miles away offered my first glimpse of Germany. I stood up in the cart and shielded my eyes against the sun as the air filled with the uplifting sound of voices singing a German folksong. "Ami, those snow-covered hills are in the land of our forefathers. Doesn't it make you feel like we're coming home?"

Her bottom lip quivered. "But Papa, Ch-Chornov is my home. That's where Semion and Gramma are."

I felt sorry for her, but at the same time, was disappointed she did not share my enthusiasm. Perhaps she was too young to appreciate the significance of heritage.

As we bumped along toward our goal, the seconds seemed like minutes, the minutes like hours. My heart missed a beat when the whine of a diving plane suddenly disturbed the still air. "Run!" I screamed, desperately trying to alert the people in the other wagons. We jumped from the cart and pitched ourselves into an artillery shell hole near a grove of trees. As if from the bowels of hell, Soviet planes buzzed overhead, spitting streams of lead onto the road. The acrid smell of gunpowder and aviation exhaust assaulted our lungs.

When the smoke and dust cleared, Star lay on the ground, blood gushing from her mouth. Ami shook the horror from her head and screamed, “Star! I'm coming.”

I caught the hem of her dress and dragged her back into the shallow pit. Forcing her down onto the scorched soil, I whispered in her ear, “There's nothing we can do for her. We *must* get across that bridge before the army blows it up, but it's too dangerous now. We'll wait until after dark.” As my grandfather had done to me many years earlier in the Selz town hall, I took her face in my hands and looked into her blue eyes, wide with fear. “If we get separated, don't come looking for me. Just get across that bridge and go as far west as you can.”

“We won't get separated, Papa.” Ami said, “I'll stay right beside you.”

To relieve the tension while we waited for darkness to fall, we exchanged memories of life in Chornov. Ami snuggled against my shoulder as I told her about my early school days and the nickname, ‘Hans Kisser.’

“Don't you wish Mama was with us?” she sighed. “I sort of remember the day she died. It must have been hard for her to leave behind a young child. I suppose parents want to see their children as adults, to know …” A single tear slid down her dusty cheek, leaving a clear trail.

“Of course she really wanted to see you grow up, but dying wasn't the hardest thing she did. Sometimes …” My words were lost to the memory of a difficult time long ago.

“Papa, what did you mean when you said Mama did something even harder than dying? Dying has got to be the worst! And tell me the truth, I'm almost eighteen, you know.”

I had vowed never to reveal Katie's last request, but if my life ended today, Ami would never know the truth about her mother's selfless act. I fought to control my emotions and slowly began to speak. “All parents want to give their children a boost in life, a gift to ensure their future. But the communists left your mother with nothing to give, so she wished to turn her death into a life-saving gift for you. Both your mother and I loved you very much, so in the end, she trusted me to carry out her request."

Ami furrowed her brow. "You're not making sense, Papa."

How would I tell her what had to be said? "She offered *herself* for you, and after she died I made sure—"

Ami grasped the lapels of my coat and shook me with such force that I wondered where she found the strength. "Papa! You *didn't*. Tell me you didn't keep me alive like that."

I loosened her grip and kissed the hand of the person most dear to me. "I did it for you and for your mother. And maybe for myself, too."

"Why didn't you just let me die? Oh, God, I hate you. I'm going to throw up." She crawled to the far side of the small crater, her body convulsing with sobs.

My head drooped while sitting in anguished contemplation. Had I disclosed Katie's dying wish in order to reveal the depths of her motherly love, or was I no longer willing to bear the dark secret alone?

The rumble of distant gunfire roused me from my daze. "Ami," I began, before realizing she was already running toward the road. "Ami, come back! It's too dangerous!" I yelled, trying to catch her, at times dropping to the ground amid bursts of gunfire, but she was either beyond earshot or chose to ignore me. A loud clopping of hooves alerted me, and a frenzied woman, her face rigid with determination, whipped a foaming horse as she hurried by. Her possessions and three children bounced in the back of the rickety wagon. As the outfit passed Ami, a redheaded girl leaned over the end gate and extended her hand, pulling my daughter in beside her. The wagon disappeared among the retreating army vehicles.

"Lord, give me strength," I prayed, and ran until the devil's claws raked my lungs. I crested the riverbank and spotted the wagon in the long line waiting to cross the bridge.

Three army trucks roared alongside the motionless wagons.

"Don't follow us," shouted a sentry aboard the last truck. "We're blowing up the bridge right after we cross."

The wagon drivers cursed and dropped their horses' reins—all except the renegade woman. She cut around the line and charged onto the bridge. The thunder of hooves pounding on the wood planks resonated like a death knell.

"Jump Ami, juuummp!" I screamed. *Boom … Boom … Boom*. The bridge exploded in front of me. Debris pelted the frozen river, while a cloud of smoke obscured the twisted girders, the toppled columns, and the opposite shore. I sank to my knees. "Amilia! Ami, I'm sorry …"

Soviet vehicles careened toward the destroyed bridge as I wrestled with the overwhelming guilt that my daughter may have died, all because of me. I plunged down the steep bank and zigzagged through the wreckage covering the buckled ice of the river, the *chat-chat-chatter* of automatic weapons ringing in my ears.

33

DON'T SCREW IT UP NOW

Berlin - September, 1945

I found no trace of Ami during my hurried search through the rubble of the bridge that horrible evening in January. Clinging to a slim hope, I frantically searched the German countryside and the towns bordering Poland, then the war-torn streets of Dresden and Cottbus, always managing to avoid both the Soviet and German armies roving the area. The end to the war in May renewed my hope of a more certain future, more freedom to look for Ami. On the outskirts of Berlin, darkness surprised me with its swiftness, and an American curfew patrol, scouting for displaced Eastern Europeans unable to prove their citizenship, arrested me, slamming my head with a nightstick.

I regained consciousness sprawled on the dirt floor of a refugee center. My brain throbbed in time to my heartbeat and, weak with fatigue, I could do no more than flop onto an empty bunk. Despondent, my life passed over me in a wave, a powerful and vivid collection of memories, both happy and painful. After three days of languishing in a depressed state, I convinced myself Ami was worth more than my self-pity. I paced the compound like a caged dog every morning for two months, waiting in vain for my release, desperate for my freedom; I had paid for it dearly. But leaving was not an option. Well-armed patrols routinely checked along the razor wire fence that enclosed six crudely built single-story barracks: four for families, plus one for single males, and one for single females. An acrid aroma from trenched latrines in two clapboard buildings graced various sections of the complex, depending on the direction of the wind.

My salvation was the collection of 'lists.' The Red Cross

posted names on a wooden bulletin board in the center of the compound in a humanitarian effort to reunite families. The first column showed the names of missing persons who had been located and their whereabouts. The second column was for suspected war casualties. Those reported by several sources as 'perished' ended up on the third and most dreaded column: Dead. We inmates referred to this column as the 'D' list. Maria Hummel, a frail, white-haired woman whose only son, Vincent, had failed to return home after the armistice, often accompanied me, or rather, I accompanied her, to the board. Our dependence on the ever-changing lists bonded us.

One sultry September day, while scanning the 'D' list, I read the new names: Gilbert Bosch, Erwin Dresser, Vincent Hummel—Maria's son! A fist closed around my breastbone. Maria gasped; she too had seen the name. As she crumpled beside me, I bent to cradle her in my arms. "There, there, Frau Hummel. Vincent was a good man and he loved you. Now, wipe your tears. He wouldn't want you to be so sad." I said what I believed would comfort her, but to be honest, I wondered if I could go on living should Ami's name appear on the 'D' list, especially before we had a chance to reconcile. Fighting to control my emotions, I escorted a devastated Maria to her barrack.

On the way back to the bulletin board, I plunked down on a pile of empty armament boxes, closed my eyes, and dropped my chin into my hands. Why did the Lord allow such tragedies to happen to innocent people like Maria and her son—and to me? I had tried all my life to be kind, honest, and thankful for my blessings, to be an honorable person of whom my family would be proud.

A grating voice intruded on my reverie. "You're Hans Gerein, aren't you? A man's waiting to see you over there." I raised my head and glanced at a wiry, middle-aged inmate pointing to the comptroller's office. Perhaps someone had given my name to an agent seeking information on missing persons.

When I entered through the open doorway of the building, my visitor stood gazing out a window at the opposite end of the room, his hands locked behind his back. Judging from his build, he could have been Balzar, except he wore an American army uniform. "Good morning. How can I help you?" I said, in the rudimentary English learned in the center.

He turned to me, and the color drained from his face. "*Johannes*?" he said, low and hesitant.

"*Ach du Lieber*! *Kurt*?" His hair was no longer blond and curly, but the thrust of his chin and the piercing blue eyes were unmistakable. My legs refused to move and my knees wavered. Kurt rushed to me and we embraced in a giddy mixture of laughter and tears. Unable to bottle my excitement, I wrapped my arms around his waist and lifted him from his feet. He clapped my shoulders until I set him back on the floor, allowing him to regain his breath.

I studied my brother from head to toe, and realized that something set him apart from me. Perhaps it was the assured look on his face, or how his muscular body filled out his uniform. His appearance verified that he had lived a good life, while my scarred face and sinewy limbs conveyed the hardships of my years.

I let out a whoop, not believing this day to be real. Kurt and the major exchanged salutes after Comptroller Major Edwards poked his head into the room and asked if there was a problem. Upon learning we were brothers kept apart for thirty years by the Russian Revolution, he said, "Well, congratulations on your reunion. You must have lots to talk about." He pointed to an office on our right. "You're welcome to use it as long as you want."

After closing the office door, Kurt slaughtered our Old German dialect with an injection of English words. "*Meine dear Bruder*, you can't imagine what this means to me," he said, tears dripping off his nose. He kissed me again on both cheeks.

"I certainly *can*, because it means just as much to me. All the time I was growing up, I dreamed of this day. And as an adult, I've thought about it even more." Unable to suppress a smile, I withdrew my hand from my pocket and placed an object on the desk beside him.

Kurt cradled the little red pocketknife as one would a newborn babe. "Hans, I don't know what to say. Papa bought it for me from the gypsies."

My words dripped with sentiment. "I treasured it more than I can ever tell. But do you remember what I gave you when I chased after your train?"

"Of course. It's on the mantle at home. Every night, I'd look at that slingshot and remember you tossing it to me. That picture never left my mind." He ran his fingers through his hair and turned away, his voice breaking. "My God, Hans. All the companionship we missed out on, and all the hell you've been through. When I think of it, I have to cry. *Thirty-one years*." Facing me again, his lips bowed into a grin. "But, we'll have the next thirty together." Come here, you big brute!" We both chuckled when he stood with his back against mine. "And how did you get to be so much taller than me, Hans Kisser?"

"Not from eating good American food, that's for sure! But Kurt. I'm wondering how you knew where to find me."

"My unit was stationed in Berlin after the armistice. I heard about the evacuation of the Germans from the Kutschurgan, and checked the Red Cross lists every day for almost five months." He grinned and withdrew a wrinkled piece of paper from the inner pocket of his jacket. "Here's something for you. A letter from Ami! She located me through the army. She's safe."

I collapsed into Kurt's arms, feeling at peace for the first time since her disappearance. "Safe! I've prayed every hour of every day since we were separated to hear that word."

"*Ya*, she's living in Saarbrucken in the French Sector, far west from these refugee centers."

"Let's go right now! It won't take me long to pack."

He held up his hand. "Wait a minute. God help me, I don't want to leave you here, but Major Edwards needs signed papers before he'll release you. It'll take me a few days to get them."

I grabbed him by the lapels of his tunic. "What do you mean? I'm going with you *now*!"

"Calm down, Hans. Don't worry, you're in good hands here. Our army's in control."

I knew from the tone of his voice that he misunderstood the seriousness of my situation. As calmly as possible, I sat down and gripped the arms of my chair. I described my sentence in the gulag, the years of deliberate starvation and the communists' total disregard for human life. Kurt, his chin quivering, listened in silence. At times, his face went blank with shock. I stood up and edged near so as not to be heard outside the room. "You Americans are allies with the Soviets, but they still scare the hell out of me." I placed a hand behind his head and drew him close, whispering as if the walls had ears. "Their agents have been coming around asking questions. If they find out I'm from Russia, they might send me back, probably to a labor camp."

"Hans, that's not going to happen. You're here in an *American-controlled* camp."

I detected a slight gruffness in his reply, and briefly considered what he said, but cold fear still pumped through my veins. "A friend told me he's planning to escape and I might—"

"And what if you get caught? Then what? You are so close to freedom … don't screw it up now. Hans, promise me you'll stay here until I come back." He grasped my arms, his eyes aglow. "I *guarantee* your freedom."

I swallowed hard before replying, "If you say everything's good, Kurt, I'll stay here and wait for you."

On the day Kurt was to return, I awakened at dawn to the public announcement system blaring, "Gather your belongings and assemble at the main gate in one hour."

How would my brother find me if I was moved from this camp? I kicked open the barrack door, and with my shirt clutched in one hand and my suspenders dangling, I dashed to a secondary gate at the far end of the compound where I had often peered through the fence, dreaming of freedom. This time, a guard prodded my stomach with his rifle barrel. "Get back right now or you're dead, my friend," he snarled.

Baffled at the change of atmosphere in the camp, I stalked back to the barracks and, reluctantly, folded my extra set of clothing into a bundle, reprimanding myself for my unfounded fears. As Kurt had assured me, the camp was under American jurisdiction. For God's sake, we weren't criminals; surely they were taking us to a processing center for our release.

Maria Hummel and I joined a crowd of detainees chatting in the shade of the bulletin board until the soldiers guided us under the stifling canopies of military trucks. The drivers veered through the streets, dodging artillery shell craters and jagged piles of bricks blasted from nearby buildings. Panic gripped the pit of my stomach when the trucks ground to a halt in front of a rail station. The air filled with the smell of fear radiating from my fellow detainees, and we exchanged nervous glances while searching for avenues of escape. A unit of American soldiers herded us from the trucks to the station platform. Some cursed, others were silent and could not look us in the eye. Major Edwards opened the door of a jeep parked beside the locomotive. My worst fear was confirmed when he saluted the captain of a waiting Soviet contingent, effectively turning us over to the communists.

Soviet soldiers, Camel cigarettes dangling from their lips, rifles and clubs in hand, prodded us into four stinking cattle cars, a soldier jabbing my arm with a bayonet when I attempted to slip away. The doors rolled shut with a clang. I elbowed my way between the press of bodies in the semi-darkness, grasped the bars of a small ventilation port high in a corner, and hoisted myself onto tiptoes. Soldiers moved alongside the cars, double-checking the latches.

My heart pounded against my ribs when a jeep roared around the corner. Kurt jumped from the driver's seat. "Is my brother on that train? I have immigration papers for him," he shouted, brandishing a thin folder.

"Kurt!" I screamed at the top of my lungs, pulling myself further aloft. I thrust my arm between the bars and waved my hand frantically. "Kurt, I'm in here. Get me out!"

His hat blew from his head as he ran toward me. "Hans, I see you!" He jerked at the door handle, then smashed his fist into the latch. "The damn thing's locked!" He whirled around to face the Soviet captain. "*Yop filla mut*. Who's got the goddamn key?"

The captain flicked the ashes from his cigarette and pointed to Major Edwards. The major began to strut away, but Kurt confronted him, tension crackling between the two men. "My brother is—"

Major Edward's voice, steady, but sharp, echoed across the yard. His abrupt words cut into my soul like the lash of a whip. "General Eisenhower ordered that every Soviet citizen be sent back home to Russia. That's what I am *obliged* to do, and that's exactly what I *will* do."

Kurt grabbed his arm. "They are not going to their *homes*! They're going straight to a *konzlager*! Are you a Nazi? Sending people to their deaths?"

A sneer curled the Major's lip. "I have specific orders. Now release my arm or I'll have you court-martialed!" He turned and climbed into his jeep.

Clink, clink, clink rattled down the line as the hitches engaged and the train jerked into motion. Kurt charged back and reached for my hand extended between the bars. As our fingers touched, the Soviet captain slammed his rifle against Kurt's head, sending him down into the dust; my immigration papers drifted in the breeze created by the train. He shakily pushed himself to his knees, the captain's bayonet keeping him at bay. Kurt's tormented voice rose above the grating of the iron wheels. "Hans! Hans. I'm *so* sorry."

My chest heaved with despair, my mind reeled. "I forgive you, Kurt!" I shouted, praying my despondent brother would hear my plea. I withdrew the knife from my trouser pocket, softly kissed it with quivering lips, and then squeezed my hand through the bars of the ventilation port. I opened my fingers. The red and silver object clattered to the cinders along with my boyhood dream.

Tears of pity for Kurt welled in my eyes as he limped after the train. "I promised to free you, Hans, and I will. *I will*!" he yelled. He stooped to the cinders, and then frantically waved the little red pocketknife above his head.

Sincerity rang in Kurt's voice, but in my heart, I knew this was the last time I would see my dear American brother. I pressed my forehead against the freight car's gouged wooden wall … and my world went blank.

AUTHOR'S NOTE

In the early 1800's, Czar Alexander I, the grandson of Catherine the Great, cleared the Turks from Ukraine's Pontic Steppe north of the Black Sea. He granted colonists—the majority of whom were German farmers and tradesmen—free land, tax concessions and freedom from military service in exchange for settling the newly acquired fertile land. Within half a century German Russian enclaves dotted the expansive territory from Romania to the Caucasus Mountains. Czar Alexander II recognized the emerging political influence of the colonists' descendants and, beginning in 1870, he methodically rescinded their privileges. Over the next forty years, hundreds of thousands of disgruntled German Russians flocked to the American Midwest, Canada and South America in anticipation of homestead land and political stability.

Their friends and relatives who stayed in Ukraine condemned themselves to years of misery, especially during the crisis in 1932 and 1933. The harvests were adequate, however, military brigades collected virtually all foodstuffs from the farmers to thwart Ukraine's bid for independence. Millions of tons of the confiscated grain sold on foreign markets funded Josef Stalin's insatiable desire for an industrialized Union of Soviet Socialist Republics (USSR) while an estimated seven million citizens died of starvation during a time of plenty in their own country.

In 1944, hardship struck again before the German Russians had fully recovered from the starvation period. Hitler demanded they abandon their properties and follow his retreating soldiers from Ukraine to Poland. The Soviet Front's rapid advance across Poland in early 1945 prompted another uprooting of these displaced people—this time to Germany.

In anticipation of the war's end, the representatives of the Allies—Franklin Roosevelt, Winston Churchill, and Josef Stalin—had already signed the Yalta Agreement. Perhaps unknown to Roosevelt and Churchill, and to this day, a black mark in American and British history, a secretive clause 'Operation Keelhaul' allowed Stalin to reclaim those Soviet citizens who had fled the country during World War II. Allied soldiers herded the people into cattle cars for the long, torturous journey to labor camps in Siberia, where many perished from exposure to the harsh elements, forced labor and starvation diets. In 1946, the Americans and British ceased sending former citizens back to the USSR.

Stalin imposed a ban on communication between the detainees and the outside world; their whereabouts becoming known only after Nikita Khrushchev rescinded their exile in 1955. The German Russians were forbidden to reclaim their former properties in Ukraine and in the Volga River region, and were restricted to settling in the desolate eastern regions of the USSR, mainly Kazakhstan and Turkmenistan, or in existing German settlements east of the Ural Mountains in Siberia.

In the mid-1970s, the USSR opened their borders for supervised visits from foreigners, but emigration remained closed until *glasnost* and *perestroika* introduced in the 1980s by Mikhail Gorbachev allowed more freedoms.

The collapse of the USSR in 1991 finally opened the floodgates. Germany welcomed virtually millions of ethnic German Russians back to the land of their forefathers, allowing jubilant families and friends to celebrate the end to 46 years of separation.

****

Thank you for reading DEAR AMERICAN BROTHER. Your review posted to an eBook site, or the contact section of www.dearamericanbrother.com would be greatly appreciated.

ACKNOWLEDGEMENTS

My heartfelt thanks to the many persons who helped compile this novel. To name only a few: Kim Aker, Theanna Bischoff, Sr. Elizabeth Elder, Joe D. Elder, Lorna Elder, Paul Elder, Odelia Ell, Christiane Grieb, Bill Hossack, Dan Hossack, Josh Hossack, Pat Kozak, Betty Lang, Rose Marie Leeb, Tamara Rutley, Anne Stang, Krista Wiebe, Andrew Wilmot, Keith Worthington.

I sincerely appreciate the valuable editing, proofreading, suggestions and advice.

AUTHOR'S BIOGRAPHY

Joe J. Elder spent his formative years in a German Russian community in Saskatchewan. His penchant for history took him to Germany several times to record the experiences of the relatives who survived the Stalin Era. A self-organized tour by train from St. Petersburg to Gulag Camp Perm 36 in the Urals, and 1989/2006 visits to the ancestral villages near the Black Sea in Ukraine were highlights in his quest for first-hand information for DEAR AMERICAN BROTHER.

Joe co-produced and wrote the narration for the acclaimed documentary *Germans from Russia on the Canadian Prairies*. Several of his articles have appeared in magazines highlighting Germans from Russia, one winning a prestigious Story of the Year award.

He enjoys an active, full life in Calgary, Alberta. His passions are writing, playing sports of all kinds, adventure travel with his wife and, most of all, spending time with his family.